FRACTURE: A MEMOIR

Arlen Rundvall

Also by Arlen Rundvall

The Bipolar Guide to the Gift

Order this book online at www.trafford.com/09-0175
or email orders@trafford.com

Most Trafford titles are also available at major online book retailers.

Note for Librarians: A cataloguing record for this book is available from Library
and Archives Canada at www.collectionscanada.ca/amicus/index-e.html

Printed in Victoria, BC, Canada.

ISBN: 978-1-4269-0424-0 (soft)

*We at Trafford believe that it is the responsibility of us all, as both individuals
and corporations, to make choices that are environmentally and socially sound.
You, in turn, are supporting this responsible conduct each time you purchase a
Trafford book, or make use of our publishing services. To find out how you are
helping, please visit www.trafford.com/responsiblepublishing.html*

*Our mission is to efficiently provide the world's finest, most comprehensive
book publishing service, enabling every author to experience success.
To find out how to publish your book, your way, and have it available
worldwide, visit us online at www.trafford.com*

 www.trafford.com

North America & international
toll-free: 1 888 232 4444 (USA & Canada)
phone: 250 383 6864 ♦ fax: 250 383 6804 ♦ email: info@trafford.com

The United Kingdom & Europe
phone: +44 (0)1865 487 395 ♦ local rate: 0845 230 9601
facsimile: +44 (0)1865 481 507 ♦ email: info.uk@trafford.com

10 9 8 7 6 5 4 3 2 1

This book is dedicated to bipolar people. We are not alone in our affliction. I hope that you find the courage and wisdom to live life.

Thank you RosaLee for helping me find my gift.

Thank you Alex Browne for your wise editing.

Thank you Tracy Sim and Kathy Siemens for the great art.

ESTEEMED READER:

This book is a celebration of the soul's endurance. You may think that I went through bad times, but it could always be worse. I have much to be thankful for, mostly that I am transforming this life challenge into a positive. We can change our reality by changing our perspective.

The names have been changed to protect the innocents around me. The style stretches language in a poetic way to capture the challenging subject matter. I hope that this gives you a glimpse into addiction and living with bipolar. May it help you to stay out of the ditch and on your desired road in life.

Arlen Rundvall 2009

"He who fights with monsters should be careful lest he thereby become a monster. And if thou gaze long into an abyss, the abyss will also gaze into thee."

-Beyond Good and Evil, Friedrich Nietzsche

PART ONE

THE ENIGMA FRACTURE

SHELTER

Wired with a headlamp and Walkman, Arlen biked the night trails. He flew through the curves and the rush to navigate the corners and miss the trees. He biked down by the river. It was dark with occasional lighting from the streets above—the bridges crossed the river. A flash of movement in the thick grass and reeds caught Arlen's eye.

He stopped the bike and shut the headlamp off. It was a hundred feet away and too far for the lamp to penetrate. Arlen's eyes adjusted to the pale glow cast from the streetlights above on the bridges. It was a person taking a few steps forward and a few steps backward. Arlen watched the machine-repeated movement.
"Are you all right?" Arlen called out.
"No." It was a high-pitched man's voice.
"Do you want help?" Arlen asked.
No answer.

Arlen swung his leg free from the bike and pushed the wheels onto the grass toward the man. The grass stopped after sixty feet and turned to wild grass and reeds. The man remained stuck in his rut in a lower depth. He was chained in place and had broken and bent reeds but was held captive by the vegetation.
"Can I help you?" Arlen asked.
"I'm stuck," the man said.

The shadow outlines became clearer as Arlen set his bike down and crunched through the vegetation. It was strange to see a person stuck—the guy looked like that old TV commercial where the cat walked forward and back. "Chow, chow, chow."

Arlen shook his head. It was odd. Arlen broke through into the clear zone that the man had trampled.
"Hello," Arlen said.
"I'm stuck." The man turned his face to take in Arlen.
"I'll turn a light on," Arlen said.
Arlen turned the headlamp on and looked down at the angle of light. The bare, bleeding, swollen feet looked beautiful and tender against the broken reeds.

"How long have you been walking?" Arlen asked.

"Don't know—days." The man kept up the pacing—forward and back.

"Stop, just stop and turn this way," Arlen said.

The river licked at the shore ten feet away. Arlen thought of the beaver and his own flip that had been a couple of hundred yards up river. He wondered how many people the river had trapped.

"Can't get across the river." The man would not stop his machine repetition.

"Stop and turn this way, I'll get you across the river." Arlen reached out his hand.

The man slowed.

"Stop!" Arlen grabbed his hand.

It felt dry and cool. The man's feet stopped. Arlen pointed the lamp at his face. The eyes dwelled in amongst the reeds, they were terror and pain and suffering. This was a broken man incapable of causing someone suffering. He was the epitome of self-inflicted cycle. Arlen looked away.

"Let's go—what's your name?" Arlen asked.

"Jason."

"My name is Arlen, can you walk out through this?"

"Maybe."

Arlen let go of his hand and pointed the light for Jason to see. Jason struggled with geisha steps. His feet were incapable of much maneuver. Arlen grabbed his hand again and walked backward trampling the reeds to make a path. It was a struggle.

"You can make it," Arlen said.

The man started telling his story in a gentle matter-of-fact way. He was distant from his own life. The hospital had turned him away. He was looking for the men's shelter. Arlen believed that the man had walked for days. Bare feet were not a good choice for long distances.

They triumphed into the grass slow and sure. The cool wet lawn felt good to Jason.

Arlen thought of doubling the guy on the back of his bike—there

was a metal pannier deck that would support him. Jason had the body
of a boy.

"I can give you a ride to the shelter, it's just a few blocks," Arlen
offered.

"Okay," Jason said.

"You'll have to hold on to my jacket sides and balance; we don't want
to drag your feet."

It was a challenge to get Jason to straddle and sit with balance. Arlen
stood on the pedals and pushed and wobbled to gain momentum to go
straight. Jason retracted his feet from scraping. They gained speed and
followed the paved trail.

"I have to get speed to try to get up the hill to the bridge," Arlen
said.

Jason held on.

They struggled up to a toppled stop. Arlen stepped off and pushed
the bike with Jason still sitting. Jason told the story of his father abus-
ing him as a child. It was like he was talking about someone else. On
the bridge flat, Arlen pedaled again and proceeded to navigate through
the same area where Arlen remembered walking barefoot. They rang
the bell at the shelter and Jason was allowed in.

Arlen rode back to the river shaking his head at the odd experience.
You never know what is occurring in the corners of our civilization.

COMPASSION BORN

Arlen darted his eyes up and down Banff Avenue; he was being watched. Arlen reached for the payphone, pulled his fingers back from the monster, pocketed his hand and turned to the sidewalk. Winter tourists walked the street, shopping, sucking in the cool air to exhale billows of condensation. Skiers represented the colors of the rainbow in their thousand dollar suits.

A tourist observed Arlen insert his hand into his pocket and retreat from the payphone. Arlen took a cool deep breath and looked at the pyramid shape of Cascade Mountain. He barely remembered climbing it the previous summer. He twisted back to the phone and stared it down. The phone won. Arlen retreated further to charge up the avenue.

He bumped into packs of "Gorbies." This was the derogatory word for tourists. Some resorts call them terrorists. In the 1980's, Gorbies was the 'in' term for Banff.

Arlen bumped into the purple and red clad shoppers. He stopped and looked at their faces. They smiled. Arlen did not. He left the street and entered the first door, into the Hudson Bay store. The heat hit him to shiver in his cellular level. The bright displays of the Christmarketable-child still leered for dollar attention. Arlen stopped and thought of the need for that phone call. As it was, he would not last. Hours maybe, overnight was hard to conceive. Each moment exploded in a magnitude of torment. The clock scribed each minute into his skin—branded in suffering.

He thought to turn back out the door but thought better of it. Those skiers were waiting to assault him. He headed toward the back door. He felt exposed in a night trouble sort of way. The shiny steel of the glass doors framed the experience of entering the alley. It required all of his strength to push the door out—the building heat system and the cold wind conspired to trap him in Ladies Outerwear. Arlen leaned through, the seal broke and momentum rushed to catapult him to the alley. Cold—he was always cold these days, but he actually felt this. His shame with what he had to do froze his internals. He looked across the parking lot. Car engines ran to taxi him off to safe exile—away from this self imposed insanity clause.

Arlen walked toward the gallery, through the lot, and stopped directly beside a vehicle driver's door. He turned to face the door. It was unlocked and idling. The windows were clear of frost—it had been warming for a journey like his. The car sat patient. Arlen waited for a signal of intent—he needed the door to open of its own accord. Arlen glanced sideways and behind and refaced the door.

He thought of which way to drive. Vancouver? The mountain crossing scared him this time of year—Roger's Pass had claimed enough lives. Calgary and open prairie were the way to go—it was what he knew—all his safe childhood warm fuzzies emanated from that direction. Where would he go? What would he do? He knew that he took his enemy with him. It would follow. Like cougar hounds chasing and baying the treed call—those damn hounds are bred to follow and kamikaze the kitty to cower in the tree. Arlen had his tree; it hung him now. His gut would soon be warmed with the death shot. The hounds barked the gallows to follow. The dogs would not be muzzled—that was certain. As long as he lived, they would follow till he broke the pattern. The lattice-woven puzzle required his heartbeat to remain.

Have to call. No hope. The snow desert; the water lay in crusts of delicate crystals and his bones were dry and brittle—they grated in walking and wondering. Trapped in the valley of eye candy: Prime Rib, Alberta Grade A Beef. Bus tours. Fondues. Gondolas. Rental cars. Chairlifts. How to escape these trappings that alleviated the skin for a moment but remaindered the soul rotting and crazy?

The alley claimed Arlen. The car still waited, ever warmer. The driver knew not of the tropical delight he had dangled for the escapee to steal. This would be no joyride, this was a matter of survival. Automatic pilot ruled the roost. Destination seemed routed, hardwired to the core. Lap after lap—there was no end. He was a lifer, a tourist hanger-on living off the backs of the happy holiday panacea. They promised no end of these people.

And Arlen burrowed deeper into his turmoil. He had tried to escape with many means. He tried to join them in small jaunts and outings—it

always ended the same. Back in his cell—in the steel bunk. He would
rub their shoulders and share in their pictured memories. He would
shoot the happy couple.

He often wondered of the tourists showing their videos and slides
and photographs to their loved ones. He would be there in his red
Patagonia jacket. He'd saved up for that coat—his coat of one color—
he was bleeding to death in the Gucci of protective outerwear. Would
anyone from the outside hear this subversive cry for help? HEY, it's me
inside the valley here. HEY, you in Europe, in Asia, can you see me—
it's me in the red coat? I know you're out there. Last summer you sliced
an image of my existence—you took me home through customs. I must
exist. Don't I?

Arlen shuffled down the alley. Patches of ice claimed his grip. He
shot across the sheets like a hockey puck—he could flip over and not
make full tracks in the snow. He was far from full weight. He had this
internal distress perpetual spin that moved him—no, it claimed him as
a surrogate set of feet—it carried him ever onward, in circles.

It was the only thing that held him in comfort—he knew he would
be back, knocking on that door, he had to receive the package. It completed his ache. It had become him. He was an extinct animal from
prehistoric times. His skin stretched taut and dry about him. He was
more hollow than the badlands of Drumheller. He wanted to walk off
into the mid summer desert hoodoos and bake. No, it was not distant
and foreign enough; his skeleton girders came from the badlands of
China—they looked the same but felt different, more alien.

Arlen's feet ground solid—the sidewalk claimed him. It had been
scoured and slip proofed from legality-inspired recourse. The Post
Office was on his right. The river slept straight ahead through the park.
He had to cross the river to get back to his cell. Arlen turned left back
toward Banff Avenue—it lay in the evergreen wilderness like a misplaced Las Vegas.

It was foreign from the elk and the cougar and the grizzly bear. All
around town stood de-spirited forms of this wilderness. In name and
in statue they integrated safely with the moneyed populace—they sold
film and appetizers. Bears loomed large and harmless—they posed.

They also traveled on film through customs to distant living spaces. The wild animal statues garnered more attention and conversation than the bleeding man Arlen.

Arlen focused on the intersection, green light, red light. He stayed on the street side of the sidewalk. He was safe there from the window-stalking shoppers. He had to negotiate the streetlamp poles, garbage cans, and opening car doors. But that is what he did as an employee— he navigated the uncultivated edges to smooth the utopia holiday bliss and hold it intact for the credit card-signing tourist.

He turned left again at the corner. He was right handed—this seemed appropriate—he strove subconsciously for balance. He struggled to let his body achieve homeostasis. He could not trust it—it rebelled against his needs. His wants had taken over. He ran for distant cover, by capitulating in this moment of space.

He again negotiated the obstacle strip of sidewalk adjacent to the street. He had to turn sideways to miss the gaudy colored smears of trendy outerwear as well as the concrete receptacles and car doors. The phone approached. Arlen vowed to win this time—he would not let it escape. He focused and spotted it through the bodies. It leered closer. Arlen lost his outer balance and slip-streamed through the scrum. He ferried the Gorbie River to reach the store alcove wall.

Arlen cornered the phone, grabbed the handset with gloved hand and placed the cold plastic to his face. It was a frozen intimate act of attrition. He waited for them to close in on him. He thumbed the cradle switch and faced the phone—his confessional booth posed pretty in this town that swelled to entertain and prosper. He waited for eternity.

"Hello, Operator, how may I help you?"
"I would like to place a collect call."
"To what number please?"
"306-874-2314."
"Your name please?"
Arlen had to focus, and remember what they had called him. What did his nametag state in this place? It was from a distance that he willed the breath and articulation to mould his tongue and lips to spew:
"Arrllen."

He knew he had formed it too large, it still resounded in his skull to mock. When was the last time he had spoken?

"Hello?"

"You have a collect call from Arlen, do you accept the charges?"

A cough. "Yes."

Arlen waited for the judgment to fall. He embraced it perversely. It must be this way.

"Arlen, is that you?"

"Mom, I have a drug problem."

"Arlen?"

"I need help Mom, I'm sorry."

"That's all right, we'll get you help."

Silence.

Arlen felt the tsunami wave of shame slam him to the concrete. Feel it weigh you to the ground and below the frozen earth. Permafrost thaws to swallow you and your memory deeds, and reflection pools cover you over and freeze solid dry, as the desert winds parch your breath for cover of balm—soothe Arlen. No, you must have none of that peace salve—you dead stick, brittle bark, crack, fall down. Breakdown. Nutrients enter the forest floor grid cycle.

"Arlen?"

"Mom."

"I love you Arlen. Call your brother."

"Okay."

"Call him now, Arlen."

The brother and sister had had a quiet Christmas, unusually mundane and restful. The call was placed through and received to rally the troop. The duo possessed peace and joy and love. The fruit of the Christian spirit dripped ready to coagulate on any known wound. Festering sores have been known to retreat in the wake of this smooth, warm place. The quiet cool moved in this Ford sedan as it traveled westward to rescue this stricken brother of disarming trouble. The plain was devoid of life—pavement and gravel arteries fed the cocooned souls in vehicles to seek destined discharge.

WAIT FOR RESCUE

The connection was made, the direct pick up intention to one-way rendezvous unknown at this time. Banff is no metropolis WE WILL FIND YOU stuck in Arlen's head like an iron prod. It numbed and did not let go, with its constant reminder. What else is there? This concluded hope—it hammered its presence to be felt and heard. The mantra continued to grow in Arlen like an island in the distant Pacific Ocean. You know it exists, you have heard of it mentioned in passing—it must be real. Unless you go there, it is in a bit of faith that you find the occurrence of reality. THERE IS AN ISLAND. Hang on to this shred of real tangible hope. They are coming to get you.

The receiver slammed against the metal cradle. Arlen felt the whole of earth look at him in this awkward spot of place and planning. Insanity and death are the promises of dedication to this sport at the Olympian level. There is no drug testing here—you strive for the podium as you dare need to. Rapidly—if you are gifted in disregard, you can do it in a year—your podium remains a statistic, forevermore your legacy in a databank. If you are not a sprinter—if you like to suffer long and promise big returns in your cycles—you could live to seventy with a twenty-six a day. You could be sneaky and steal your number away from the alcoholic column. What joy—you died of a heart attack.

Everyone that hones this sporting life will face the end if they continue. The cause will claim them. Perhaps a spouse is needy from their childhood passage of dependency—this crutch of relationship may help the user live a shadow life. The two are hollow, twisted shells that together keep the mutant addiction safe and secure, and exceptionally operational. It is sustaining and needful of this campaign of deliverance. Salmon in a cannery are beheaded and gutted and steamed and canned. The supply is endless till the doors are closed. Commerce is open to profit quarters increase. Addiction is open for business and is a steady leg for our economy. Another is born this day.

Enough nattering about addiction—we have a semi-sane blood-pumping addict still with us. Arlen, where did you go? Down the street, there you are—the red jacket gave you away. Where are you going?

Away from all these people—out of town—watch me get away from this main drag of sales. Through all these streets named after mammals, past the cemetery on the treed slope. Through the Banff Center where the gifted ones study and shine.

I see now the shoulder you mount—the Tunnel Mountain you climb. Why there? No one can help you. Forest and rock promise nothing. Turn around Arlen, TRY THE HOSPITAL.

Arlen backed through the artistic endeavors, past the gravestones lining for attention, through the mammal streets, to grab the avenue by the bank before the river. Cross the bridge—you are exposed Arlen. Jog across this open girder bridge deck. Get it done. That's it, good boy. On the other shore, the parks administration building faces you down. Quickly left, that's it, puppet string walk now to the big H.

In the door by the Spray River—enter the public domain of treatment and bliss.
"I have a drug problem, my brother is coming to get me, I don't feel safe, can I stay here?"
Atta boy Arlen, you spit it all out. This haven might work for you and your affliction to settle you in for the cover of darkness to fall. Look at the shadows grow. You can feel it Arlen.
"I think we can help you out, do you have your health card?"
"I'm sorry I don't."

Arlen thought of the system grid tracking numbers and names to hold up the service to maintain dignified grace. Arlen kicked himself for not having his card. He reached in his pocket. His trusty hash pipe was there cool against his thigh ready to brave the elements and deliver Arlen through the valleys.
"That's all right, we can find that out, come with me."

The hour passed with Arlen settling into the scene that helps the hinder to soothe. He realized his place and accepted the people to be. The meal was served—he sat to engage the colors and tastes. Hospital food. Arlen poked his right index finger into the metal lid hole and felt the steam, the warmth triggered saliva and the aroma teased, he lifted it to see the hospital food menu tonight had, on its main plate as a side dish, mushrooms to please.

Arlen flashed solid resolution—the poison was ready, they followed him here. Away you must flee, freedom gain, bust out the gates, out of the ward and through the front door. Quick like a bunny for fear of them see. Not a word that they trick to find you. To the forest, up the mountain, Saint Bernard to rescue you with brandy this night.

Arlen turned right down the sidewalk. He lost details of the passersby people—they blended in the night with the enemy position condemning and pointing. He must get out now. Cross the bridge and back through the mammal streets; chimneys delighted in smoke twirling warm inside fire. Up the trail by the cemetery, the lights sporadically staged details. The center of art was quiet; evening had claimed them indoors to reverie and delight.

This time we could not call him back from the shoulder of this small mountain. Arlen climbed in his boat shoes up the dim trail. His guts prospered in carrying his bones through the night. He had forgotten the savior Ford sedan was on its way. Step by slippery step he gained the height of Tunnel Mountain on this New Year's Eve.

The revelry abounded below and around. Thousands gathered from around the globe to party this midnight through. Where Arlen stood, not a party favor colored the scene. It was a cold wind that greeted him at the top and sang 'Auld' through the evergreen tops.

It was evening—not midnight yet. His clothes were shy of protection from these mountain elements. He felt the end was near and reached out his wings—to accept the wind that passed right through. He gave all to receive: the wind took none. Or did it take all? Arlen stood and leaned and numbly felt the wind rip his depths. Nothing withstood this power of touch. Shreds. The experience left him as he was before—still something to do, to fall.

The wind left Arlen calloused. A fresh abrasion blew raw upon his soul. He turned toward Rundle Mountain. The cliff invited him and fell to the trees hundreds of feet below. The treetops waved as shadows and said hello—he liked the look of the evergreen swell. Perhaps this was the prescription needed. Arlen was so far gone that consequences masked themselves and hid to blend in.

Arlen peered over his destined demise one thousand feet to the verdant spears. He could even surmise the first contact point—the epicenter of his torso felt correct—he could imagine his limbs flailing earthward, his gloves would stay on, but his shoes would pierce the snow crust. Arlen could even see the dark fluid enter the dry bark of the trunk. The force of impact liberated snow from the tree—the white dust would float for moments.

Arlen rubbed his ribs and felt himself go over. It had to be this type of body disposal; it had to end—this crazy tornado of self-bashing and paranoia had to cease. This was a mercy jump that claimed him as sacrifice. He had no other choice, the wind had blown clear through him and left nothing but earthen metatarsals, and they crept to the edge.

GRADE TWELVE

The school hallway buzzed at eleven o'clock—most high schoolers were now awake.

"Arlen how's your dad doing?"

He's fucking dying of cancer you schmuck, that's how he's doing. Thanks for asking though.

"All right."

The bell rang. Huddles shrunk and filed through doors that closed. The hallway floor shone in emptiness and the still fresh wax from summer maintenance.

The school bell rang for lunch. Arlen's stomach growled. Algebra books slammed shut, equations fell from the bubble spaces that students form above and in front of them. Sneakers squeaked on the floor. Girls clutched their caches of books to their chests. Boys gripped the book deposits on their hip. They surged to locker and homeroom to ditch these formula books.

The hallway struggled to squeeze the hungry teens through. The country kids ate in classrooms. The town kids headed home. This was the time before eating out and the school was too small to have a cafeteria. Imagine all your school years eaten out of brown bags or lunch boxes. What do these people eat now for lunch? Do some eat the very same lunch their parents made for them? Do they go out of their way to eat out? Do they make themselves late for work to avoid the taking of the lunch?

Arlen headed past the principal's office, past the staff room. He felt the eyes of one teacher—they knew his dad was dying. What can you say? What can you do? Arlen thought of hunger as he headed out the door and past the flagpole. He smelled autumn in the air and looked to the colors. The leaves blew to tickle the street. Arlen was happy that appropriate winter approached. He looked at his feet.

He walked on—this walk could be taken in sleep. In the mornings he was asleep as he walked across the schoolyard. Arlen looked up and saw a police car in the driveway of his house and leapt inside to fright. What is it? Is it dad? No, it couldn't be. Arlen picked up the pace. He was frightened to arrive, but too curious and too needy to avoid this meeting.

COMMUNION

Psychedelic Led Zeppelin and Pink Floyd posters lined the two-person cell. It was dormitory style—a sink and mirror, steel beds and wooden dressers that had held how many people's underwear and socks for decades? There was a window. It was covered with a Pink Floyd flag. The occupants had shopped at the concert tables.

The washroom and shower room were down the hall. This was a maze of institutional residence dwelling. It was cheap and social. Arlen wore a leather string around his neck—his room and mountain bike keys were tied to it. He had learned his lesson. He hated blacking out in public—it was a tough locked out recovery, and harder to get to work.

The room was lit with a red glow from behind two of the flags. Six people shared the campfire of this room. The warmth emanated from the shared focus. Four sat on the two beds and two sat on chairs. It was a circle. It was Friday night for the six—their weekend promised eternity. It was actually Tuesday night—no one in the room cared which days they had their weekend on. This was Friday; Mushroom Friday—an hour from now the magic mushrooms would arrive.

The door was closed. They would smoke bongs of hash as the appetizer. It was decent hash—they had done some the previous night. The family came together after work to share this circle of brain enhancement. Music drove the focus. Led Zeppelin simmered in the walls. It looked the same in this inner room any time of year. From summer solstice to winter solstice, the red glow was ready to show direction.

They chatted about this girl and that. Some of the six darted glances at the posters, but that would come later—the mellow melt of contemplation would hold them to it. This was the service; the priest was in court, the saint held the drug in his hand. All eyes in communion watched the ritual and gave reverence. The priest set to prepping—it was joint time; the bong needed a rest. He took a cigarette and rolling paper and with fingers and thumb making the sign for money, he fed out some tobacco to make a nice long nest in the fold. He took a chunk of dark hash, a good quarter gram, and stuck it on a pin, and lit a match to dry the delight. He fingered the batter and crumbled it to nest. It felt warm to his touch—like a homemade bun out of the oven. He broke it open and the latent heat escaped. The dark hash sat ready in the tobacco strands. It was packaged like an important breakable with paper and Styrofoam. It was ready.

The priest was good—he one handed it to his mouth, to kiss it with spit, his tongue slid across the glue strip. He then used the other hand, and with both he rolled it; not too tight, nor too loose, perfect. He tore a match from the matchbook, tamped the loose end in. He tore a strip of matchbook and rolled it and inserted it in the spliff. He placed the filter in like a fuse with explosives. The matchbook paper's memory forced it to uncoil and meet the paper's internal circumference. It became a perfect filter—it filtered nothing; but it allowed the six to inhale directly to match cover. They would not waste any of the precious. It was time. The priest smiled.

All eyes were on the sacrament; the bread and the body, the joint is divine. Something was missing and this held the promise. They salivated and anticipated the high—their first, their millionth, they all want the same.

The priest lit the match—the mini fireball flared. The smoke rose up in harshness. The priest touched the papered goodness to his pursed lips. It stuck. The priest glided the fire to the paper and sucked the air. The paper end crackled and grew to take cherry dimensions of description. The tobacco and hash ignited and smoke billowed airborne. The paratroopers jump. Static lines sever. The priest lingered his inhalation—his head lopped off. He quickly exhaled and deflated his diagraphm. His chin hit his chest. He replaced the joint to his lips and drew back. He grew in stature like an inflatable clown. He arched his back, and pulled till the end. He closed his eyes and pulled the stick from his mouth and blindly offered the baton. Fingers mingled and confidently dispersed and accepted. The priest was in glory, he held onto the clamorous chest. It swam and skirted through his neurons, synapses fog mute firings. His muscles relaxed and soon he must breathe. He billowed the room to reek of this potion. He opened his eyes and smiled at the group. They smiled from the other side—they knew they'd soon arrive in that kingdom.

The service glowed—smiles all met. The moat of today was behind

them. Before them promised relief: a respite from all that was not here
with them. The tunes man rose from his bed. How can he do that?
Arlen wondered of his might. The music was raised to drown out the
plane of verbose. It floods and washes and cleans. Smoke filled the
room; from the ceiling it invaded the heads, the waists, the knees. With
this first encounter of the night, the feet and shins are still clear air.

Everyone forgot about the psilocybine. Can this mushroom poison
be the solution? Is it needed beyond this simple repose? The posters
were gazed and worshipped and oohed. Frozen ghosts pandered for
additional dust that settled the score. The peak settled and asked for
more. The priest offered the goods and passed the honors to his right
hand man. He rose to the occasion and prepared just one more.

PRECIPICE

Arlen is numb—comfortably could be disputed. He is cold beyond belief and unaware of this fact. Is he hypothermic? Perhaps. We know he is doomed up on this cliff. He may think he could burrow away from this state that he mixed. You and I know there is no quick fix.

Save the leap, the toss the body into the darkness routine. It has been done before, and will be attempted to perfection. Addicts do end up there—can we ask them when they jump, what is over there? Do they know at this point? Is there anything of promise? What stops them from turning back? Is it genetic how one can leap to body bag?

Arlen, are you there? Can you hear me? Those shoes look cold man. Arlen slips and falls forward, just slightly; don't stir, don't breathe, don't shout. Whisper.
"Arlen will you do it?" Can you care? Does anyone care? Will you make it on your own?

Arlen with intent tossed himself off. Arlen threw his hands in the air. His feet anchored. He was stopped by something, someone. For a moment he lingered at the apex. The wind blew. The mountain eroded. The river slept. The trees rested their sap. Arlen stepped back.

You could see his breath rise and disappear—the wind stole it to cease. He took another step back. Was it done, the duties at this polarity place? It was hard to believe. Arlen was on missions from an entity. He turned from the cliff and sauntered north on the summit. He did indeed feel an odd spat of peace. He knew he was done up here, no wait, what was that? To the east. He faced his directional escape route. The spirits of the people that roamed these valleys. Arlen tore down and scattered to the winds—he picked up vibrations from a different dimension. Is it always there? Arlen, do you know? Are you at the overpass to another side? Are you in the gap for a purpose? Is knowledge any worth? Or are you simply being and is that the best? Are you being Arlen?

There you are. Remember they are coming for you this night. They drive that Ford sedan. Willing and ready to pluck you, you rotten fruit, before you smash to the ground.

Flash forward, slip, slide grip your way down this little mountain. Through the arts center and by the cemetery, you enter the mammal street names. Stop. You're the one that they chase. You are shame, you are evil, and you are outcast all the same. Run, you pitiful, loathsome mutt. You dog of despair, you have run amok with your youth and your gift potential. You are stricken with a vision of paranoid 'beware, they are watching, they are following you now—run through the streets.' Like a dog, you must cower and respect the master's brow. Beat me down. Chase me. Yell at me. I see you push me with your violent, intense glares.

See Arlen run, he is bones pounding and sinew stretching and nerves pulsating and misfiring synapses. He is stricken of fear itself. He runs to nowhere, for the cause of pursuit and avoidance. He stumbles and carries on in his mongrel berating of self-id and odd it is, he that must fight. He cowers and flowers tear out their colors, his heart bleeds this night. He wanders on the outskirts of the resort city. Not too close for warmth of fire but far enough to escape their blows of derision. The hours pass.

The cold is final and at distance, he solidifies. He mellows. A spark of warmth flashes hope of rest. The police station presents itself—he has done nothing wrong. I have a problem; they are coming to help me out. I am not a criminal. Please help me to sort this mess, that I am, out. There is an entrance. A conveyance. Push the door. No. Push it harder. Lean with your might. Whoa, don't fall in, to the floor, they might balk.

Feel the warmth. Set you down, on the floor. Eyes close. Safe. Secure. Hold you now. Thaw—tips of fingers and crown of head. The ice crystals smooth and flow to water. Still parched.
"What are you doing here?" The officer looked stern.
"I have a drug problem, my brother is coming to get me."

Arlen, are you warm, are you there? Did you have that conversation? You are still here in the warmth and soothing safety. Hold on, they're coming. Let the cozy take you. It steals you away to a flaccid place. You droop and dribble, shut eyelids tight. Your tailbones rally the cool floor; your feet push the rubber mat. You nod off.

BUTTER KNIVES

This has been going on for weeks. Your roommate, and you, Arlen, have been binging on the hash, hot knifing. You two have discovered that hotel butter knives make beautiful administrators. You are passionate about your pursuit of the blackout.

Arlen, your throat feels like a well-used tail pipe. The hits continue to cycle you down. A couple of kids in a playroom, you knock yourself out. You help the other to suck the medicine. Arlen, your ski wax torch blares flame to heat the stainless blades to glow. The balls are ready to provide their magic puffs. One by one the soldiers go to their dutiful grave.

The room is padded, and Nurse Nancy does well. The hits wander and focus on brain popping demise. Look, the two of you are rolling in daze. More—focus on red hold the knives tight. A few more, that's it, take it in, all the way, suck it up. Now it's got you by the tail and flipping you right. Turn the flame off as you go on down.

The next day is a day off for both of you, is it a Saturday? The day's blue sky invites an adventure from the cell into the bright light. Your roommate is a rock climber—he even has the fancy rock slippers. No carabiners or ropes or anchors though. That's all right; you have hash to hold you up.

Arlen tears some hash and rolls the little balls and sparks up the ski wax torch. Four hits should do it, you take them in now. One, two, three, four. Four for you and four for me. That's it. Let's go. Out the door of the upper annex and past the lower annex. The stonework grabs your attention. You look back up to your left to see the glorious hotel. You stumble to mount the walkway down to the golf clubhouse. Your body falls and submits to gravity, you think of wheels, and how nice that would be. Let yourself go, in no time you'd be at the bottom, quarry in the river cool and clean.

Is it ever hot this day in June. The cool mountain morning air has given way to that dry heat. The sun cranks its brightness when it picks out your sensitivity. Arlen, you are thankful for your glacier glasses, and with their side protection, you look like a bug.

They stepped onto the golf course road and walked across the bridge. Arlen looked to the right, up the valley, up the creek. They walked down the road, hole one sat to the right. The exercise had mellowed the buzz and threatened to turn to drudgery. They walked on. To the left, by the rivers edge rested an elk protest. They grazed and posed on the fairway edge.

ARRIVAL

Arlen thought back to the previous fall. To the night he had arrived on the bus from Calgary. He had hitch hiked west through the prairie. His last ride had been from a diamond drilling bit oil patch guy. He drove out of his way and dropped Arlen at the bus depot.

The bus had arrived in Banff at midnight. Arlen wandered around, the shadow giants of Rocky Mountains stood like proud shadow sentries. The night mountains were too large to enter. He was short of cash, and looking for work. He searched a bit, and discovered warmth from the cool night in the post office. The mailboxes repelled any sense of comfort; the hard floor was temporary removal from the large landscape. Arlen was not the only one—there were four others hiding from the wilderness under this federal tax paid roof.

They told where they were from and gave tips for jobs and travels and chat-napped through the night. In the brisk cool mountain morning, Arlen walked the road to the hotel. What a beautiful place. He could stay here a while. Look at those mountains, what adventure for an eighteen year old. The personnel office had just opened and sure he could work for them—on the golf course, the very next day. He was processed and housed and fed and lost in the under level maze of tunnels.

The residence was connected to the grand hotel via tunnels. Arlen took several tries to landmark each twist, each stair. He took a wrong turn through a door—and entered the art adorned wall and red carpeted floor that the guests trudged on.
"Oops."
He reentered the door to step on bare stained concrete. The walls and ceiling left open for ease of utility access. This was a crawl space that one walked through; this was the domain of the cart pusher—the laundry, the garbage, all things unsightly found their way through these tunnels.

The laundry plant was between the staff residence and the hotel. This was a winter blessing—it was a cozy, moist nook to walk past, an industrial tropic from the dry Alberta air. It was through the laundry that Arlen explored, someone had told him it was a shortcut to the pool. Arlen felt odd to walk through this workspace—people folded and sorted and loaded and unloaded the large machines. Steam steaming, presses pressing, washers washing, dryers drying. The radio played.

The workers wore shorts and tees, dressed light. They turned to watch him pass by. Their robotic digits and arms memorized their task. They did not have to look down but to glance. They knew what he was after, which mouth he needed to find, to exit this factory of cleanliness. A lady smiled, motioned swimming. Arlen smiled and nodded. She pointed further on and to the left.

Arlen thanked her. She smiled. She could not hear him but knew. Arlen caught a glance of two others performing the laundry sheet five step—in and out they weaved, hands meeting to transfer crisp lines. Like winged birds their hands flapped. Back and forth the sheet shrunk in geometric shapes. The one set of hands always held high while the other set saved the folded end from the floor. Arlen thought of the train carrier for royalty. The person bowed slightly to dignify the robe. Arlen did not see the hardness of wrists and hands—the mastered pain that rose again.

He found the corridor; and entered the tube through the swinging doors. It was hot. He stopped in his tracks and looked onward. He was inside a machine; he could be five miles underground. The steam lines and pipes were barely overhead, and to the side. The lighting was minimal—a faded light hung at intervals. You could read as a teen by this light. A gray adult could not read a page.

No one was designed to linger here, except those wizard trades people that spin pipes and wiring; we as commoners respect their design, their talents, their kingdoms of backspaces and ceilings and walls and floors. We might change a light bulb or clear a drain, but never forge past this point.

Arlen decided to push on through the tunnel, he was getting too warm now, a little claustrophobic. He trudged up the concrete grade. He could see the crest in the middle and was a quarter way there. Doors opened at the other end—an awful screech and the sound of steel wheels rolling threatened toward him. Arlen considered turning but sped up instead. Over the crest, he saw the laundry cart and the hunched back of the person pushing.

As they met, Arlen offered his back against the piped wall to give clearance. He was careful not to touch the pipes, some still felt hot. He wondered what creatures had respite under the bottom pipe in the blank space. Arlen pondered rats chewing his ankles. The pusher looked up at the last moment and smiled. It was a woman leaning to mount the concrete incline.

Arlen stood and wondered. He was a ball, bouncing inside of a gigantic pinball machine. He scurried to the other end; the length was at least a football field. He noticed the scraping the carts had done on the bare wall. He heard the woman crest, the sounds mellowed and then increased as the cart physics accelerated. He could hear her—she wouldn't be leaning forward now.

Arlen could see the door, the exit from this hot tube. He lunged through; he squinted his eyes at the brightness, the painted walls shone. An elevator waited at his left. This was weird; the transition to the decorated threw him off. Surreal. He smelled chlorine, the pool was near. He heard video games. Arlen walked through the corridor, the games lined his right. Clusters of family played. Off-duty uniformed employees raced and shot the light.

Arlen made it to the pool—its size impressed him. He enquired at the desk. He could and would get a monthly pass, it was cheap. He walked back through the tunnel and smiled at the same laundry woman. Back in the annex, he climbed the stairway. He walked to his room and sat on the bed. He wondered if this was the best place for him; he would make the best of it. At least one year.

FIRST DAY

He planned his first day of work. He would wake at five thirty. He woke and dressed and made his way through the tunnels to the staff cafeteria. He had to ask once for directions. He took his tray and toast and cereal—he didn't usually drink coffee, but he needed one. He paid the nominal price at the cashier and entered the cavern of tables and stood. He noticed clusters of same dress at the tables. The tables were not even a quarter full. Like uniformed tended to eat with similar uniforms. He was still asleep—he looked down and saw that he had no uniform. He saw a table of that type too. He headed to safety, the only bridge in the room. He did not want to sit by himself.

He stood and asked if he could join them.

An older man said, "Fill your boots."

Arlen focused on the task of eating. He heard the shop talk. They joked easily. He had played the Sesame Street game of which one of these ones belongs with the other? He had won the game.

"You the new kid?"

"Golf course—Arlen."

"My name is Sam." He reached his hand across the table.

Arlen thought it was a gnarly weathered hand that had touched places.

"Good to meet you."

"We can give you a ride, just stick with us."

Arlen focused on the food; he really did not feel like eating but forced it down.

"Don't worry Arlen, we'll be easy on you the first day."

Arlen smiled.

POLICE ENTRANCE

The door opened. Cold air rushed into the entrance. The brother Jake looked at Arlen on the floor sleeping. Jake looked at the next door with the buzzer button. He wondered if Arlen pressed the button and talked to someone. It doesn't matter. Arlen is still on the outside so everything must be fine.

Jake and Carmen had driven around for half an hour looking for him. They had been happy to pull into the police parking lot and spot the body on the floor. Jake nudged Arlen in the knee with his foot.
"Arlen."
Arlen looked up and could not believe it. Jake was here. Everything would be okay. It would be good, he was safe now. A wave of warmth came over Arlen.
"Let's go."
Arlen stood up and followed Jake out the door. The cold darts of air were dull now. The Ford sedan rescue unit idled. Carmen sat in the navigator's seat. Arlen climbed into the back seat. It was amazing—this comfort and safety felt warm. It felt odd to be in a motorized conveyance. Arlen released a layer of protective guard from his body.
"Thanks for coming to get me."
"No problem, we had a quiet Christmas."
They found Banff Avenue and turned toward the bridge. A flash hit Arlen—are they taking me back to work, do I have to stay?
"Where are we going?"
"Get your stuff."
"Oh."
"Is that all right?"
"I'm not going in there."
"I can go in."
Arlen felt the barbs start. He darted his glances around—out the back window, the sides, the front, the back, and so on. He was a trapped dog that needed to get out but not back on this side of the river. He needed to get out of these mountains, and soon.

Arlen loomed as a fearful animal, caged and scared of the outside. This backseat appeared like the animal's domain. To Arlen, he was a dog—a mongrel of shame. He had taken a good mind and body and destroyed it—he had done this to himself. He was worse than death. He was living remorse and damaged brain. He was livid craziness.

"Where is your place?" Jake asked.

Arlen had to turn and focus on the front.

"Keep going straight."

Arlen peered left and right. He shrunk from sight. He would burrow in the ground if he could. He took the blankets and wrapped in them and sunk.

"To the left."

"This building?"

"Yep."

Jake stopped the car and left it running.

"What number is it?"

"One thirty seven."

The three sat waiting.

"The key Arlen?"

Arlen felt for the key at his chest. The steel next to his skin felt strange—heavy. He found the leather string on his neck and pulled the string up and over his head. The keys caught on his chin. Arlen handed them to Jake.

"One thirty seven?"

"Yep, this floor."

Arlen and Carmen watched Jake walk into the building. Arlen thought that Jake was a brave man. This was now a terrible place to stay—they were trapped in the car. It was all around them and closing in. Carmen tried to get Arlen to talk. He said little; this was distressing to see the driver out of his place. How long must it take? It is only twenty doors down on the right.

The hallway was dim and sallow. This was survival living. Decades of resort troops had rallied through these halls. Adventure had been waged and won. Innocence met with the dorm and grayed a bit.

Jake was surprised by the smallness of the room. He found Arlen's side by recognition. Jake made two trips to glean the items of value—the mountain bike. Arlen's roommate would return to see some of Arlen's stuff gone and would never see Arlen again.

This was the busiest night of the year; Auld Lang Syne was sung and past. Arlen had missed this shift—his teammates had to pick up the slack. Where did he go?

Arlen felt exposed, danger hinted at penetrating his soul. The two trips that Jake made to the inside were brutal. It took forever. The door lock and handle screamed at him to open, to run, to hit the valley and not look back, cross the ice, run to the plains—out of this tangled mountainscape.

FIRST DAY GOLF

Arlen spoke when spoken to, and offered no more information. He did not know what to say yet to fill gaps. He did not know how to question people, and listen to them talk and yammer for hours. He would learn in time that to get others talking about themselves would be easy—listen. Time would pass and you would be considered a great person—and you had not said anything about yourself.

The truck bounced down the hill from the castle to the course. At the clubhouse they picked up more of these seasonal groomers and cutters. These were the keepers of the course. They continued across the bridge and passed into the course depth. Left and right, the cultivated green hinted at perfection.

They turned left into the maintenance area. Arlen was inside now, past the caressed green. He was with the machines and the stockpiles of dirt and gravel and fertilizer.

Arlen felt at home in this place with these men and women. They worked the land. They were straightforward. The land spoke back to them and through them in honesty. A morning meeting was held. Arlen met the man, the head greens keeper. He seemed like a good guy. Direction was given. The troupe dispersed to load and start machines.

The fairway headman directed Arlen. Arlen was taken to the bunker trike—it was a small three-wheeler with a rake on the back that could be lowered into different positions. Arlen smiled at this task; it was like a boy in a sandbox, this job was all right.

"I will see how you are doing in a bit, start at number one and keep going."

"Where's number one?"

"Back up the road and on the left."

"All right."

The hardhat felt funny. The plastic was cool at this time of morning. Arlen headed to the first bunker. It felt good to be driving something. It was fun to figure it out. It moved fast. He left the road and entered the fairway of number one. It was all his, nobody else was in sight. He headed to the sand bunker and raked it. It was later when the golf balls rained around him, that he was thankful for the hat. He became accustomed to the balls dropping. He liked to see them fall and bounce.

The waves of sand were great—he imagined he was surfing. The time passed. The next day he raked new holes. His time sped up.

THE WALL

Arlen walked with his roommate—the hashish wore down. Arlen wondered how long ago he had worked on this course. It seemed like years. Did it even happen? A truck met them on the road, the driver waved— Arlen waved back.

A ten-minute walk past the bridge, they came to the shoulder of Rundle Mountain. They left the road and headed into the trees to the right. Boulders sat in the trees. Like grated chunks of cheese that crumbled, the huge mountain dropped blocks that waited for erosion to wear them flat. Arlen and his roommate looked up, the false summit teased, an eon away.

"This is a great wall to practice on." Tim the roommate smiled.

Arlen managed to unfurrow his brow. He was no longer sure this was a good idea. He wanted excitement though. Bring on a plate and pass the salt.

Tim stopped at the toe of the rock sheet and sat down and pulled his rock slippers on, and tied the laces. Arlen looked down at his own hiking boots and wondered of the comparison. How would he do in this straight up a rock face? Sure it was not straight up but Arlen wondered at the lack of ropes. He was more comfortable blacking out on drugs and hitting the floor with a flaming torch than this mountain rock and tumble and fall to your death. Do it for experience.

Tim took to the rock like a kid to ice cream. Arlen followed like a kid to water, a child that respected the liquid. There was something there that lurked to do harm.

LUNCH POLICE CAR

Arlen picked up the pace. One step in front of the other. He had lived in this house for fifteen years and had never seen a police car in this driveway. He had seen them pass by on the road many times but never to stop at his house. He needed to know what it was.

He glanced inside the police car—it seemed too official. Too cold. Arlen walked by the dining window—he could make out the uniformed shape. He was sitting at the table. Where food is meant to be eaten. And conversation. Nothing else. No bad news, no crimes, and no guns.

The air felt different to Arlen. Something had transpired and changed. Was it blood? Arlen felt his feet climb the steps, and his hand turned the knob. The door opened. Shoes removed. Arlen was no longer hungry. He wanted to forget what he had seen, and simply head straight ahead and down the stairs to his room—to avoid the scene to the left. Arlen's will pointed straight past the event but his duty prevailed, he turned left. His mom sat at the table with the uniformed man. Arlen saw on her face the look of transgressions that had passed by her—and left their mark.

She said nothing. Arlen sat to listen. The man in his role spoke, and said the unspeakable. Arlen looked at the cold steel of sidearm hidden with leather and rivets. Brandon his brother was dead, and by his own hand, it was horrible, and I am sorry. Nothing could be done. It was too late.

NINE DAYS OF SEPTEMBER

Lunch sat on the cupboard and stove. Unfinished. Arlen left the table and took the shortest route to the basement. He lay there on his bed in the far corner from the table. In the silence he craved the cop to leave. There hear it now—from the basement, the steps and the door open and close. The bearer of the news departed—his news lingered and stewed to leave its sting and horrid taste. The house smelled of tragedy—it was tight and hard to breathe. The whole world was tightening about this basement room. The ceiling squares held his mind in this dim of light. No artificial light burned. The rectangle window pointed a shaft of light relief. It touched the foot of his bed and lingered.

He thought of his schoolbooks, and where he left them. He had no need of these afternoon classes. Nor the next. It could never be the same. His whole life had changed in glint of color hue—people stood in a different shade. They had faded. He would ever more be in touch with a darker side of human. It was he, and he was able to see inside of people like no other—he could not have done it before these fateful days of September.

What honor is there in days of death? Is there wisdom in the house of the dying? Can it be true? Arlen lay upon the bed—a steel framed bed. He pondered this sentence—was there no pardon? What was the purpose in this dying?

Arlen was sensitive to others—to what they said and did. They had teased Arlen, of Arlen and Arlen's dad. Taken to heart, it festered inside of Arlen—he thought that yes, indeed, what the others said in childish rank and testing, was true and to be weighed.

Arlen had indeed weighed and found himself lacking. He weighed also the teasing of his dad—who had certain movements. He was the cadet commander; this marching and short hair was to be mocked. Arlen in his hormones had taken it to heart and wished his dad to be done with this and gone. The news of the cancer had come as a start. It was horrible, this sentence: could be three months, or two years. Who were these freaks who sentenced another human being to six months to live? Is that power? Compassion? Is it to motivate? To prod?

It was in this time of how-long-to-live that Arlen had come home for lunch. His dad was done with the workplace—he was, indeed, re-tired—nothing but breaths and pain-free existence. It went from fish-ing at the lake in retirement in a couple of years to, 'Can I get out of bed on my own?' Back to the hospital. Now. We radiate and toxify your cancer. Kill it to contain. Limit its spread. Sorry, you have no hope left. That is that. This is it. You have to live. You have to live. Each day to find joy, love and peace.

Who should tell the father that his son has died before him? Arlen did not think of such things. He fell into the basement and stayed there. He thought of where he had placed his books before lunch. He thought that they could stay there, he would not go back, and he could never go back.

In such cases the family gathers, and this is no exception. The days pass and it is discovered that no, Brandon did not commit suicide, it was an accident. How do you adjust to this turn of events after visiting the suicide realm? The siblings visited the man who was with Brandon when it occurred. He talked of discovering Brandon, the shotgun blast to the chest. The old gun caught on something as he pulled it out of the truck toward himself. The geese were eating the crops. They were harvesting. Brandon drove the grain truck and scared off the birds. The man went looking for Brandon when he did not come with the truck to get another load. He found him slumped against the truck.

Brandon stood mostly under his own strength. They called an am-bulance and drove to meet it. They drove fast. Brandon was lucid and assured the man that it was an accident. They met the ambulance and transferred the chest wound. The ambulance raced toward the hospital.

Years later it was discovered by the family that when the ambulance personnel laid the chest wound down, he proceeded to drown in his own blood. This was back when this was procedure. It was the way it was done. Can one accept that certain occurrences are meant to be? Is there, when is there, the point that you give in to a situation? You fight and plead and pray and wail. You keep the body going, breath-

ing, pounding the chest. Do others have to pull you away, only after
the body is cold?

Arlen lay in bed in a numb place. He decided, by his subconscious
and reality, that it was all too much for him. Too surreal—it had passed
into the imperceptible: how could one digest this material about one's
family? Arlen burrowed inward toward the hole where nothing sat,
and built his castle in the basement—he dug a moat first to keep the
others at bay. This was to act that all was all right—he was fine and
working it through. This was the way it was. The days passed in construction. Arlen was working on the castle walls when people dropped
off flowers and casseroles and goodies. It was important to eat well
while working construction. You had to stay strong.

The evening of viewing came and found the family at the Funeral
Home. It was a special place—Arlen had never stepped a foot near the
entrance before. This was his night to enter the quiet repose of mourn.
The family trudged along toward the room where Brandon lay in casket. It is funny that when you enter, the casket looks peaceful and in a
way wonderful—a cozy, protective cocoon. At first, you cannot make
out the person inside, if it's an open situation, as this night was. The
pew benches were sat upon. It was of course all a blur.

The entourage passed by the gaping coffin. Arlen waited till the end
and felt duty call him to his feet. Everyone was doing it; he felt like he
should, it was important for some reason. Arlen rose to his feet.

CLIMB ROCK

"You sure about this, Tim?" Arlen looked at him.

"It's a blast man, come on." Tim grabbed the rock and headed up. His shoes stuck to the rock like glue. Tim looked back down at Arlen and gave him one of those huge smiles. It gave Arlen confidence.

Arlen thought back to the other night and smiled. Tim had placed a tall chef's hat on his head and lit it on fire. Arlen took pictures. The flames rollicked a foot high. Tim smiled—his eyes shone to stardom. The pictures will be great. With Tim you had a sense that everything was to be grand—attitude prevailed.

Arlen arced his back and stretched his legs. The rock face felt cold to the touch. There were plenty of good hand and foot holds. This was fun and easy. Arlen got into it, it felt great. Hand over hand, foot over foot—it was great. He looked down from twenty feet and smiled.

Arlen headed up further. He heard Tim hoot with joy. Time was cruising. The angle was easy to climb. Arlen carried on. He looked down from fifty feet—it looked different from here. His hands sweated. He kept going. From a hundred feet he could look to his side and back a bit to the castle of tourism. He was well above the trees—it felt wonderful to be free of the earth. A hundred and twenty feet up. No ropes. It did not even cross his mind now. He was free. He felt fatigue in his limbs and appendages. He carried on and up.

He was in a rhythm now, in the groove, with no plan of how far to go. The rock made his fingers the same temperature—a cool numb. His heart pumped warm blood. Arlen sensed the urge to look up. He looked up in time to see a human head sized rock catapulting straight to his own forehead. He flattened to the face, it was hard to not lose grip. The rock breezed by his shoulder blades. It hit the face below him and thudded onto the forest floor.

Arlen shook now. Sweat poured. Where did the shake originate? It was in his legs and arms. His body was still; you could feel the blood rush his core to flight. He had to get out of this. He could not fall—that would be it. Get it together. The shake torqued his elbows and knees. The wrists and ankles had to counter and stay hold.

Which way? Up. Down. Sideways. Arlen! Get it together. Find a new hold. Move somewhere or you will perish. Grab on to something. Where are the holds now? Shake and sweat. A cool breeze. The view of Arlen had erased all about him except this five-foot radius of rock. It was his moment of challenge. He had to get it together.

Arlen looked up and down and beside himself, he shook. *Get it together.* You have to. He breathed and settled his limbs. His core pumped to escape. There to the right. Try it, a new hold, to the right, you can do it. Let go. Reach over and take a new hold. Let go Arlen. The hardest thing he had ever done. To let go of a sure hold, and shaken. To reach over to a new hold. His body ached in acid lactic move. Reach Arlen.

He reached and reached and broke the hold. He did it. Up and down he meandered to the right. He could not go straight down. He was too shaken. He had to go to the right. There, the band of trees. It is sanctuary. Meander-focus your shake and sweat your muscles to respite. There you did it Arlen. The trees feel good. An escape chute of branches banded to the ground in the gap. Feel the bark. Trust the roots to hold you. Rest those appendages. Good job Arlen. Remember the trees.

MAGIC MUSHROOMS

Arlen popped the mushrooms and hopped on his mountain bike. The morning was cool and fresh. Snow still lay heavy on the mountain crags. This was a solo journey. Arlen pedaled the flat by the soccer field and tennis court. He coasted the avenue and gained momentum toward the hospital and bridge. He braked to make the corner and crossed the bridge into town. The day was still getting busier as he headed direct down the main drag.

He wanted to go somewhere new. He thought of the airport, he had not been past it. That was where to go. He headed beside the school and carried on. The psilocybine brewed in his stomach—it ate at him. Arlen grimaced and coasted for a minute. At the end of the strip, by the last hotels, he felt a change. It was slight but hinted of more to come. A psychotropic stirring. It was visual—it twisted him to view things aloof yet enhanced.

He slid into less awareness of his legs pedaling and more into the scenery and his internal. Arlen blew by the airport and the cadet camp on his right. The waterfall was rocking up to the left. He carried on. The hallucinogenic lifted up on his skull—it expanded to take in all around him. He climbed onto a shoulder of Cascade Mountain. It sucked him onto the grassy hills. He dismounted in amongst the ruins of a mining scene.

The drug hit him in full waves. It washed over him and left him a different person. He turned around and it washed that way too. He looked across the vista at distant Banff. It felt great to be off the beaten path. Not a soul was in sight. He didn't even hear the Trans Canada highway.

His water bottle sat half empty—he was losing touch with his bodily needs and ways. The sun shone deep into his head and warmed it— this was nice, a perfection. Nothing else in the world existed. Only this bike, this drugged mind and this mountainside. He wondered of the reality of this mining place. He did not know of its existence before, why had he not seen or heard of it? He would have to return.

The forest called to him. He heeded the beckon and entered the forest on a trail. He headed away from Banff, to the north around Cascade Mountain.

The trees swallow this stoned young man. The evergreen-needled hands brush him and wave him on. Through the trees, the hill drops sharply to his right. The mountain towers above his left ear. He stops and listens, nature booms—the effects weigh upon him. It is tight; a squirrel looms large in chatter. The scene looks new in this light of poison that courses through his veins. He is fully stone.

He looks at the trail at his feet—it is down to a mere deer path now. He looks at his feet—no hooves hammer the trail. He wears boots—light hikers. He pedals on. The forest closes in on him; he dismounts and pushes the bike.

He hears the stream—it babbles its presence. He pushes the bike midstream, ankle deep. He reaches down to the water, it is foreign, this water that touches nerve endings—somewhere Arlen senses relief from an unknown plague. He cups water and anoints his neck and shoulders. They drop in soothing. He feels his head, it is sweat—has he run this way? For how long? Where was he headed?

The nature drug was full upon him now.

He emptied the water bottle into the stream and filled it—the air bubbles exchanged his attention. He poured it over his head and shoulders. He filled it again and set it in the bike carrier. His Ray Ban sunglasses spot liquid. He touched his wet lips with his tongue. It moistened his mouth. He craved booze. He couldn't drink water. He grabbed the handlebars and pushed onto dry trail. His boots squished with the excess water and left a trail. Soon the trees closed in further. Branches tore at his calf flesh and thighs. His arms tore.

The first cobwebs that hit his face had been all right. But now their intensity grew. They seemed stickier after the water wash. It was near impossible to block with a stick or his one arm and push with just one. He was no longer capable of rational applicable thought. He pushed on and the webs slammed wrap onto his eyes and ears. They stuck in his hair. They moved him to move faster—it was upon him now, this bad trip claimed him and these hours upon the mountainside. It roared its breath upon his emotion.

He tensed and felt a fear that was more urgent and removed from his reality. It was primal and base in its core—it entwined and spun him deeper. He was mere reaction now.

The trees closed further. He had to twist the handlebars past the trees. He might as well be carrying this bike now. The trees ripped slight trails in his skin, red slashes straight and narrow remained. Blood and non-blood raised grooves.

The cobwebs stuck constant now. He was always wiping them clear of his face—he could not separate from the whole web. Another stream—shin deep this time. He pushed on; it was barely a trail, a line in the moss and rock. He lifted the bike over the fallen timbers.

Arlen turned the handlebars sideways and negotiated the narrow that much easier. He pushed the bike as a constant. The minutes passed into the hundreds—the cobwebs kept track. It was a constant wiping to be free of them—they whipped him into a froth of sweat and panic. It raged within him now this bad trip. Feel it clutch at you with sharp but soft webs that cling. The cold snow water rushed the six crossings thus far—they grabbed at his bones. The whips of sticks cracked upon his flesh.

He was oblivious to a certain level of this, yet on a different plane he took even more in upon himself. It was a sickened rage that consumed him now. He had to be free of this bush, this steady web that stuck to his head and shoulders. He wore a tank top and shorts and sunglasses—that was it. He still drank no water. The bottle sat jostling and warming in the early summer's day.

Arlen jogged and pushed and wiped the webs. He especially hated it when he could feel the spider on his skin. The spider knew its prey was too large and retreated—the human flicked it clear to lay another trap. The webs and the streams and the trees passed. Arlen was in a space that had no exit in his condition. He bad tripped it onward.

His ankles angled down to the right. He was not aware of this. The bike was always on his left—it was easier to push it this way, at a higher spot than himself. How far did he have to go to extricate himself from this web bush clutch? He had no end in sight. The drug wore through and onward. It pulled him in an empty hull shell.

It came upon him suddenly. Past exhaustion with the webs, he arrived at another stream. Another runoff from the snowy peak above him.

"This stream goes somewhere."

It could have been a voice. His voice. A whisper. A scream. A thought. His first rational thought. It stopped him in his tracks. He focused his eyes on the spider web that would have draped his face if he had taken another step. Arlen looked at the spider's face and turned down hill to follow the stream.

"It must go somewhere."

His voice sounded odd. He said it again and again.

"It must go somewhere."

He stumbled down and through the trees. It was steep in places and it was all he could do to stay upright. He straightened the handlebars and used the brakes to anchor it. The brakes squealed. Arlen ducked to miss a web.

It was a change, this following the stream down its course. It was a struggle to negotiate the bike through and down. The slope lessened and the going became easier. The stream leveled off and hit steel—a culvert, a road. Arlen reacted—this was a good thing. He mounted the road, the gravel felt slippery and solid. His knee locked. It was flat and there was room for the bike too. Arlen looked over at the river that received this stream and every stream he had crossed. It danced in the sunlight. Arlen was still in the shade of the mountain above him.

"Follow it out."

Arlen had no idea how far he had gone, or how long it would take to get home. He felt good about the road and the direction that the river flowed. The road.

He mounted the bike seat and pedaled—it was smooth and easy. The decline pulled at him, he geared up and let gravity claim him. The

speed thrilled, and he just sat there. The wind drove his body temperature down. His sweat dried and caked salt upon his forehead.

The first patch of sunshine felt glorious. By then he was almost too
cool and the solar heat soothed his soul. This road was mostly downhill momentum. He reached down and took a drink of water. The desert that was within, blossomed an oasis of moisture.

He followed the road to pavement and town and home. By the time
he hit the Banff bridge he was mostly back to his human form. The hill
climb back to the upper annex was a chore and he dug deep into re-
serves he did not know he had.

He pushed the bike again into the building. He knocked at his door;
his roommate opened it and checked Arlen up and down. Arlen was
dirty and scraped and dried blood. He smelled.
"What happened to you?"

THE CHANGELING

Arlen communed chemicals with variations of the same tribe, or by himself. The exceptions were with certain individuals that liked to talk and get high. They would ingest the chemical twist enhancement and visit many topics.

It was hash that flavored this meeting. Arlen faced his friend and shared the pipe. It was small talk that grew into lofty ideals and paradigm shifts. The clutch slipped in one of these shifts and threw Arlen into a dilemma. The hash was laced with unknown.

Arlen turned into fear and respect. He watched his friend melt away and transform into the fire spewing Satan. There were no tails or pitchforks. There was the undeniable fact that this creature existed in fire. Arlen did not wonder why this creature sat across from him in a chair. Arlen could not look at the face. He rode out the laced stone on his ass looking at Satan's feet. They were cast for thermal and the odd aspect was the inclusion of ingrown toenails. All the toes had been modified in surgery; the small ovals and circles of imbedded nails were inset. The valley walls of flesh were a molten metal of pink. Arlen could tell that this valley flesh was the weak point. He could stamp upon the flesh with his feet and cause great suffering. Arlen respected the wrath and meditated on the toes till he could get out of the chair and leave the room. There was no sense of time elapsed—Arlen knew that he could not look upon the face or turn his back. He could not move till freed from this rut of chemical splash.

ELK PARTY

Busses shipped the staff out onto the end of the golf course—past the last fairways and bunkers. It was the end of summer party—the wrap up; you made it through the busy season, atta girl, atta boy. Party hardy.

Arlen drank around the fire having a good time. He had not sat in front of a fire for a long time—it danced against the black tree backdrop. He had taken the mushrooms nearly an hour before. It was time, he could feel it. He was hoping for a good trip, like the first few times. He had paid his dues and it was time to receive some interest. It was overdue. He had not taken them since the bush bike and web trip. He thought of his first good trip on mushrooms—the moon dripped in fullness, he could reach out and touch it, he could taste and feel it. He needed a good trip.

He drank two beer in the wait for the good vibe of shrooms. It didn't arrive. He slipped away from the fire to the outskirts of the party. He placed his beer on the ground and slipped into the trees.

The darkness claimed him—he had to stop to adjust his eyes. It was tough to slow down—he needed to make some space from the people behind him. He felt the trees and made his distance from the party.

He walked in nature—the stars were bright. He heard a bull elk call in the night. It was powerful and eerie. This night was different—he slipped to the ground as he walked and rose up on all fours as a hoofed elk. He moved on, more wary of the humans that took his wildness away. He had to stay away and keep to the grass and forest. The roads were to be avoided. The time in the dark passed into full elk fruition. Arlen rubbed his head up against a tree—he could feel his antlers. This golf course of grazing elk claimed him. Headlights in the distance froze him; stay still or they will spot you. Stay away from the road. Pass through the trees. Through the Spray River, the water cold to your groin. To your room hide away to hash—turn it to black. Turn it from this wild animation to human sleep. Sleep Arlen.

THE INK POTS

Arlen and his different roommate Brian decided the night before their day off to bike to Johnston Canyon early in the morning. They readied their bikes and drug supply. It was a pavement highway ride to the base of the canyon. They rode along the Trans Canada—it was flat and easy going. The turn off onto 1A was a welcome change—the traffic lessened. The dozen miles passed by easily. The road turned more and changed elevation.

Elk on the side of the road looked at them. Arlen thought of the animals in the park—they belonged to a union and came out to work their shifts to entertain the tourists. They each had a quota of pictures that they had to pose for. They were put into rotation—they would pose up front for photos. The background posting was a nice change from the reacting tourists up front. It was the down time seniority that they worked for and were rewarded with; they could roam the backspaces free of people.

Arlen and Brian pulled off the road at the Canyon. It was a climb ahead of them. They took turns in the wooden outhouse. The other watched the bikes. You could see the trees when you stood up inside the outhouse. Arlen took his share of the cocaine first. He snorted it in three lines. His vision jumped to the upper reaches to see the stimulated trees. He was nowhere near the floor of this piss-laden receptacle. The outhouse door swung open. It was Brian's turn to mount up. They passed the baton of paraphernalia and supply.

Arlen floated past Brian. He was good to go. He felt like he could take on the world. He was power and energy. He was right. He could fly. He could pedal straight up the mountain. He waited for Brian.
"What's taking you so long in there?"
"I have to take a shit."
"Can I head up without you?" Arlen asked.
"Can't you wait a few minutes?"
"No." Arlen tore at the ground with his boot.
"I'll catch up to you."
"It's the stuff man, I'll wait for you in a bit."
"Go hard."

Arlen leaned Brian's bike against the wall and grabbed his own bike. He was huge in energy. He felt like he would explode—with a massive smile. Time to move. He had been building in deed potential. His sense of place moved and gained momentum.

His feet hit the pedals and cranked. He was through the parking lot and up the trail in a flash. He weaved between the people. They blurred by.

"Excuse me."

They would move.

"Thank you."

Over and over again. They would have to move or he would hit them. He was polite. The trail followed the groove that held the river's intensity in spring. It had cut canyon. Arlen geared down to climb. Trail turned to walkway—attached to the canyon side. It was a smooth way up but narrow. Arlen pushed his way through.

"Hey." Brian caught up to Arlen.

Arlen turned. "You were quick."

"Like a bunny."

"This ramp is cool."

"Narrow."

"Nobody's really pissed off yet." Arlen looked ahead.

"That's good."

"Weave them through."

The gobs of tourists thinned out as they climbed. In granny first gear they approached the falls. The noise and moisture vapor soothed their hot flesh. This water still cut canyon through rock. They dismounted and walked to the cave lookout. They smiled at the moisture and rage of nature.

They resumed the drudge of climb—it became the way of the revolution, souls of feet spinning to triumph against gravity. They stopped and snorted more. This catapulted them through the tourist heaviness and onto the fire road section. They turned right and flew up to the valley plateau. It was Eden with the mountain blue sky against the ridges of rock. The river babbled through this valley. But it was the inkpots that clutched at the eyes and soul. How does the neon blue water sit in such perfect circles of feminine lined pools?

Arlen and Brian rode around the inkpots and collapsed on the earth. They drank water and smoked marijuana. Their bodies drooped onto the ground. They smiled and looked at the sky and summit ridges. They laughed of endorphins and chemicals. The ground dirtied their clothes. Munchies claimed them to dig in packs for grazing and gorging. They had pedaled fifteen miles and two thousand feet.

They rested and nodded off to the restful space. It was high summer and this was a tall valley of content. The hours passed and they mellowed to the day's return.

They left the grassy fertile inkpots for the dry trail. They followed the fire road that headed steeply down the mountainside. It would claim them quicker than the ramp tourist trail they had climbed.

The view opened to them—it tore at their hearts. They offered the bikes up to the heavens. Speed grabbed them to concentrate on the surface of gravel and rock. They launched off of rocks and ledges. They clutched at the brakes to settle the pace from suicide. The road curved and ate up descent. The trees whizzed by on both sides. Bear scat challenged the road's passage.

Minutes transpired to steal this descent. Time warped and stole the eternal ethereal from them. Flat road required their pedal. Pavement found them. They passed by the outhouse that snowed them up.

They focused on the work of getting home. It seemed so mellow after the sights and feelings of the day. This place was such beauty—it spoke to an inner place within them. It spoke through the drugs that assisted them and held them down. It raced and soothed and meditated upon their minds.

On the flats a third of the way home, Arlen felt his left knee twinge in pain. He stopped and rubbed it and stood for a while. He stretched and pained.

"Have to go slower." He mounted and pedaled to find a pace of pain-reduced comfort. The damage was done in the past; the pain was blocked and just now arrived.

The miles passed into highway and town and home. It was difficult

to make the knee comfortable. They smoked hash. They sat there for
the body to rest. A cold beer was heaven to last.

KICKED OUT

Arlen headed back to his room after breakfast shift. He was tired and wanted to sleep. It had been a busy morning. He was ready for the little hash pipe. He thought of where it sat in his room. He was proud of the imported drug box that he had purchased in a shop downtown. He headed toward the pipe in the box.

He climbed the steps and walked down the gray hall. He opened the door and discovered Tim was packing.
"They're booting us out for a month."
"Who?"
"Room search, burned hotel butter knives, ski torch, not happy."
"Were you here?"
"They woke me up."
"What did you say?"
"What could I say, not happy?"
Arlen read the notice of eviction, effective immediately. He made a game plan.
"What are you going to do Tim?"
"No money, have my tent, I'll be all right." He laughed that contagious laugh and grinned.
Arlen felt better to hear this. The plan took form.

Arlen gave his key back to security and felt true remorse. He stored his stuff at a friend's place and took only his bike to find a place to stay. He headed to the hostel. A month would be fine. He was thankful that he was making good tips, and he had just been paid. It was in the residential area off of the strip. Arlen had no time to nap that afternoon. He was back to work in bow tie and tartan vest and locked his bike in the trees.

The word spread. The next night, his headwaiter said, "I thought your eyes were red from swimming."
Arlen smiled.
The days passed. Arlen ran into Tim after work and they took a trip to Tim's abode. Down the hill and through the golf course. Cut across fairway number one and into the trees. What a spot. No one was near by. Above the little green tent Mount Rundle rose to its heights.

They sat in the tent and smoked hash in a modified two liter plastic soda-pop bottle. You sucked the smoke from the usual drinking spot. A chamber of pipe was built in toward the base. Arlen thought that this was falling down living. He wondered where he himself was heading and where he had been.

CLEANING THE NIGHT

Arlen and Tim had worked together the last winter. They were night cleaners. The golf season had ended and there was no work to be carried on. Arlen had transferred into the hotel for the cozy winter. He could stay inside for the whole season and not come above ground or out of doors.

They had cleaned the kitchens at night. They were the only ones around. It was spooky and a delight. The stainless steel kitchens gleamed. With not a soul around the main kitchen looked like a science fiction scene. The dining rooms sat spooky—you could imagine creatures hiding under every tablecloth.

It was on night two that the ghost stories came out on break to play.
"Have you seen the bride on fire?"
"She caught fire on the steps and died on her wedding night."
"They closed the steps off in her honor."
Arlen headed down to assist the boss in the small kitchen. He got confused in finding it and ended up in the back of the dining room. He entered and walked between the tables. He could feel the slimy hands grab his ankles.

There was a view of darkness out the windows to his left. The tables were set to provide opulent French dining. Arlen saw the kitchen corner, or so it promised. He walked on but looked to the right. A wide marble stairway arced gracefully into the ceiling. It had indeed been closed off. It spooked him that no one was anywhere to be seen. He could picture the lovely bride, in white and flames engulfed her. Her screams curdled his blood.

Arlen hurried to the kitchen corner. He could see the rectangular portal from linen and candles and silverware to stainless steel and heat. The entrance was around to the right. Arlen entered. Good. Mel was scrubbing the grill. Company to warm the chill that crept up his back.
"Mel, what do you want me to do?"
"Wipe the surfaces, make em shine."

"Still warm in here."

"Cozy." Mel rowed the brick foam. Brick forward and back to scrape the grill free of food matter. He used his whole body. Arlen admired the athleticism involved with Mel's level of cleaning.

They finished and stood back to admire the gleam. Even at three a.m. the artificial lights made the kitchen surfaces shine.

"I'll show you a new way back up."

They walked out the front entrance of the dining room and glanced at the lobby on the left. One Doorman and one Front Desk Person stood ready; their heads were down reading something. Oblivious to the world that moved about them—it wasn't from the lobby doors.

A sound to the right. Mel and Arlen looked at the old elevator doors open. Nobody stepped out. The car called to them. Arlen shook the shiver from his shoulder.

They walked through the medieval hall. The pale light cast its hue on the cool furnishings. The huge fireplace sat waiting. They turned and walked up the spiral staircase. Mel pointed out the fossils in the marble. The torch style lights carried them up and into the bar area of the dining room. The wood was rich and deep on the bar.

They entered the red, black and white dining splendor. Eight tables in the center were set with tablecloths—it was the off-season. It was only open for special functions through the winter. Wall lighting added to the spook. It was a grand empty room. Shadows promised surprises.

Mel looked at Arlen. "You like it?"

"Yeah."

"Let's get back to work." Mel walked toward the kitchen door and swung it open. There was a fifteen-foot long room of storage. He swung the next door open. The kitchen glared in its brightness. Look straight ahead and you can see the entrance to the next dining room, it seems like a football field away.

Mel turns right and around the corner is Tim cleaning in the pastry section.

"Tim, show Arlen what to do here—help him out, Arlen."

"All right boss."

Mel disappeared in the sea of stainless steel.

"Hungry?" Tim asked.

"Sure." Arlen smiled.

Tim headed to one of the pastry freezers and popped the door open. The fog shrouded them in mystery. It billowed and cooled their faces. It cleared to good visibility. Tim reached in and plucked a fruit filled custard tart and smiled at Arlen. Arlen grabbed the same.

"I like to dip mine." Tim headed to the decorating section.

Arlen followed and watched. Up on the back shelf sat a square metal box. Tim lifted the lid and dipped his tart in the molten chocolate. He raised it triumphant—Arlen rejoiced and thought of 'Willy Wonka and the Chocolate Factory.' Tim took a bite. Arlen reached and dipped his own. The chocolate cooled quickly with the hardened frozen tart. He raised it—the chocolate contrasted beautifully against the strawberry and kiwi colors. Arlen chomped it in half and moaned; it was good, very good.

After work, Tim invited Arlen over to his room for a toke. It was Arlen's first hash. It hit him hard. It was the missing link; it relaxed his muscles and mind. Arlen enquired as to where to get some. He was told the room number and first name. That was his plan when he woke up.

Arlen discovered the fresh buns and pads of butter. He would rip the bun open and place two butter pads and close it up. The crumbs would threaten to fly onto the red squared kitchen floor. Arlen felt like he was doing something wrong when he ate the hotel food.

Scrubbing and wiping the kitchen passed the fall into winter to arrive. Arlen's eyes watched the dining rooms. They looked great— he could get into that, and more money. There were women to work with—they looked great in the tartan and black skirts.

RED COLLAR

Money and women prompted Arlen to appeal and present himself to the powers that be. He was directed to the uniform cache room. It was on the way to the residence, the upper annex. He signed the form and took over his first uniform. The white smock with red collar announced the busboy.

He had to turn his clock around. He had to start at six thirty in the morning. That was awful. He was only off one night. He was still awake at three a.m.. In the cafeteria, he trayed his food and entered the institutional dining room. Again he had the uniform clique experience.

The Busboy dressed table was to the left—there were a dozen of them sitting with the plain black smocked Busgirls. The black and white trimmed dresses did not flatter. Arlen looked to the right at the dwindled barebones golf course staff. It had been a while, Arlen headed to his old table. He was not quite ready to dive into the mix of new workmates.

"Long time Ar."
"Hey guys, how's it going?"
"Got yourself a warm job."
"First day, I was night cleaning."
"We thought you had moved on."
"Still here."
"Bussing is better money than cleaning."
"Hope so, what do you do in winter?"
"Snow removal and outdoor odds and ends."
"Lots of snow."
"Lots this year, you coming back in the summer Ar?"
"I don't know."
"Bet you won't with all those girls."
Arlen smiled.

Arlen headed upstairs to his warm job. He walked through the kitchen and into the dining room. It was fully lit with black windows. It was festive with people in it. The preparations had begun for breakfast. Arlen reported to the head waitress—Tamara. She smiled—Arlen smiled. She paired him with a bus girl to learn the ropes.

Amy was cute and knew her job—she was all business in carrying out her duties. She was in the midst of preparing the liquids for the section. Arlen watched her fold a small white tablecloth into a plastic bus pan. She then went to the ice machine and deposited ice on the bottom. They filled six pitchers with juice and placed them in the ice pan on the side stand. They had the section closest to the kitchen. As they walked around, Amy pointed out locations of equipment and food and drink. She showed him the automatic toaster by the backspace window—the air was chilled and the hearth of the toaster felt nice. The sunrise waited behind the mountain; it tarried and slept in—it felt like everyone should still be cozy in bed.

They filled pitchers with ice and water and filled all the glasses in the section. Arlen struggled to find the proper grasp on everything—it felt new and different—the edges were hard and his flesh was putty. These dining props would later become extensions of Arlen. They performed a table check for the proper setting and accessories. They poured coffee from the reservoir by the kitchen into carafes. The chefs stood ready in the exposed kitchen.

The cooks stocked the buffet table. Bus persons attended to the fruit and pastries. The doors opened to the guests. Arlen was nervous. He poured his first glass of juice and coffee. He cleared dishes and reset tables. He was nice to the guests. Orange juice and coffee were the usual requests. They reset the tables for lunch. The morning rushed by till ten o'clock. He received his cut of the tips from the morning section. He smiled; he liked the freedom that money provided. He also liked working with women. This was a good career move.

He received his shiny name tag—he was proud of it. He looked at himself in the mirror. He was part of a presentable front lines team.

He was off work till five thirty, a split shift day. He went home and slept a needed nap—he lived two days in every one for most of the days thereafter. It became routine—this breakfast and dinner, and Sunday brunch.

He loved working Sunday Brunch. It was exciting to set up the food extravaganza—the ice sculptures looked great. The champagne and orange juice spoke of celebration. The view out the windows of the hall made him feel special inside, this was a unique place and he was part of it.

The bus people kept the tables stocked with food. The huge round receptacle that held the eggs benedict was the crown. Word spread when it was time to replenish this delight. The bus person would receive the laden tray of hot, fresh egg bennies in the kitchen and would head the back way past the service elevators. Two or three receivers would intercept and liberate a tasty delight each. They would then rearrange the remainders to have no space.

Hundreds of merry Sunday revelers partook of food and drink. It was a destination event; people would drive from Calgary to enjoy. Tables would linger and drink and celebrate life. It was well into afternoon by tear down time.

PROMOTION

The weeks passed and Arlen found himself trading his bus shirt for a green tartan vest and black bowtie. White shirts and another pair of black pants found his wardrobe. Between laundry days, he washed his three pairs of socks in his room sink and let them hang dry. He had money for more socks but other things called his name. Like drugs.

He embraced pot and hash as a friend. It was a shelter, an impediment. He worked with great wonderful women. He would flirt and enjoy their company but he could not act upon it. They liked him but he could not break through to go out with any. He reinforced blocks into walls with the drugs.

Arlen opened his first bottle of wine for a customer in the alcove of the dining room. He shook inside. The couple sat gracious and accepting. It was a delightful experience. Arlen shone in grace and servitude. He had been watching while he was bussing. And he knew who took home more money.

The first night went great—only some confusion with the billing. He just had a few tables at a time. At the end of the night, he gave his tip share to the bar and bus persons and the remainder in his pocket made him smile. This was a good gig—cash daily, enough to up the lifestyle.

On the way to his room, he knocked at his dealer's door. The door cracked and a smile gaped in recognition at the steady customer. Arlen purchased two grams of pot at a reduced price. Life was good. He toked up and received the munchies growl of incessancy. He wandered down to the fast food staff joint and ordered his first chicken sandwich with extra mayonnaise. It was loaded with taste that touched his sex. He had a hard time to not moan. He felt self-conscious, darted his eyes and dived into the juices deeper. This was pleasure.

TRINITY

It was his substitution for lack of the opposite sex. Drug, food and pleasing himself were the trinity that protected him sub-consciously from the labia pleasure. Sex and hedonism raved all around him. It was a celebration better than college—no studying. Put your time in at work and the rest of your twenty-four was yours. Have at it. Do as you please as long as you are hurting no one. Live life fully, take huge bites and choke it down.

"Two to the zoo." The cabbie radioed in. You had crawled in from the cold. You were drunk like a skier carving down Banff Avenue feeling the verve of booze. Your friend and you had apexed with shooters and barely made it out of the nightclub. You hailed a cab and blubbered, "Upper annex."

You slid up the hill to the castle in amongst the trees. The cabbie exchanged the funds for transport. You fell out and slithered to the door and up the dingy stairs. The steps were worn with thousands of passages such as this. Round and round, hold on to the rail. You decide, your addiction decides to top the inebriation with a hoot or two. The mix claims you to another place as your brain cells pop and skitter.

Arlen wakes to a dark amnesiac slate. Curiosity prospers him to figure out the night's events. There are gaps in the linear close. Blackness dwells over and above him. It is a safe predictable place, nothing changes; nothing promised but nothing and nothing gained. Black is the springboard from which nothing leaps.

Arlen starts his day off with a joint. The marijuana crackles and pops dry sweet smoke. That black place eases as he lies back on his bed and transports to intricate worship of the ceiling. Arlen wills himself to not drink as much—he can pursue the drugs in depth and not have the physical sickness. They only leave the dull head.

LYSERGIC BALL

"Is this your first time Arlen?"

"Yep."

"California Sunshine, here's your hit, it'll take an hour to take effect and will increase like five hours before you come down."

"That's a long time."

"Enjoy."

Arlen opened his lips to the tab. He wondered how something so small could have effect. It entered his system and brewed. He checked how he looked in the mirror—he was in plainclothes and looking good. He walked out the bottom of the annex underground and into the bowels of the hotel. He surfaced in the carpet close to the lobby. He climbed the carpeted stairs and passed by the lounge on his right. His feet hit the marble floor. He entered the hall and immediately saw fellow employees. It was strange to see so many in one place. This was the Christmas Party with close to a thousand staff imbibing drink and food.

Arlen felt thirsty and headed to the rum and eggnog. It tasted fine. He sipped and stood and chatted at the periphery. The meal was to be held in forty-five minutes. The eggnog reception was filling up. It was a special place of decor and warm extravagance—the fanciest party that Arlen had attended. He stood and drank his second glass and nogged to a different place—he was changing with this hit of acid growing in his bloody mind. He was slipping with the marionette strings—they grew from his back shoulders, head and arms. Arlen concentrated on the drink and to blend in. It was becoming increasingly difficult to carry on a conversation.

The hall filled to the brim. It was nearing time of the ballroom. The festive lights drew Arlen in to gaze. Slam thud, the sick sound of human body hitting the marble floor—it jumped above and beyond every milling crowd sound. It had been announced by the glass smash. Arlen missed the body fall but he now saw the scrum of help. What had happened? The clean up crew wiped the milk from the floor.

The man eventually rose and walked from the party. He left rumors that circulated the room.

"Bad mushrooms."

It whispered from person to person. You could tell who had taken them. The panic spread amongst the devoted following—it clutched at them to ponder prostrate down upon the stone.

The message had hardly finished when the next began its course. "Bad acid."

Arlen could not avoid this one. It hit him hard and he needed no encouragement, he was transforming into somewhere and someone that he did not know—he was celled in, handcuffed to the experience now. Have to ride it out. He pushed out the wave of fear and discontent. He concentrated on his glass—it was half full. He could tell its fullness but he was losing touch with who was holding it in mid air. This was bordering on something he had to react to and not observe in this astronaut state. He willed himself to polish the liquid and dispose of the glass in a non-breakable fashion. It was like a space walk. He performed it without flaw and climbed back into stand and gaze.

The puppet strings were growing taut and pulled at his head. The ballroom was ready for the throng. Arlen waited for the majority to pass through and he joined the tail end. The portal grabbed at his consciousness. He could feel the drug roar and sensed there would be bite to follow. It was barely an hour and this was huge.

He entered the ballroom in all its finery. He looked up at the oblong ceiling inset. The white and gold shone. The hardwood gleamed. The tables sat gorgeous. Arlen forced himself to find a seat and sit. It was beyond sitting in the wrong movie theatre—a horror flick audio played over the Disney video.

The wine bottles drew his attention, that and the settings. It was done right. But he knew vaguely the people that were around his setting—he could affect them. The lighting was peach yellow. This was wrong and he was wrong and this drug was wrong. Arlen. What are you going to do?

Arlen calculated the time. This was one hour and a bit. By hour five he would peak. Arlen made a director's decision and yanked his own strings. No food would enter this puppet gullet. It was time to leave this situation before it became something that others told you about.

He excused himself with no explanation. The strings pulled him up to walking height. His feet turned and articulated steps beneath him. Arlen became aware of the float—he was on a plain of slide parallel to the floor. The strings carried him through the hanging art—his head swiveled to see the frames. He was the ant in the closet. He was carried down stairs through the scarred corridors and corners to his domicile. The door allowed him sanctuary of cell and closed him in.

Arlen ripped his clothes off and lay prostrate upon the bed. His heart pounded and surged, the sweat flowed. The ride up the five hour jet trajectory was well underway. Seatbelt signs were nowhere to be seen. It was cleared now for take off. This verge of clearness spoke to him and he turned the radio on to sweep along on discourses and eddies of tangent. The intensity tightened beyond these five senses of experience. The hours blurred and rocketed him on.

In an instant, gravity claimed him to the bed. He was down and all right. He felt great—it was relief to be sullen in charge of ride. It was peace that transposed him now. His body wash cooled. He was drawn to the window. It was snowing large flakes. He needed to be out in the cotton.

He dressed and exited the panic stage and entered the bliss of mild snow falling on his brow. Each flake pricked and melt-shriveled its sharp edges to flow a bead of water. They hovered and plucked at his dry skin. The flakes tickled and made his nervous system tingle. He felt his feet on the ground. The snow scrunched underfoot. The streets echoed: devoid of automobiles. Arlen gloried in the winter land—he walked to the bridge and back.

The castle looked otherworldly through the trees. It made him feel warm and excited to find good things inside. This was adventure. This stone building held what he needed now. He felt like drinking and dancing. He shed his outerwear in his room and headed through the tunnels with purpose. He was reborn; he had survived. The best part of this acid trip was merely getting through it. The relief was stark, and swelled with gratitude.

He jogged to the party; it had dwindled to a small room. It was easy to find from the noise. The ballroom had closed. The end of the dining room was partitioned and held the booze field of party. The hard corers remained at this late hour. It was an aquarium, Arlen swam through alcohol like a fish and stood strong and true with gills. It too became a blur but a positive one painted against the naked intensity of the trip.

Somehow he ended in bed and entered a sleep of sorts. Few hours passed and he was awake to reality. He was alert and could feel the chemistry experiment gone awry in his cranium. It was soup and slurry. But he felt good, odd, he felt no physical illness from the excesses of booze.

DEALER

"Do you wanna try it?"

"Is it good?" Arlen asked.

"Best you've ever had." The importer knew that it was better than anything sold in these parts.

"I'll try it." Arlen said.

"And think about it?"

"And think about it."

The importer was in the early stages of recruiting himself a cocaine dealer. He liked Arlen for some reason and thought he had the stuff, a little dangerous, and a head for the stuff—he could be a disposable one, if need be.

The razor blade chinked rock to powder on the mirror. Arlen pondered the blade and mirror. He was still a little stoned from marijuana. He had smoked some cocaine and had snorted a few times—he liked the feeling. But these lines were different. It was huge and in your face with ego—it stretched and tore to new acclaim. Wonderful. He exploded open to possibility. He felt like he could do anything, and had to do it now.

The importer worked the pleasure and binge buttons.

"Is it good?"

"Best I ever had."

"More where that came from."

Arlen thought and enjoyed the pleasures of this trafficking pursuit. He pondered the outcomes. It felt too good. Too pleasurable—he still needed to be hard on himself, for what he did. This was the wrong vocation—he had crossed his limit of danger. He was a waiter; he served food and drink.

"I don't think I'm your guy." Arlen looked him in the eye.

"You sure man?"

"Absolutely, I'll buy some though."

"All righty."

The importer was an entrepreneur through and through; he could roll with the punches and still smile to make a dollar, even if it was less than he planned. You had to be flexible in this profession.

Arlen felt massive but there was little around him to take the handle of. He felt like exploding in some purpose and had none. Confidence billowed and sagged like a spent balloon.

PADDY WAGON

Arlen had roamed downtown without being stoned for a change. He was trying to stop. He bought a couple of items and ate at the health food nook. He walked back up on the main sidewalk. He was in a drudge. Usually he would take the forest trail by the river in at least one direction. Halfway back up to his home, he realized he needed some simple hash.

He had let his supply run to nil. He usually did not buy huge amounts because he found that the more he bought, the more he smoked or ate. By now, Hash was his favorite. It was the dirt that kept him down and dirty, his feet dragged on the ground where his spirit lingered. He needed to dwell in this place of mud.

His eyes wore on the sidewalk as the castle appeared on his left in the trees. He was close now to his pleasure button being pushed. He picked up the step in anticipation. He passed the hotel and looked both ways, and crossed the street toward the upper annex. He looked up to see the police paddy wagon parked under the arch of building. Arlen panicked and felt self-conscious but continued walking. He passed within five feet of the wagon. His eyes met his principal and secondary dealers. Desperate looks. The dealers inside faced their demise. The user outside faced the challenge of scoring.

Arlen felt bad for the guys but soon focused on his own dilemma and solution. It was a situation with no other approach. The room numbers of the two dealers passed through his head. Then his toking buddy's numbers flashed and tractor beamed him to knock at one door after another.

On his third try he was able to share a joint of hash and tobacco. Arlen sat in the chair and grabbed at the armrests, as the combination sent him upward to spin. He did not smoke cigarettes and it sent his head to twist. He settled back into the chair with gratitude. His friend had saved him from this day of dryness.

"Thanks man."

"No problem, we'll get through."

TUNNEL VINO POLO

Arlen and his roommate headed up the mountain with the bottle of red wine. It was noon and late August. The sun promised heat and came through by the time they lingered on the summit. They looked down on the town site—it was a different angle to open and drink from the wine. The red glowed spiritual in the sunlight. It was a special liquid that would enhance their take on being waiters on this fine mountain.

They drank their skulls marinate in the sun and heat. They smoked marijuana and swam the delights of such a place where sky holds the mountains in the air. This rock that banded and arched and cracked, rested perky and detailed in a million complexities. The blue sky flowed ashen by the rock faces.

They stumbled merrily down the mountain and through the town to the castle. It was soon time for the foursome to play golf. It was a great evening to be the last group on the course. Two carts held four people to conquer eighteen holes.

The tee off was up, a demanding hit over the creek. Eighty yards would place you safe. All four hit clear—surprising that none played regularly. The first fairway played serious. After the cup pinged with four balls and the flag was replaced the first bottle, a Southern Comfort was freed from its golf bag and shots were downed. The second tee was more relaxed with giggles released. A drink per hole set the pace and mood. By the time Mount Rundle seemed straight above, they glowed. By the time the back nine arrived, the second bottle died and the marijuana came out.

This could be a solution for taking your score too seriously—get drunk and then stoned in such a way that you lose track of the score. Greg hit the ball against a tree—it bounced back and just missed him. He hit the deck face first. Everyone shook deep in laughter. Arlen thought he might piss his pants he was laughing so hard.

The driving of the carts melted to drive bys while the shooter was set to hit the ball. Sabotage on the course. Inebriated golf at sunset became polo. It was Randy that hit the ball from the cart first.

"Keep driving Arlen, so I can hit it."

Arlen steered the cart toward the ball and slowed. Randy reached out and arced the iron over his head and down. Snap—a clean hit.

"Yeah!"

It was a precedent to be followed; it was required to play like wise. This included the blubbering switch of cart drivers to allow each person to hit their own ball. Weakness of laughter claimed Greg from hitting it clean. Sylvia slammed the ball and looked like a pro from a horse.

Everyone placed on the green and hopped off. It was a good climax of crazy golf. The putts in took place in near dark. The sun was deep behind the mountains. They drove the carts back to the clubhouse in laughter that subdued to a presentable level.

They stumbled and partied till midnight. The next day they were thankful that no one saw them playing the polo, they could have lost their jobs. Fall was upon them and a memory of this fun time would help them in warmth through the winter.

SUNSHINE

The gondola ride into the alpine steals the heart for beauty. The trees lessen to behold the beauty of snow ridges and sheer cliffs. The relief of scale is beyond compare, it takes your breath to ponder the adoration of nature—it is wonder, how can such a place exist?

Arlen and his buddies ski and take frequent breaks to adjust their chemistries to suit the scene. The base drugs of alcohol and marijuana are mixed and tweaked to ease into the jump off. A set of jumps situate themselves close enough to the bar to be a focal point. It starts with spread eagles and increases to pain inducing acts of gravity reclamation.

They pummel and twist their bodies into the air and through the gift of adjusted brain cells; they soar bolder and fearless of consequences. They are hammered into stones that fall and roll down the hill in impossible ways. They are beanbag toys thrown to the snow. They laugh and wash their faces in the white. Pain lives in straight people. These guys are invincible in solvent courage and possibility smoke. Like the inebriated guy who steps out of the back of the camper at sixty miles per hour, they are drunken graces of accident.

CHRISTMAS PARTY ATTEMPT NUMBER TWO

The food and beverage department threw their Christmas party out of house. Pay someone else to throw the party—it was at another hotel at the other end of town. It too was a nice place, brand new in comparison with the castle.

It was a nice energy party that started out fine for Arlen. He drank with the others and chatted and enjoyed being with the people and not working. Arlen picked up the pace and had to include a toke or three. It was toke number two that threw him onto the hall floor in a state of nauseous undertow—it bowled him over and gaped his stomach free. Arlen thought of the nice carpet that he puked on. And that was the last thought he had till the next day. He found himself in his own bed.

He went to work that night and felt sheepish—who had seen him? It was embarrassing. How did he get home?

It was a busy night that stole his mind to concentrate on the duty of serving food and drink. It was toward night's end that the cashier gave him a strange glance.
"Is there anything wrong?"
"You don't remember?"
"Oh that, what happened?" Arlen asked.
"I took you home," she replied.
Arlen smiled a naked smile of thanks.
"Thank you."
"No problem."
They exchanged money and receipt and that was that. Arlen could have gotten a date, perhaps. He did not pursue her. He thought she was cute, he would like to go out with her, but was constrained by the need to stuff himself down with more drugs. He already had his mind on what he was going to do and in what manner. It was a work night and he was just going to toke hash in his little decorated stone pipe. He liked how it heated up and gave him warmth. If he kept it busy it would be too hot to the touch.

He needed the haze and dullness that the smoke gave him. He tortured himself and needed to kill and inflict pain. Arlen had wanted his father to die and then he had. This was the mantra that played its tape over and over. This was how he slammed his body in mountain biking. He used the anger fuel to push the oxygen to explode into muscle. He would pump and pump the pedals with this self-consuming rage.

He could not have a girl, a woman. He did not deserve one. They were all around him, ripe, and dripping, and he could not allow himself this pleasure. He could hear them laugh in the group hallway showers as he passed. Sex was in the air he breathed. He was trim and lean from the heavy trays and cycling. He wanted them and thought maybe that they wanted him too. But he wasn't sure enough to act—it would take one that could be the initiator.

She was from the Maritimes, an east coaster. She was a new cutie busgirl. She took the initiative and a shine to Arlen. She asked him to go to town. It was spring, they had a nice time and walk by the falls. They sat and heard water through the cascade. It was magnetic. They climbed up the hill and in her room she took her top off. Arlen choked and awkwardly excused himself. He wanted her but felt he shouldn't. It was wrong and he did not deserve it.

Arlen went to his cell and got stoned and masturbated. This escape stole the girl's initiative. There were other men that would want her.

GONDOLA

It was decided to escape the kingdom of posters and Led Zeppelin for a smoke in. The tribe rode the gondola up and mingled with the other continent people—it is unnatural to be plucked and dropped into another geographical zone. Whoosh and you are up above the tree line. All in snow and rock, flighty at this height. You swoon with the sights that sit below you. They take on a different light and slow down.

The human developments leave an odd mark that is sometimes beautiful but quite often strange and temporal. It is out of place with the beauty of nature. It messes with the scale of earth; constructed things are too close together. It is a quick study in construct. The town waits for an act of God to change it.

The boys of the bong seek out the distance due to legality. They hike out into the snow and rock looking for shelter of sight. They are victims of a plane crash; they are out of place in the skins they wear, they could not survive up here with joints and lighters. They find the nook of rock and smoke it down. The cliffs fall away to dance and mesmerize with lofty awareness and discovered nuances. They are the gifted seers. If only they could transpose from their perceived minds to realities of renown and contentment.

SOUP

The summer staff headed back to university. The boys of toke had made their own plan. Save enough tips over the summer and have a time of it in Vancouver. The plan was conceived in early July. The tips found their place of travel fund. It was a great summer for Arlen in the Spanish dining room.

He was in charge of a section and had his own waitress and bus-girl. They were a great team. They focused on getting the job done and money made. Each night began with finding if the executive chef was on duty. If he was in, then Arlen would work the front and per-form the drink duties. If the chef was not in, Arlen would work the back and serve the food. It broke up the duties between the waitress and Arlen.

It had happened months before, when Arlen was a new waiter. He was deep in the hot and steamy kitchen. The air hung with heavenly savor. Arlen ladled soup in bowls for a table of eight. This was a tour table and an athletic event: to serve and clear the appetizer, soup, salad, entrée, and desert. And the drinks.

Arlen spilled soup on the kitchen floor. The executive chef wit-nessed the event. The chef screamed and ripped Arlen open. It was a travesty of biblical proportions. It required addressing. The chef needed a stress relief valve—Arlen became that valve. It was a ven-detta between a general and a foot soldier. The foot soldier learned to stay away from the venting general.

Arlen served the soup to the table of eight, and noticed that the one lady was turning color. He noted to keep an eye on her. He cleared the next table and returned to see the lady worsen. He could feel her need. Arlen grabbed a wine ice bucket and handed it to her. She turned into her lap and faced off into the metal receptacle. It echoed and turned the appetites of the surrounding diners.

She finished and handed the bucket to Arlen. She smiled half-heartedly and excused herself to the washroom. Later heading out the door, the lady thanked Arlen and bowed many times.

VANCOUVER SEPTEMBER

The day had come to pack in the room—it was epic to escape. There had been talk of becoming a lifer. This was not a good thing at this level, not an enviable condition. One needed to escape the Banff. The lifer term referred more to the state that one was in, lonely and pitiable, than the fact of living forever in Banff.

The Trans Am was loaded with John at the helm. Arlen had rolled several joints and had stuffed a bottle of Bailey's Irish Cream under his seat. His throat was taking him to desert cracked proportions. He had a need to let loose and toke. John hammered the car onto the highway. Arlen lit the first joint of the road.

This trip to the Okanagan was windy and aggressive. The curves slammed Arlen to the edges of his seat. The hours passed and found them at their first destination. It was a stopover to refuel and store possessions at a relative's house.

They picked up another guy from last years toke brother's group. The highway wandered left and right and up and down. It was a long day that ended in Vancouver. They found an apartment in East Vancouver. They posed as two persons, as the third waited on the side. Documents and money exchanged hands. The third snuck in. The Trans Am was tucked into the underground. Arlen was amazed at how many keys were given for the building access. This was a different place than Banff.

They placed their sleeping pads on the carpet in the living room and stuck up a couple of posters. The focus was on partying and seeing Vancouver. They dwelled in the edgy affordable section. Life teemed in this neighborhood. Arlen had not seen anything of this nature before—it was like a foreign land to him. They stoned and drank. They drove around.

Downtown loomed large while stoned. The buildings looked ready for eruption, they had sprouted from the ground in spectacular fashion. Arlen mesmerized the sights in through his drug-induced gaze.

Stanley Park was the day's adventure. They parked the car in the lot and walked the sights. The ocean rested ominous and promised something that Arlen did not grasp. It left him wanting more of something, but he wasn't sure. They toked up in the rain forest. The spiders and slugs watched them change to gaiety and laughter. The trees stood huge and worthy of yoga back bends to take in the full height—they stretched for sunlight. They walked back to the car—it was locked with the keys in the ignition. Shit. And John did not have a spare key, nor did they know how to break in. The spare was back in the apartment. It was a long bus ride that took their stone and covered it with many stops.

GROUNDING

The three prepared for the drive by smoking more pot—it was good pot that energized you into an appreciative state. John drove as he always did. Arlen sat in the front seat slouched with his knees on the dash. Ed sat in the back behind John. They were driving a new route when they saw it.

The Expo ball stood on their left—it was just being built—in its polished stage it shone for your attention. All three sets of eyes affixed left while the car sped forward. Arlen stared at the rows of bicycles in racks, he had never seen that many.

Ed screamed, "Look out."

All eyes forward: black van with brake lights pleading. John slammed on the brakes. All they see is the black hurtling at them, at the slightest of angles. All bodies move expertly according to physics. Meet the two together. Arlen's back twinges. Crunch of bumper on grill. Forward slam, return back thrust rebound. Nothing else in the world exists in this slow motion, quick exchange.

"Fuck," John yelled.

John pushed on his door. "Fuck."

Arlen pushed on his door.

"Can't get out."

Ed wants to get out of the back seat and further out the door. John and Arlen push with their shoulder, still nothing. By now the van driver is out parading his righteous anger for all to see. The light turned green and the traffic flashed by on each side—at a safe distance they ward off the evil happenchance—necks twist rubber and turn to pivot stare. The steel flowed past the scene. John and Arlen finally get leg power involved to extricate themselves. The power of the thigh counters the door hinge meld.

The three stand on pavement, their hundreds of ponies under the hood are silent. Antifreeze flowed for these three dogs to lick. The van man cooled—the damage was done. His bumper needed replacing—no doubt about that. But he cooled to see the red car was dying—the boy's toy had broken. Look around at the world pass you by. Talk about a downer. These three kids thrown straight to effect from cause. They were unaware of the cities approach to the accidental situation.

"Do we call the cops?"

"Let's exchange numbers." The man pulled a pad out of his pocket.

That was an awkward request to appease. The three did not set their priorities to include a phone.

"I'll give you my parent's number." John twitched—his face screwed up in a serious intent of deliverance. His baby steamed and moaned. The white bumper had obliterated the grill and hungered to push the fan into engine. The front quarter panels had slid back to engage the doors shut.

This was goodnight. The three gave their report to the police station and the car was towed and inspected to be totaled as far as insurance was concerned. John dealt with it all, and with his parents, the insurance company was in his hometown.

Ed and Arlen assisted John in overcoming the odds of being carless—a tough transition in a utopia month such as this. It was a humbler to get to know ones street intimately. To walk to the local bus stop and stare the details down to a memory. The dead car was a piece of this party gone. How can you have a bash without transport? How do people gather? They never did fully regain that sense of goodness.

GASTOWN

They fell into Gastown one night. Its dark pit reflected nothing at two a.m. on the weekend. These clubs hinted at a shady past. They heard stories of the sixties when tables were set up at the entrances and the drugs flowed. These toke brothers missed this era. They went back to their apartment with the Led Zeppelin and Pink Floyd posters. This was their haven. What was missing was structure—there was too much time on their hands. They filled it with drugs.

Arlen bought mushrooms outside of the golden arches downtown. How many served? They were freshly picked and slimy in tinfoil—just plucked from their wet home. It made Arlen's head shake sliding down his throat. He wandered into Stanley Park mid way through the night.

It was a wild place, an epic journey along the seawall trail. The moon was pregnant and swollen—it pumped its heart at Arlen. He stopped and looked up. Behind him, the forest yelled.

The mushrooms wore on into the park. The forest swallowed Arlen to illuminate. He felt one with the trees; they were bark and sky and moon. They were black and green. The totems scratched their heads. They gazed at the shapes against the moon. They wondered how they arrived in this place. It was purposeful and timely, these bastions of First Nations Story. It was in this place that the dawn arrived to place Arlen back into his cranium.

STEEL RAIL

These fall weeks wore on with visits to friends. There was talk of getting jobs in high end dining establishments—bring the money on. Arlen decided to depart. His time had come. He stored some possessions in North Vancouver; this included a set of binoculars that Arlen's Dad had lifted from a dead German Soldier in World War Two. Arlen thought nothing of leaving such things with abandon. He was self absorbed in cycles of emotional perversity—it led him onward into night. Arlen was unsure of where he was going, getting out of this place would improve things. It had to.

Arlen entered the train station and waited and climbed the steps of the train. Arlen searched his soul, the windowed view held his meditated grasp outside of his hold. He reached but could not find what he needed. He thought he needed to quit the drugging. He had to end it somehow. This VIA Rail Train headed east toward night. It sped up the sun's decline.

The side to side rocking soothed him toward sleep. The movement took him back toward the womb, his mother was walking and he was bouncing fore and aft and side to side. This night approach was pleasant. Arlen wished it would not end—he could be the food for swallow. The juices would eat away and he could sleep final—without interruptions. The mantle fell upon him.

Sunrise peeked over the mountains. Roger's Pass astounded the passengers. Their faces glued outward and, flashes stole moments, attempted to penetrate the glass that stood between the rage of nature and this cocoon of rail comfort.

Arlen rode coach and wandered the train. He passed by the berths and wondered of the caves inside. He passed through the glory of the Rockies in the sky car. The windowed observation ceiling made him feel like he rode in a cathedral place. Not one person could stand the passage by reading a great book. The vista grabbed at your periphery—you had to revere it. It required your respect.

The staff were allowed by the great rail mountain gods to focus on their task of hospitality. This agreement had been cast after many passages. The scenes grew indented in their spirits, their souls had the full set—it was warm in their hearts to remember these places. They would carry it to their deaths—this beauty and inhospitality. This passage had been paid for with hundreds of lives to build the rail. And this allowed the staff to focus on their work instead of gazing with the others. It had claimed a piece of their soul.

Arlen thought of the danger of the trestles—he thought it would be great to walk over one someday. It was wild to be hundreds of feet in the air. You could look out and down and see nothing but space. It was akin to flying, and throw in the elliptical motion, and side to side. It was wild, and lovely—a special route of steel.

The train with Arlen approached Banff and he did not know what to do. Should he get off or continue to Calgary and beyond? He had bought a ticket to Banff, and here it was approaching. Was he ready to embrace his Banff life again? He did not want it like it was. On the right side of the train, he looked ahead and up at the notch of Mount Rundle. It was to the left of the summit. He likened it to the notch of the quarter moon. He had spent many hours embracing the sight of this arc from his room in the upper annex. It had become reliable—it never changed, except for the snow that came and went. The frosting served to enhance its beauty in nooks and crannies.

Arlen thought of the golf course and the memories of blackouts and bad mushroom trips. This geographical escape that was Vancouver reverted back, what had it solved? Had he changed? He was hardening his arteries of free will. The routes of addiction were paving over his fertile gardens of youth. Barbed wire was hardwired to push the fix button. That was the daily need and requirement—to get stoned on something, it didn't matter what.

Arlen thought of his dad and brother. It was fucked up, nine days apart. Arlen felt like the victim of the guillotine raid and hang master all the same. He had convicted himself to death; he needed to suffer for his guilt of wanting his father to die. It was so for a reason—he was the chosen to suffer now. Someone chose him for this path of denial and stone.

The train brakes screeched and the thousands of tons subdued to a stop. Arlen jumped from the train. Elk grazed up the tracks. Arlen ran into the station and bought a ticket down the line, to the place of Louis Riel's trial—Regina. The hanging verdict seemed a rightful place to hop off. Arlen tasted again the flavor of international tourism in the Rockies. A herd of paparazzi mounted an attack on the grazing elk. Arlen could hear the 35 mm camera mechanisms at a hundred paces. He climbed the steel steps back onto the train.

HOME

This was the trip to the homeland. Maybe he would find the missing piece. Perhaps it had worn down enough to fit into place. Years previous, parts of him had ruptured to odd shaped proportions that did not fit in with that region of living. He had to get away and be in a different land to sort it out. Now he was returning for some purpose, maybe just for the contrast of place. Vancouver had been out of his comfort zone. He was spread over three provinces, he needed to pilgrimage back to the place of beginning—where the fracture first appeared, and it was there that he could learn something.

The train ride to Regina passed too quickly. Arlen loved the in between places feel of the track and train. It was a bit of community and place on the train cars. The landscape was the royal court—it soothed him to look out the windows at the miles rolling by, the ground shifted in shape and line. He found his conceptual mind returning to his game as a kid.

He would lay in the back seat of his parent's car. They would be driving down the highway and Arlen would follow the power lines as they arced and pendulumed between the poles. Like Spiderman's swing, the lines would dip and peak. He would follow them to the end. He imagined himself safe back in the seat. And the falling to sleep, and dad carrying him into the house. That was living as royal. Parents to carry you while you slept. Arlen loved that feeling.

He blurred out the window at the lines and terrain. In Saskatchewan, the pepper clouds of ducks and geese grew. The winter was ready in the wings to take stage at any time. Leaves composted to provide nutrients in the soil. The sun drooped in the sky, closing in on winter solstice. The frame skeletons of trees posed to rest and interpose—they drove Arlen to introspection and bleak outcomes. He knew not what to do or how to do it. He was drifting like a winter blizzard. The fingers spread only to cover what will exist again next season. He avoided the essential archeological dig of Arlen. Yet it was the only procedure that would suffice at this level of demise.

He had to straighten out—no drugs, no booze. Was he ready to continue in that vein? He had had nothing since leaving Vancouver. The only lines he did were these steel tracks. The landscape held him tight—if he could stay tuned to it somehow it could be his salvation, but he had to interact with the people and his past. This was his stumbling place.

Arlen stepped onto the platform and retrieved his bag and sauntered into the station. He wanted to keep riding for eternity; it was a palatable place of purgatory—if he had scenery to look at, he could make it.

One week later Arlen was back on the train heading to where he had come from. His thoughts returned to the outsized oddity that his pieces had become, he did not fit in at home. He felt lesser for the fact. He was a wound that needed a place of healing; he festered with this wandering for solution. He needed not a new drug but an inward cleanse and wiping of his ass. It was time to face the movie—this was he who needed the face in the dirt. What would it take?

Arlen, we are waiting to help you. The whole world is there poised to help you. When can you pull your hand out and open? What will it take? Remember addiction ends in insanity and death. Those are the promises that will be kept if you allow this dominant matrix to succeed in forming your outcome. Arlen, wake up! We want you to make it out. Why are you going back? What is there that you are looking for? Did you not get your fill at the decadent buffet of soul succulence?

Arlen meets a man that has just been in Madagascar. He claims to be a Paramedic tripper who experiments with the different drugs around the world—he is a regional connoisseur. Bold and enlightened, he designs his adventure well. He was just in Montreal and has some killer hash. The man carries on to Vancouver; as they depart company, he cuts two grams of hash from his bar in his waist pouch. Like a timely apparition the man appeared and provided the means to an end. It was set in Arlen's mind to diverge—this providence gave the final nudge.

DISEMBARKATION

Sickness follows you like a cloud, it rains upon you as you cross the provincial border and remove your body from the train. The walk across town is a lonely defeated step. The job waits for you like a sentence. It comforts you in familiar strokes and strikes you, diminishes your soul in steady wearing of flesh. It sears your dreams and hopes.

Arlen! Can you remember your dreams? You had dreams once. Can you touch them now? Go ahead, fall down your mountain. We have to let you go. You stupid boy. When will you learn? Do you need tough love? I think so. Chew on you leg trap. Have your fun, it's your life. How long will it last?

Arlen walked across the bridge and blurred through the familiar surroundings. But the mountains felt different now. They were signposts, parameters of his imposed chemical exile. He had been clean for close to a dozen days and his next knock on the door was already planned. He hoped his dealer had not been busted or moved.

A position was there, waitering back in the dining room. It was special function season, and Christmas was approaching. He was set with black vest in hand. A room was entered in the upper annex, he didn't even unpack his bag, Arlen reached into the bottom corner and retrieved his pipe. It was like an old dysfunctional lover. He lay back on the bed spent but left wanting and wondering why he came back to this door. Sure he had gotten off but where was he now?

Arlen you are working the dining room again to buy drugs and anonymity to pursue the addiction course. You scrape razor blade to mirror and catch glimpses of your eye, you avoid it and focus on the crumbling dust. You don't bother with a hundred dollar bill to snort with. Anything will do—a dirty one-dollar bill. The taste reminds you of ether—it excites your primal thrill to explode out. The spectrum of rock precipice keeps you in the valley.

You mix it with hash and revisit the bad mushroom vacation spot just to make sure it hasn't changed. It has worsened, it is seedy and characters linger in alleys. It left its mark upon your skull, jelly. The coke has inserted the fear of out there inside you. Arlen you did not need more fear of the regions, fear of man. What are you doing Arlen? You work with people, and serve people.

On a day off you eat a gram of hash. Not the stuff Madagascar man gave you—that might put you in a coma. It had hit Arlen like a meteor and he'd stumbled around in the crater. That stuff had changed the ground around him.

On this day off, the hash was not of that quality. The quantity made up for it. Arlen liked the taste of hash. It reminded him of the garden as a child. Maybe when he put dirt in his mouth as an infant, he was preparing for this appreciation of chewing grit. It did not flow down his gullet. It stuck and needed a rinse. Just a little rinse and music to wash over him. He reclined and settled into the chair like putty. He melted and drooped to gravity. His DNA regrouped—sheer physics mixed with relaxation to slab him to peace. A piece of raw sirloin slapped on the counter. He zoned and entered the dot on the wall. It was epic, these hours in this wall, utterly in the moment—it consumed him to meditate, his Zen trip. His lifetime to this date was summed up in this dot on the wall. And in this moment our poor Arlen was all right.

CONVENTIONS

The weeks passed through convention season. There was the night of travel agents from Australia—that was a party. It was a medieval theme with the costumed head table locked by their arms and heads in stocks; and finger food was thrown at them. The Mead was sweet nectar to Arlen at these events. He was glad to be scheduled for more of the historical ravaging. Arlen was impressed with the debauchery and passion. A layer of food clogged underfoot as he navigated the room. It was perfection after dressing up in lederhosen the previous year.

He had felt like a dork traipsing around in the strapped suit. The hat on his head was too much. But he had entered into the spirit of it with the others, for money. There had been a sexual energy about the Oktoberfest theme. It had been the first time that Arlen had his ass pinched. He kept walking and looked back to see the cougar grinning at him. He smiled at her and carried on. She was deep into a bottle of wine. Each time he passed her by he smiled. The size of tip grew.

Christmas had come and gone. The dining room staff had spent a lot of time together, spreading the special Christmas cheer to the guests. The staff grew weary and Arlen was tired. It was a huge team working together setting up after lunch. The uniformed staff bowed to the tables and gave fresh linens and settings and glasses.

Pete worked his way through the crowd. Arlen saw him writing something in his pad after talking to people. Arlen was indeed curious. Pete arrived at Arlen's side. He carried a bar tray with a few things on it. To an innocent, it looked like he was working.

"Benny order, want some bennies Arlen?"

This was not those delicious Eggs Benedict. This was a stimulant, a huge coffee effect, and a mild speed effect.

"Sure." Arlen said.

"How many?" Pete asked.

"Five."

"I'll put you down for five, should have it for New Year's Eve."

NEW YEAR'S EVE

That is how synchronicity worked for Arlen—it just came to him. He thought it worked out great in this way, he was an open vessel. It took a couple of days. He did not even care where it came from. How many hands had the drugs passed through to fuel the select few amongst the staff?

It seemed to Arlen like the enhancement drug of choice. It would help him perform to serve better and make more money to provide more little helpers. It was a vicious two step—move forward to make money—spend it on drugs and step back.

That first New Year's Eve opened Arlen's eyes. It was wild in the dining room. The whole place housed a few thousand for the festivities. Arlen was paired with a waitress; they had a shitty spot in the very back corner. They decided to make the very best of it. She wanted to do the food angle and Arlen would do the drink. The bennies percolated in his system, perfect for the relaying of alcoholic beverages—from beer to bottles of wine and champagne. They only had three tables. It was good because you could hardly move in there. Arlen went the long way, snuck out the door and into the entrance by the bar.

Much of the evening was spent in lines. Arlen bought himself a few B52's to celebrate and found a happy place from which to serve. Their two smaller tables were low maintenance. Arlen focused on the table of eight. They knew very little English. It began with bows and sitting and drinks. Arlen decided this was the fun table for the night.

He opened the champagne with grand show and respect. The table ate up the service—time passed the party to glow. It passed the food stage and entered the drink and dance.

Arlen stood by the bar and was surprised to see ladies climb on tabletops and dance—this was a grand party. Arlen headed back to the tables and danced with the Japanese women. This was a night for letting go. In the end Arlen was handed the largest single table tip he ever received.

THIS DECEMBER

But this was a new December of innocence misplaced. It was the twelve days of noel bleeding on the soul. It had blurred since the arrival time by train to this festive season. No bells rang in Arlen's heart. It was heavy and dark, withered and cracked. He was ready for the end—he needed this drug treatment to cease. He had taken it to its full course—was he ready to perish for the ideal of his castle? He had built it from the inside. He did not even know what it looked like from the outside.

He was at home in his basement bedroom when he drew up the initial plans. He would pretend that everything was all right. Maybe they would leave him alone. He could get away from his family and continue the castle project. It would be his full time pursuit. He had to lock up his mangy little secrets in the dungeon. He could go and visit them but no one else was allowed. It was his castle and he was serious about maintaining the walls and moat. Stay away from Arlen please. He has a hidden place within that is ugly and diseased. Back away from the stricken.

Arlen patched the crumbling walls in his pursuits of the blackout. No impasses of communication could pass through from the outside in these times. No runners were employed to pass messages. This Arlen strove to become his own-country exile—it was his need to cut himself off from the others.

It is hard to see Arlen in the last weeks of this year. The chemistry experiment had no guidelines—it was off the rails with no laboratory guidebook; no notes existed of where Arlen wandered. It was off the map. The spiral tightened and left insane mortality.

He was promoted to the French Service dining room. It was the cocaine that gave him the confidence to pursue it. It was a victory off place, he was out of his element and too old of a dog at twenty to learn anything new. The synapse firing range was fogged in and not shooting true.

The walls crumbled. Arlen could not contain himself—control had vacated. The Food and Beverage Manager entertained clients and Arlen had the table. They ordered drinks and Arlen returned with the wrong set, this was a bad scene of shine. They re-ordered and Arlen returned with the wrong set again. Was it sabotage of the path he was headed into this desolate garden? He uprooted his own transplant.

The damage done, Arlen was threatened to work in the deli. A head-waiter rallied and took Arlen back in the upstairs dining room. It was relief—the deli was too drastic for Arlen, too much of a fall down the hierarchal chain. Not to mention the pinch of drug choice.

This headwaiter had seen Arlen in his career prime—it was only months before. Back when he had perfected the foot deflection move—if a glass dropped within range, Arlen would deftly deflect its force to roll and not break. He had used himself up. Arlen was a shot fighter pi-lot, smoking engine, spiraling to earth. He was still alive in the flames waiting for impact. He knew deep down the grounding was imminent. It was required; he needed his wings to be clipped: he could not be trusted to keep his system clean.

It was a season of need: trained employees were at a premium. The days blurred as Arlen binged the brain cells dry. His work was unin-spired. He could have stayed on the train. A mix of drugs and booze scrambled Arlen's brain to incubate—it warmed a new head to birth; it had control and its own purpose: Arlen was simply the vessel for this pschycotic ride. You're coming with me boy! There is that certain point where the crazy old man makes you sit on the back of the motorcycle. You are suddenly there with no escape, two hundred miles per hour, and you are naked. Do you touch him? You can't step off—it feels like death. The panic and servitude take hold. You answer to him alone, the old man of psychosis dispenses no mercy—he rides you hard, grinds your meat to bones. Ashen you blow in his wind. He is a pitiful, parent-less old codger that has not known love, only pain. He is your mentor, Arlen, as you pass these twelve days of Christmas.

SHIFT

Feel the judgment you passed upon yourself reap. It is true, and prepared to grind you to demise—final breath and body bag. Arlen you
had to steal yourself away. Why did you have the breath of dignity?
The wherewithal carried you twice to that phone, through the herds
of shoppers. You called for help. We came for you Arlen. Can you hold
it together long enough? Can you make it Arlen? We have your stuff
in the car now. Hold on to the blankets. Feel the Ford sedan rumble.
It will soothe your rash. Keep those doors locked. Can you close your
eyes? Have you slept? We'll leave your castle now. Can you leave it
here? Arlen do you have to bring it with you?

"Yes I need it!"

I suppose you're accustomed to it. Bring your blanket of mistaken
thinking and guilt with you. Your self-condemnation is your companion, if you have to Ar. We want you to get better, let us help you. Settle
back in the seat, rest your back against the seat. We are leaving Banff
now. There's the last hotel. Forest. And highway, feel the smooth. Is it
warm enough for you Arlen? Why are you still shaking? We are taking you through the valley. Out of this world you have clasped onto
and into a different place—where should we take him Jake? Saskatoon
should have something to help.

It became a decompression journey for Arlen. His ass did sit fully
on the seat as his thighs released their clinch on his forward motioned
toes. The darkness held him in the Ford womb of passage. No distrac-
tions of sight cut at him. No faces of people, of dogs chasing him. His
back touched the seat—the clinch was releasing.

The motel in Calgary was secure. He was safely stolen away. Arlen
thought of cult documentaries he had watched in previous years. It was
he that was intercepted and removed from his created fold. He was a
dying boy that needed light, and warmth. The brother Jake and sister
Carmen found a Christian program on TV. Arlen found himself in the
shower and could not get warm. He had been freezing for days or was
it weeks? He was freezer burnt—the shower bounced his heart and
threatened, the fight of flight was beaten by the warm water. His feet
cracked of ice, his hands pooled snow. His blood warmed and surged
erratically. Too cold too hot, it mixed in flashes and leaned him against

the tiles. He touched his head to the wall. The water caressed his homeostasis to wobble and weave. He settled in to a whisked warmth, it was fleeting, this wave that warmed him passed on to other places. He dried off. It had flashed over him, all the while he was showering he thought of being deprogrammed and wondered what it would be replaced with.

He may have slept that night—it was all the same: this racing dream world blended and tossed with reality. It was restless reaction—he was processing the events of weeks previous: it all passed by his casket now and viewed him, and clutched at his senses and feelings; he shrunk into fetal awareness and his body curled from the attack. It was just this fight—he was reaping what he had planted in the dirt, this was the corn creature in the horror flicks, it was the pillow at night, it was the head that thought and felt; it was Arlen.

The morning passed from city to badland to rolling plain and scrubland. A light cover of snow smoothed it all into one. Arlen slipped for moments into the safe passage of the train. The Ford sedan was steady in movement—the train allowed itself to wander and comfort. The car focused on a line and destination. Arlen talked and blithered and yammered the mile down.

A scenic church grabbed Arlen's eye and he pleaded with them to stop. Jake navigated the four doors into the churchyard. It was midday and a beautiful sky opened upon the scene, warm and inviting. Jake and Carmen sat and waited for Arlen to exit from the car. Arlen wanted to pray in the church and die. His fingers plucked the door lock to unlatch. The metal popped up. His fingers caressed the handle. He felt the hope and peace—he pulled the handle like a trigger, he waited for the proper moment in his sights. A wave of fear and condemnation struck. His hand found the other side of his shoulder, and held him fast.

"Let's go," Arlen said.

Jake drove onto the highway.

SASKATOON

They arrived in the outskirts of Saskatoon at nightfall. Nothing was open—no facility existed. They did not want to go to the hospital but Arlen worsened. He panicked and needed help. They drove up to the emergency parking. It is an otherworldly space to enter—different than the outer world. There is a serious intent in the air and a callous observation of suffering. It is calculated and triage-designed to save the human. Arlen is seen and prescribed Valium—it is the solution.

Jake and Carmen pluck Arlen free from the pharmaceutical. They decide that he does not need another drug to replace the last. He needs to get clean. They stay the night at Carmen's sister's place. It is the basement that comforts Arlen: he performs better below grade. Arlen is cold. They point an electric heater at him. He huddles in the covers and focuses on the red-hot coils. The fan cuts in and out. Arlen discovers the shared rhythm and lets his heart match the electrical thermostat. His heart stops when the heater stops and his heart beats when the heater engages. He is enslaved to this machine. He has lost his autonomy—he has no latent involuntary muscle ability. Somehow he has crossed over and his nerves have taken control of his heart and he has no endurance to continue the beat.

Arlen you should have left the control to your body, you had to interject your experiments and leanings. Look where it has taken you. It is too late to meddle. But it would be better to drive this soul to safety. Can anyone help him out here? Any suggestions to unplug him from the machine? The lights are out and he is left in the basement. He has never read Frankenstein but he is kin. He is the freak in basement that is unfinished. The rhythms pass into hours. Arlen lays motionless for fear of recompense with his heart on the machine. Morning falls into the basement and he is pulled to dress and breakfast and the sedan. The calls were made and the vacancy found.

They are off to the Detoxification Center. It is a cold morning and Arlen finds himself shivering again. He wants to run. He feels his muscles tighten and breathing deepen. He was not and is not hungry. This is a final door of exit from the land he has dwelled in.

The center is in a basic housing area on the wrong side of the tracks.

The sedan stopped and the engine died. The front doors opened but Arlen is back in the train not wanting this ride to end. Always forward the momentum carried the focus to point ahead and never within his experience. It must not be pointed inward—never could the scope see the guts of his crater. He would crumble and fall.

Jake and Carmen waited for Arlen to swing the door open.

"This place will help you," Jake said. They waited.

The door creaked free and allowed Arlen to emerge. He looked at the deep piles of snow with trails cut through to allow passage. The house was large but non-descript. It too had its special going-ons inside. Perhaps Arlen and the house could match on this note and play a song. Carmen shivered and headed beside the house. It was the only trail cut in the snow. Jake held out his hand, after you. Arlen met his fate—his fight would come.

DETOX

The house felt warm and moist. Voices conversed at most corners. Chopping sounds on a cutting board. Coffee smell. Arlen's eyes soared upward to find the first plaque, "God grant me the serenity to accept the things I cannot change, the courage to change the things I can, and the wisdom to know the difference."

It captured his brain and would not let go, the word 'accept' kept rolling over and on. Arlen's shoulders dropped a quarter inch—maybe he did belong here. Jake and Carmen talked about him to the lady in the office. Suddenly Arlen's gaze was ripped from the words and he found himself to be in an interview—the focus was on Arlen. This was the strangest job interview he had ever had. He did not like being the center of attention. He heard the minimal answers spout out of his throat. The chosen and used substances were noted and his file was conceived. It was January Second. This was home.

Jake and Carmen left him there with his bag. He was given the tour. It seemed a wider, larger house on the upper floors than the bottom. The bottom housed the large kitchen, a bedroom, office, storage, and the smoke room. The smoking walls were dark yellow, like dirty bee comb—the smudge was keeping the black flies at bay. The characters were excessive and chain smoking: it was a feat to slam that much smoke and coffee into one's system.

The bathroom was the next room by the stairs. A man sat and shook, tremored like he was on a paint can shaker. His hand's radius struck three feet. When they were heading up the stairs, Arlen asked why he was shaking.
"Valium, twenty years, it'll get better."
Arlen wondered at being on Valium for that long.

The second floor consisted of all bedrooms with one bathroom. Arlen was given a bed at the end of the hall. There were two other beds in the room. The third floor consisted of more bedrooms and two bathrooms and a large meeting room that was now being used as a TV room. Arlen had noticed that sprinkled throughout the house were more plaques of inspiration and encouragement. It was soon possible for him to always gaze at one. There were few spots without a plaque.

The tour was complete and the lady released him to his own devices.

"Eleven o'clock tape in the smoke room."

"What?" Arlen asked.

"We listen to a tape at eleven, you have to be there."

"All right, thanks."

"No problem."

Arlen walked to his room and sat on his bed. His only roommate was in—he lay on his bed reading a Louis L'Amour book. He was a happy man: he still seemed like he was on something. But so did Arlen, he was different and aloof and scared—he was the druggie. The reader was an alchy whose name was Wil and Arlen had not seen him go through D.T.'s. They exchanged pleasantries for such a place and Arlen placed his head on the pillow.

This seemed rather harsh: this place was rough. He thought of the happy button when he used—that would fix him now. He wanted a drug, any drug; this place gave him desire. He crawled under the blankets fully clothed. He was just starting to get warm when Wil rose from his western.

"Time for the tape pardner."

Will stopped to pee and Arlen continued downstairs. The coffee preparations were on—this was a prerequisite for tape time.

Two guys of Arlen's age were laughing and slamming tablespoons of sugar into their cups. They sounded like cartoon characters, and their frantic actions looked the part. Too much acid amongst other substances, Arlen would later learn. They were here by the court's request. It was this or jail. And this was their fifth time.

Arlen poured a coffee and the kitchen staff guy introduced himself as Earl. He was sixtyish, tall and lean and his intentions led him around the kitchen leaving a whirl of activity performed. Arlen soon learned that looking your age in such a place was deception. This style of living was age in a bottle. People came in looking like death and they would reverse through time. Perhaps they may morph back to their approximate age.

Arlen was not capable of fully grasping how he himself looked. We saw him to be pale and weak and fearful. He was timid skin on bones. It was easy to see that he put his drug of choice before peanut butter.

TAPE TIME

"Tape time Arlen." Earl checked the coffee station.

"Thanks." Arlen walked down the hall.

The smoke escaped into the hall. Arlen did not smoke without drugs and chose a chair by the door. It was a motley bunch—all ages of more men than women, from teenagers to seniors.

The tape was this guy who gave his life story before A.A., the finding of the twelve steps, recovery, and sober living. It was a different language; it was shoptalk of the program. He heard things like, "Finding the program, let go and let God, higher power, insanity and death, find a sponsor." Arlen wondered what the sponsor was about—would someone pay him to live? Through second hand smoke, Arlen massaged that same part of his brain with nicotine and caffeine.

By the end of the tape, Arlen felt better. His chemistry had soothed. The voice ended and the tribe rose. It was lunchtime. Arlen followed behind the group. The kitchen filled up with bodies at tables. Arlen sat. It was Earl's homemade soup and sandwiches and sugary juice. Arlen ate some but could not taste anything. It made him feel slightly better, which was still horrible—but he had just entered that first country of suffering.

Arlen lay on his bed all afternoon; he was almost warm when he was rousted again. Wil had read the whole time. This tape and meal went smoother for Arlen—he knew what to expect. The bed found him again. Arlen wanted to warm up and thought a shower could do it. He found the shower on the next floor up.

There was a different focus on funding in this place—a steady war was being waged for lives and new plumbing was a non-essential. There was a stack of towels and soap. The water threw his body into shock again—his insides bounced around and he held on to steady the balance of heat. It hinted at coming. He warmed his torso. His appendages ached purple and blue. The experience of water exhausted him. He felt rinsed down the hair clogged drain. He was drying off when he heard a new staff member knock.

"Time for meeting, eight o'clock."

Arlen's heart jumped into the basin. He panicked and grabbed a blue bathrobe from the pile next to the towels. He put it on and opened the door, he left his clothes. He headed to the meeting around the corner.

FIRST MEETING

He entered the full room and found a seat facing the hall. He felt conscious of the bright blue robe but it was like this for some reason. They chuckled. Arlen was reaction at this point in time, he was fodder for the throw. Anything was possible within these faded walls.

The room was filled with backs to the wall. Twenty people faced the center and together they faced the front, a guest from the outside was marked by his outerwear. He opened the meeting with the Serenity Prayer, everyone stood. Arlen kept his robe together.

The man read the preamble from the blue book. He then opened with his story. He had been here in this room three years previous. He worked the program and lived life clean and sober. "You can do it too," stood out to Arlen.

The time to speak went around the circle.
"My name is Mike and I'm an alcoholic."
"Hi Mike."
"My name is Sue and I'm an addict."
"Hi Sue."
Some seemed to talk for hours and others offered, "I want to listen tonight."
"Take what you need from the meeting and leave the rest," the three-year man said.

Arlen dreaded his moment of spotlight—he could hear, see and feel it approach. It rose in waves and clenched at his bowels—he was not even aware of shitting in the last week, and here it was—spasms and clinching. He was up. The three-year man looked at Arlen.

Arlen could feel his gaze and the silence of the room. It boomed his shoulders in from both sides. Arlen started to cry and felt like a big blue baby.
"My name is Arlen, I'm a drug addict." He cried in silence. That was all he could say. The room was silent; they all knew his pain, his tears, and his silence of shame. Dignity waited.
"Thanks Arlen."

Arlen's streams subsided—it felt good to cry now that it was ending. Something within him had opened. A dead withered perennial had sprouted. He sat wasted in the chair, exhausted. A lady came up to him afterward and thanked him.

"For what?"

"Honesty."

Her name was Bianca and she tried to talk with Arlen—he didn't have much to say.

"I'm tired."

She walked him back to his room. That was the wrap on meetings for the night. Arlen watched Wil finish a book and start another without a pause—he simply gazed at the ceiling for a few seconds. Arlen wondered if Wil was imagining himself in the westerns but didn't ask.

THE MEDICAL

The morning came with little rest for our blue boy. It was medical time for Arlen—part of the program. Good to get checked out, you never know. Coffee and morning Alcoholics Anonymous meeting set Arlen on the day. He nibbled at his breakfast. Arlen played the detox role and blended in.

His bed partner for the night had been shame and self-mutilation of spirit. He played the same tapes over and over. He was evil. He was shame. He was bad.

The staff member handed the map to Arlen. He was to follow the map to get to the wing entrance of the hospital—he had an appointment. It was an easy walk that sapped the roots from Arlen. It was cold and he was shame. He was off to see the doctor to make sure everything was fine. Arlen wished that the doctor could fix him with one procedure, one pill.

Arlen sat in the waiting room; he was not capable of looking at the magazines. He stared at the wall and ticked the moments to pass. He thought about the serenity prayer. "The courage to change the things I can." Arlen was escorted into the examination room.
"The doctor will be with you in a moment."
Arlen waited and took in the medical tools and devices. The doctor arrived and began the inspection. Arlen felt himself drift off and respond to the questioning. The doctor poked and prodded.

It was the abdomen palpitating that twisted. Arlen had closed his eyes; all was silent and then he felt the doctor scribe an X on his gut.

Flip to the new template of psychosis, it was a targeting system and Arlen felt the doctor clear and the charges hit clean—it was in him and through. They had gotten to him with his guard down, he was toast. The morph had snapped him to attention—he was a changeling that took orders from a different muse. It was a silent tune that demanded utter obedience. Arlen offered himself on the slab: he knew when it was too late to fight, this was destiny and right.

The doctor finished with few words and Arlen was free to go. But free he was not. Arlen was on trial, indicted of atrocities. This day would travel fast to noose. He walked out of the office and into the hall of the hospital. It was quiet in this wing, no one was around, Arlen did not see the striking workers out front.

Arlen was hit again with the aftershock—that was where the damage consumed, flames licked his skin. He was done. He had caused it. There was no electricity, no production, everyone had ceased to flow. It was his fault and his alone. Arlen headed out the door and looked to the sky. It was odd, the clouds covered like smoke. He felt warm— Arlen was warm.

He looked to the street, traffic trickled. This is wrong. The world is dead. I have caused it. You destroyed the world. Judgement fell to Arlen's waist. He is cut clean through. He is driven on tracks now. It is passion this locomotive scream through his soul and conscience. He must die. Arlen you must die. Yes you feel it now. Perform justice surgery on your breath. The answer is clear. You must kill yourself Arlen. Atone for the destruction of the world.

JUDGEMENT

What are you waiting for? GO ARLEN. There he goes like a rat through the streets. He scurries his way through the snow and sneaks in his detox center door.

"Everything all right Arlen?" Earl asked.

"Doctor said I'll be fine."

Arlen clambered up the steps and found his room. Wil was not in. Arlen closed the door.

It was another force that fueled his actions. You must bleed Arlen. Bleed. Arlen grabbed a chair and pulled the bed away from its pillow end. He lifted the foot of the bed onto a chair. It coursed and bubbled—this condemnation splattered, he had to serve the sentence; the judge presided over the slice. Arlen grabbed his toiletries bag and plucked out the pull type razor. He removed the cartridge from the handle and chewed to get a blade. He moved frantic—it was insane, this quest for recompense.

He had to balance and chew this limb free. He felt the plastic with his tongue and chewed. It cut his lips. He gnawed and pulled the blade free. The Cracker Jack prize. The blade was ready. He sat and felt for his jugular vein. He marked the spot and rested his other fingers in place and pushed the blade home. The skin resisted and Arlen poked. The skin capitulated and spewed blood. With all his strength, Arlen pulled a stroke and then another. The blood was warm.

He grabbed the garbage can and placed it between the bed and the wall. He had to bleed and he flowed now. He hunkered down and stretched forth to drip his blood into the can. The red blared against the white plastic. It felt good to heed the call. It was all over him now in weakness. He let himself go. The warmth fed him. Arlen blacked out.

He awoke with renewed rage. The blackout had left the guilt remain. Absolvement sought but not found. Arlen looked in the garbage can and discovered a clot of inadequacy. He was not capable of even this. He exploded and looked up at the electrical plug in. He must burn. He sat up and pulled the nail clippers from the bag. He broke them into two pieces and lay back down on the bed. This was the solution. Burn

Arlen. He inserted the short file piece into the right slot. He inserted the remaining piece in the left. It arced before he was ready. Snap. He jumped back. Instinct fought at the judgment. This was a serious fight for survival. He readied himself, arms above his head like Superman in flight. His cape was shame and guilt. He lowered his melded hands to the steel.

Zap. Feel the surge. Hear it, Arlen, rage through you. Yeah, this is it. Don't jump back. Embrace it, your reward. You need it. Feel it. Arlen, get your fingers back on there. Snap. Don't fight it Arlen. Make it yours, feel it. That's it. Hold on. You can do it. Try harder Arlen. Let it shake you silly. Yeah. Hold it firm; shake your arms and head—hold on to the bronco Arlen. Endurance. This is your marathon of pain. Feel it all. No it's numbing you. Let go Arlen. It shakes you. You like the numb. Embrace it. Cuddle the shake and blur. Now you're warm. Good boy Arlen. Take it all the way through. What is on the other side? You can find out Arlen. Push it to hold, to the ream. Arlen nerves it to dull. The snap fizzled to gray. He is done. His hands drop to drape the garbage can. His eyes close.

The smoke smells and the plug-in and wall are blackened. The darkness spit Arlen out. The snake recoiled and released the boy. He could be a man. Arlen woke and parted his eyelids. Everything remained. No change except the depth. He had reached it. There was no further that he could travel. He had dived to the murky depths. He had pushed it to the end.

He felt such deep shame. What had he done now? He swam in a wave of clarity. He felt shame too deep to speak of. It painted him, his blood pumped the color of shame. He was left with nothing else. That was that. He could not continue. He had tried to pay. He was honest in his attempt to appease. Why could he not equal the task? It had called him and he answered—Arlen thought that should be worth something.

He struggled to sit up. It slammed him now. The circle of shame tightened and squeezed him from the room. He stumbled upstairs in the blue robe and looked in the TV room. Fred Flintstone danced on the screen. Arlen could not comprehend the cartoon. He turned and entered the bathroom, closed the door and faced the mirror. What had he performed? And to whom?

He raised his eyes from the sink to the mirror and glanced in his eyes. He could not see the neck bite. That was all he could manage: a flash of eye on eye. The surface of the water reflected the glare. The beasts below the surface were not fully seen. It was there for only an instant.

Arlen turned to the tub and drew the frigid cold. His shame needed some icing to carry its theme. It wanted to grow. What you focus on will prosper Arlen. If that's what you want we have to let you drag your sorry ass through. Do you want a kick to speed it up? Is this your bottom? Arlen, get real, this is messed up. What have you done to yourself? Atoned for the destruction of the world. Like anyone is going to believe that. You are a sorry sight.

Arlen stepped into the cold water. It grabbed at his ankles and sucked him in. He stood and thought of the end. He wished his suffering could cease and he could be warm. Rational Arlen sat in the water. His genitals retracted in the shrink-wrap of freeze. This felt good. You are a sick little kitty. Bye bye Arlen. They're coming to take you away. A ha, it's about time. You are trying our patience Arlen. Are you finished?

The cold water cooled the rage of shame and Arlen stood and passed the mirror by. The door opened and Arlen returned to his bed of rapturous sanding. He lay down and shaped the bed in a way of support. He was in excruciating discomfort. He was pain and raw. His soul had screamed to its death and dragged the shards. He was now done. He fell into the mold of clothing and drifted off toward black.

INTERVENTION

Earl spun into the scene and hammered Arlen to wake.

"No, what have you done?"

He grabbed at the plug in steel and can of blood to conceal. It was inhumane to allow such sights to prosper. Not another eye should see this stage act. Earl disappeared and returned with two burly men. One sat on either side of Arlen and lifted him to stand. They dragged him down the stairs. His feet kept up. In the kitchen, they sat him down and Earl gave him juice, sugary juice.

It was an ether returned—he was body again. The sugar found its place and craved more. A spot of food, some soup, a bite or three. There Arlen, you are coming back to us, wake up, you've been sleeping.

"We need to get you to the doctor."

Arlen's eyes hinted at recognition.

"These guys will escort you."

They stood and supported him on either side. He arose and walked out the door. It was two blocks to the house that held the doctor of the head. The henchmen sat nervous and curious. The wait was short and the doctor prodded with questions. That is a desk to sit behind; you thought you've heard it all.

A pill was given and the men returned through the snow. Arlen felt his muscles sag and blossom. This was what he was missing. He needed this pill, whatever it was—the missing ingredient in this cold turkey pie. This was a different twenty year old walking back into the center.

He was hungry and drank cold soup. It was nectar to this peasant peon of addiction. This was the rebound of it all that started for Arlen. I for one have had enough of his spiral. Haven't you? He climbed the steps and lay on his bed. It was perfect.

They woke him up and into the downstairs room. He would have a bedside watch; twenty-four hours round till he left—there were no beds open this day. Arlen wondered not of where this bed would be but he thought of how good he felt, this was the solution. He was being rebuilt, they had the technology, and they had the pill. It was in him now massaging his cells to rest. His penis swelled. Arlen thought this was a good sign and smiled. The watch began. The person sat in his room and read magazines. Arlen drifted.

Arlen stood up, ignoring pleas from the watcher to take it easy, and walked into the kitchen. Arlen lost consciousness and slid down the wall to the floor. He woke in bed. This blackout within the rolling brown outs stood out. The hours passed into new faces that watched him. The brother Jake and Carmen arranged volunteers from their church. Arlen would sleep and wake to see a new face—time had passed, this was his clock face. He was blurry in how this was required. He knew not the argument.

HOUSE OF CRAZE

They had found a bed, it was afternoon. Arlen's mom and sister and brother came to pick him up. Arlen went along into the car. They drove toward the hospital. The streets raced with cars.

"Where are you taking me?" Arlen asked.

"The psych center."

"I don't want to go."

"They will help you there."

"I might as well jump out of this car."

The family sat silent for a moment. What do you say to that? He was in a bad spot. The world has one place for these bad spots that come in a myriad of shades. When you have the affliction that knows no aid, you are dumped at the Psychiatric Ward. They will help you there. It is a place that is hidden—you can go through life without meeting this friend of a place. You are blessed. But it is a rich place of life—it is on the edge that the games cease to play and true humanness beats. Raw persons walk these halls. Everything is meaningful on the sharp side of a knife.

Arlen walked down the hall with his family. They were nice to escort him in, they were worried and afraid—they wanted him through this mess. They walked beside him, but Arlen walked this hall alone. He knew that he was the only one staying on. And that the doors coming up would be closed behind him. They would be returning home.

It was a lonely walk of shame and fear for Arlen. He carried his cardboard box of possessions; it was part of the flavor he felt. He was toast, not knowing how long he would be. This hallway was long, too long. And he carried this box to his doom. It closed in on him.

The isolation that this hospital used for its deranged folk was elevation—they were five floors up and a world away from the lives lived below.

There were the doors. Arlen felt the walls close in on him in defeat. This was it at twenty years of age. The nurse showed him to the room next door to the station. It was a long one-hallway ward with the nurse's station in the middle. They had passed the TV lounge by the door and at the other end there was a recreation type room with a table tennis game. Arlen was pleased to see the table on his tour. The family bid farewell. They did not want to leave him in this establishment but it was required, this was the only place that would have him. They left. He stayed.

Arlen settled into the room. He lay in his bed for a nap. His door opened and the nurse poked her head in.

"Howdy sunshine."

"Hi," Arlen said.

"Do you need anything?"

"No thanks."

"I'll talk to you in a bit, we can have a chat."

"All right."

Fifteen minutes passed and there she was again checking on him. Fifteen minutes later she came in and started talking to him.

"I need to take your vitals."

She took his blood pressure, temperature, and pulse. She asked him questions and drew his story out. Each person in this hall had their story to tell. Arlen finished and felt better.

"Thanks, I feel better."

The nurse left the room hoping that this one makes it through. Arlen went for a walk. He had been told that he was confined to the ward— he was not to step from this place. This was Arlen's first confinement. It was horrible, he wanted to escape through these doors; he walked right up to them, stopped and looked out the wire glass squares at the hall he had walked in from. It was the ultimate challenge. He decided that he would walk out that hall and soon. He had had enough of this place.

In the TV room, people watched, chatted, read, and put puzzles together. Arlen entered and exited. He did not want to get comfortable here. He noticed a happy man who was large, approaching the four hundred pound mark. Arlen walked down the hall and peeked in the rooms. He noticed several young girls and women who were skinny and gaunt. There was a sadness about them, the ones that walked looked to be in pain. The ones that were in bed looked like they could not rise on their own. It was with passion that they had starved themselves. It was dedication to weaken your muscle tissue. Atrophied health. They were attractive girls, Arlen thought, attractive sticks. Arlen wondered how much they weighed.

Arlen himself was no prizefighter. He was a plank boy on the ropes. Those fists had done their damage on his brittle bones and spirit. His trunks had fallen to his ankles. Arlen walked past the desk and his nurse smiled at him. He attempted a smile in return. She wrote something. Arlen felt like he was being watched, and this was true. He was in a place that specialized in observing people, to protect and assess. Arlen was being protected from himself. This egg yolk quivered without a shell: these walls held him tight.

REC ROOM

He walked to the end and entered the recreation room. He felt the energy of the hyper man at the same time that he heard him. He bounced the pool balls against their rail. The cushion popped the ball back in the air to slam on the green felt. Arlen felt his violence. Arlen possessed no protection from the elements of other patient's emotions. He was a spineless sponge. He had no resistance to dramatics and strife.

And this hyper man Clarence was edge energy. His feet could not and did not stand still. He appeared emotionless and surged with movement and angst. He was the doomed man of movement. He could not sit still. Arlen watched him. Clarence had glanced at Arlen in passing and had not acknowledged him. His scan continued their eye's passage through the room. Arlen was another object of detail to be alleged and challenged at a later point: Arlen would have to respond to this creature in the room.

It was an electromagnetic event. It was an experiment to have the two of them in the room. Clarence ripped Arlen's soul to ache and tear. Arlen detested the man but could not free himself of the magnetic field.
"You play Ping Pong," Clarence said.
It was a command-question-challenge.
"Yeah," Arlen said.
They headed to the duel spots. The ball sounded light as it bounced. They rallied—both were decent. Emotion and frustration volleyed to the opponent. There was no doubt that these two were warring. It was their spirits that fought. Three minutes of play wrapped up. It was done, that was all they were mutually capable of. It wrapped up in a truce. Arlen held his poker hand to his chest—he did not want Clarence to know of his weakness. Arlen knew Clarence to be of too much energy and he lacked control. Clarence slammed his paddle to the table. This could be the monster's weak point. Piss him off and press his fleshly stomach with a ping-pong paddle and he would catch fire. The tricky part would be to escape the fire without a singe. He might have to hit the deck.

Clarence bounced into the hall. Arlen found himself shooting pool to unwind. He tried to breathe—he felt like his insides fought to throw him off balance. He thought of this guy Clarence and Arlen knew that he had to get out as soon as possible. This was the challenge: Arlen would be discharged before this battery bouncer, he decided to will this. He could catch new bungee cords that would catapult him free from this pit of suffering.

PROGRESS

Two steps backward. First there was detox and he could not even handle that—he stepped back another step into the psych ward. He needed a step forward. He disappeared from his life and job in Banff. He had not even told anyone. These seemed to be three steps backward—this nullified the two forward and one back theory. He was screwed and needed momentum. He had been clean of his drugs of choice for days now. This was his garden—it sprouted weeds.

The second evening of his stay, his first nurse gave him a book with a page opened. It was a book of triumph. The opened page told of Abraham Lincoln having to be protected from his own hands and knives. He had seen it through and survived this period to live greatly. Arlen closed his eyes with new hope. He was not the only one. He felt like he had a chance to make it out, he had hope.

The days passed with the fifteen minute checks—they were reduced to thirty. The night flashlight scans became part of his dream world. Arlen dreamt toward morning of weird and wild events. His crazed mind fought out battles with the tranquilizers and anti-psychotics. In the din midst of these dreams he saw a darkened figure shining a flashlight into his world of darkness and dream. Did they point the way out? This added credence to the reality of the dreams. They melded into a vision of strife.

A nurse placed a small paper cup of petroleum jelly on his bedside table. It puzzled him. He could not get through with the idea that she was encouraging masturbation. He pondered the dry lips and nose—this was true, no doubt about it in winter on the prairie. The amount deemed an encouragement and this is what Arlen did before sleep. It became his knockout pill of tension release. Under the covers for fear of display, he stroked the therapy free.

The drugs gained an edge on the psychosis. Arlen was moved down the hall. He was considered less of a threat to himself. He talked to the large happy man who had lost two hundred pounds. He was overjoyed to be walking ten miles per day while listening to the radio. He melted into his intended being.

Arlen talked to the anorexics and bulimics. This was a murkier solution. They had deep meanderings that tripped. It was tough work to overcome the eating disorders. The overweight struggle seemed the easiest to Arlen. This man made it happen with movement.

"I move, I win," the man liked to say.

It was inconceivable to Arlen that the girls could starve themselves to the point of not being able to walk under their own power. He could understand the drug till you drop ploy, but the starve till you die was a tough one. Arlen's appetite returned with the drugs. He looked forward to meal times—it was an adventure to see what the food would be. He was hungry and the food tasted great.

They walked in a place of voyeur exile five floors up. Arlen took to observing people in the park. There were cross-country skiers that wowed him. He thought of how great it would be to be out there, free and clear of all this.

He focused on acting every moment like this was not his intended place of residence. They continued to bring the colored pills in the little paper cups. Arlen would slam it and chase the water. He liked the medicine. It took the edge off and settled him in to a decent person again. It was the truth his body needed right now. His body did not need A.A., meetings or tapes. He had trained his body to have external chemicals. He had a lazy body and it stopped producing its own chemicals. The cold turkey electrocuting and cutting had shown that he needed a drug to get him through.

GROUP

It was expected for Arlen to go to group twice a week—that is what he did. He went to group. You want me to cut off a finger; you'd let me out? Arlen would do it. He needed honorable discharge from this crazy facility. It was dire consequential evidence that delivered Arlen here. It was desperation that goaded him to group.

After the first twenty minutes, Arlen knew that he had better things to do than listen in depth to others whine and moan and mutter incessantly. There seemed no end to the rants. The facilitator was trained and practiced in the field—they were marathoners. Arlen could sprint listen and then he crumbled and fidgeted. He was over it and the hour was a third done. How do they do it? They go on and on, they are encouraged in this. Arlen's head swam with the sordid details and attitudes of tonal verbiage. He was dead meat floating in the water. Meat that was being watched and evaluated for freedom. His turn came and he shared a little—he knew that this animation could get back to the authorities. He intended to play nice. The woman that followed Arlen went on and on about becoming the Prime Minister of our fair land. Arlen wondered how living in this psychiatric ward was going to sit with the electorate. It's been a while since Abe Lincoln and his top hat. It was a difficult hour for Arlen. It was done—he felt released from a bad place and he rode this wave of freedom for hours.

TWENTY-ONE

He was surfing about on good vibes when he opened the recreation room door. Clarence was bouncing around the room. Arlen looked down at Clarence's feet—they did seem to touch the ground. He moved so effortlessly, a tall wiry frame.

"Want to play?" Clarence asked.

"Sure," Arlen said.

Clarence sped to a side of the table—Arlen assumed it to be Clarence's favorite side.

"Game to twenty one," Clarence stated.

"Sure." Arlen picked up the paddle.

The ball sounded hollow and happy to bounce.

"Warm up."

"Sure."

The warm up became heated. The intensity rivaled game point. Arlen knew he had his hands full—but he had to beat this guy, it was part of getting out of this place.

The dead air was killing Arlen; it had been a week since he had tasted fresh air. His breaths took in recycled air that had been sucked in, heated and blown through metal. His head crawled thick with it. He had seldom in his life gone one week indoors. It was a slow death. He needed to get out and soon. It was time to fight this nemesis. One of them would lose.

Arlen loved good competition in his true health—he could get over a loss. But he wanted to beat this live wire that was always running into people and pushing them with his gruff aggression. It was not a good soul to have around in a tight quarters place—you wanted souls of peace and harmony. There was a general mood of love and healing and this guy walked through with gas and a lighter. Shoulders hiked when he came into the TV room to eat. He affected people to be on the defensive. The best defense is a great offense and nobody was capable of scoring goals on this battery man. Until now. Arlen met Clarence in a format that could effect justice.

They stood alone in the room. It was a battle of the wits and sphincter. There was more on the line than simply twenty-one points. It was war of the patient that gets to leave first. It was a battle of release from this incarcerated drug land. It was the end of seeing your almighty doctor and having to be nice and cooperative, but hating him inside for his three minutes of daily attention. This was power of biblical proportions—to smite one to extended days and weeks in such a place as this. They both needed release. Arlen wore his need on the inside. Clarence was obvious—he was too large a person for this hallway and two public rooms, they sat horizontal and he needed ladders to climb.

"Rally?"

"Sure."

Clarence won the rally and served clean, he was up three points to two. Arlen thought of strategy with a guy like this. If he could piss him off Arlen would win for sure. Arlen decided to let his points slide a bit toward the ten mark. This would give Clarence a false sense of easy victory. Then Arlen would pick his own game up, and this would flip Clarence. Arlen could control Clarence's ability by first controlling his own. They were close enough in skill that it could go either way. But, he would lose points on purpose.

By Arlen's next serve, Clarence was up ten to five. Clarence had the game in the bag—he was bouncing up and down now. He could taste sweet trouncing. Arlen served and missed the table. Eleven five. Clarence threw his hands in the air. Arlen gave him one more point; he set Clarence up for a spike. Twelve to five—it was all Arlen could handle giving him—it unnerved him. Arlen brought out his superspin serves. He crouched and put crazy sidespin on—Clarence did not compensate and the return missed the table. Arlen repeated, Clarence countered this time but still missed by two inches. The third serve, Arlen reversed spin direction and gained another point.

Twelve to eight felt much better to Arlen than twelve to five. Clarence's countenance had turned to yellow and approached orange. Clarence served; he was tight with the previous three serve losses. He missed his own serve. Arlen laughed. Clarence was full orange now. His next serve was great and the rally ensued. Arlen won the point cleanly with a topspin backhand to the right—Clarence could not reach it. Clarence served to close at fourteen to eleven.

Arlen served a spin and won his first service point. His service closed at sixteen to fourteen for Clarence. Clarence tried to direct his nuclear energy through the little paddle and fragile ball. Losing the point advantage was getting to him—he lost the lead at seventeen but regained it with eighteen. He stood nervous and clammy.

Arlen won three straight points—twenty to eighteen. Clarence miss-hit the ball: it bounced and teased him. Clarence slammed his paddle onto the ball and crushed it to dimples. Arlen smiled at him. It was the largest smile of freedom since he had arrived back in the province. This game was a symbol.

Clarence was in the red zone and lost the next point. He erupted in rage. He did not even look at Arlen. Clarence threw his paddle to the side. Arlen followed the path—it spun and glanced off the floor and hit a cupboard at five inches of height. It changed spin pattern as it bounced off. Arlen didn't even hear or sense Clarence move. The paddle stopped. Arlen turned and saw Clarence's back blurring out the door.

Arlen laughed. It was sweet victory. Arlen walked to the door and looked down the hall in time to see Clarence exit the main door. It was unlocked during the day if everyone was stable. It was also a test of self-control. Arlen smiled with assurance that he would be leaving this place, and soon. Arlen walked to the nurse's station and heard them call security. This was great fun. They called him a runner. He was marked energy—his hospital pajamas and robe flowed.

Arlen walked to the TV room and told the Clarence haters that he had run. Six sets of eyes peered out the windows and down. They hoped for a sight of him. They waited and laughed and felt great. They knew that this would place him in a different state—he would most likely be restrained and drugged to compliance. They hoped he would not get caught or would be taken to a different place.
"There he is!"
The hospital wardrobe fluttered behind him. He could run, that Clarence could make time through the snow in his slippers. The snow cover of ice cut gashes into his legs. The security team could not make it—there were few motivations for speed like Clarence's raw escape run.

That night the meal was eaten in celebration—the whole mood had improved. And maybe Clarence is still out there running.

RELEASE

Arlen was released two weeks to the day after he was taken in. It felt great to walk out and down the hall and outside. The air was moist and laden with energy. It smelled. Arlen was empowered by the experience. He was starting over in great and powerful manners.

He was born again. Jake and Carmen, the watchers, and the odd nurse at the hospital had served the Christ experience to him. Arlen knew that he had to be born again. He had killed his old self and needed newness—they promised peace, and joy and love. He had seen some of it amongst them—it looked good and right and promising. It looked easy. He joined them the night he reentered detox.

A winter storm raged outside. Arlen sat in the A.A. meeting and dwelled on his sin and shame. Earlier, someone had read him the scripture, "Though your sins are red as scarlet, they will be pure as driven snow." He thought of this scripture as someone spoke. He was shame and sin. The window above him blew open and snow dusted Arlen's shoulders and head. It was his sign—he could not deny it.

He accepted Christ as his savior. He walked around the block that night and sang, "This little light of mine, I'm going to let it shine." He had not heard it since Sunday school as a kid.

The detox house seemed casual and relaxed after the hospital. Arlen felt like a kid on his own with so much to do and see. And no one cared to watch. The meetings surged organic and edgy. Some went on in their drunkalogues but it was easier to take than the group in the hospital. It did not seem so much like a waste of time. Arlen could see the desperation in these three-year-old sober guests. Their program had saved them from horrible self-proclaimed atrocities. If you cast these deeds upon another you would stand in a court of law. These people faced the mirror alone, and their families.

A few people were still in detox from his first time. Valium man was one. Arlen was impressed with his reduced shake—his hands were down to a foot of movement. Most had moved on to the rehabilitation—it was in part of the hospital where Arlen received his physical.

Arlen settled into his new found faith and Alcoholics Anonymous meetings twice daily with two tape sessions thrown in. The programming was intense. Arlen felt hammered on over and over again. A wave of suffering came on him again—he was jumbled institutionalized man. He was pre re-hab. The Christ child birthed within him—he was magnificent, Arlen was the special chosen one. Illusions of grandeur propagated in Arlen's psyche toward delusion.

He was born again, the Christians told him. He was twelve steps and a sponsor, go to meetings, a day at a time. His mind was mush and pain and he troubled to continue. He started the mantra of an hour at a time, a minute at a time, and a second at a time. He suffered it to a millisecond at a time. He was time itself. His heart beat now on its own and kept time.

He woke in the night and walked downstairs to the kitchen. There was a spirit man there who claimed his name was Darren—he dug in the fridge. It was in the fridge glow that Darren grinned. He was odd and took a non-human form. Arlen thought him to be a ghost— he had finally seen his first ghost.

But in truth, in a couple of days Darren switched to day shift and Arlen found him to be a real person and a staff member. This was hard for Arlen to grasp. The man told him of his own drug trips that took five days to peak and come down. Arlen believed him for he looked the part—his body had evolved to skinny arms and big eyes. He had been somewhere where few had trod. He laughed crazily and existed a little distant from everything that occurred around him. Arlen wondered if Darren saw things differently. Arlen knew that he himself did. It was confusing to take it all in at once—it became too much. Arlen's cracks of thinking were held from all around. He was skilled at keeping his internal world hidden. No one knew him here or anywhere—everyone was focused on his or her own world.

Arlen learned the HALT acronym. Hungry, angry, lonely, and tired. Arlen strove to address these four and his craving for his drug of choice might end.

DOWNTOWN

It was Saturday night and time for the big meeting downtown. It was an event. Extra cars arrived and filled with detoxers. It was a cold night. Arlen caught the wave of newness and became scared and fight-or-flighty. His limbs became cold and then his whole body froze. He concentrated on a minute at a time. He hung in there till the next minute arrived. And the next and the next.

Downtown looked exciting to Arlen. They stopped by the riverbank and walked to the large church. It loomed in shadows and wings and size. It was impressive. Arlen followed the group to the front steps. They walked to the left of the main entrance and found the narrow stairway to the basement. Around the side of the church stood huddles of smokers. It was a darkened approach that through the door lightened and opened, and then a grand hall blew the cave big to house hundreds of people.

There were already a couple of hundred people who talked and hung in pockets. The hearth coffee urns attracted the most people. They huddled and dispensed coffee and talked and drank and headed above ground for smokes. Arlen was nervous in large crowds and it built to these proportions around him. He shrunk and shriveled to his walls of silent protection. No one penetrated his armor.

Arlen noticed that the place smelled of church basement. Any church basements he had been in were the same. He found a seat in the back and waited the minutes to pass. He looked at the podium and microphone—this was a different league of meeting from the detox.

The group gathered on a silent cue and the meeting began. Arlen liked to watch this scale of meeting. He thought that some of the people liked the stage light. Thirty minutes passed with the planned speakers. There was the drunkalogue guy: he was always represented at meetings. Arlen tired of the bragging about the binges. It didn't make sense why it was allowed to proceed. It made him thirsty, and hungry for a toke of hash. He salivated to taste it—gritty on his teeth. Arlen floated back to the present and the guy was still talking about his drinking. Arlen thought of group in the hospital. Arlen looked at the clock on the wall—it was passing into history. The man finished his talk and it was time for open mike.

Three people rushed at once and had to wait their turn. Arlen caught an urge to speak but fought it down to his gut. He listened half-heartedly as the urge kept popping up into his chest. Over and over he stuffed it down to his gut. It was wearing him out to avoid it. He lost. His feet found the front by the side. He waited and listened. His turn came. It jumped from his chest into his stomach and throat—it see-sawed up and down. Arlen walked to the mike.

"My name is Arlen, I'm an alcoholic and drug addict."

"Hi Arlen." The room reverberated with the name.

It felt great to Arlen. He walked out to the side and back to his seat. He felt like a noose had been cut off. He was free before the community. He had confessed his sins to the whole. He was cleansed. He was suddenly hungry and wanted to get out of this basement.

He forced himself to sit on the wooden and metal hall chair. He focused on the clock and deep in his mind, he delegated brain cells to listen. His clean and free feeling had passed out the door with the hunger and now he was dodging and kissing the darts of accusation. He had the prosecuting lawyer pacing his head and lipping to the jury about the deeds and shame of this Arlen.

Within minutes the sentence was passed without a closing statement from the defense. Arlen was bad. He looked up at the clock and it was minutes to the top of the hour. They stood and recited the Lord's Prayer. The chairs thudded and scraped the floor. Release. It was over and not a minute too late for Arlen. He rushed for the door. He wanted out of this program and into life, and now. Enough of the suffering druggie. Take those clothes off and take on the look of the student. Studying, classes, and dates. Why was he not there? Change Arlen and make it happen.

COLD

He walked up into the city-wintered night. The cold was his friend—predictable and it touched his nerve endings. It was nature's hug. It was appropriate for him now. He was the iceman. He felt it to be true. It was all he ever knew and would know. This experience was the ice age and he was ice. It kept people away at a safe distance. He walked down the sidewalk toward the river. He could feel its presence. It was friend. The silhouetted branches danced in the breeze.

Arlen waited for a car to pass to cross the street.

"Arlen!" The voice was female.

Shit Arlen. It was Bryanna. Arlen turned. She ran up to him from the dark. They stood under a streetlamp. The winter felt lonely but comforting. They needed to be inside. She liked Arlen and he liked her. It was a curious friendship—they had not said much but were kin. She was like a close cousin in this A.A. family.

"Where you going?" Bryanna asked.

"To the river," Arlen said.

"Why?"

"I was cold."

"Give me a hug." Bryanna opened her arms.

They went out after the meeting. You guessed it. To a smoking, coffee place. They smoked and coffeed another hour to dust. Arlen had a coffee—his adrenal gland secreted its limit. He listened and did not say much in this place—it was his usual format to say more one on one than in a group of people. The minutes passed to home time.

They drove back across the eastern city to Olson house. It was a party spirit that consumed the group. They were back in their element—a substituted place and a drink in their hand. Arlen was glad to be in a place of central heating. He was finding that the hot and cold still took him for rides. Maybe it was part of his mountaintop memories. Regardless, he found it best to stay where the temperature remained constant.

PILLOW THOUGHTS

He approached the office for his nighttime meds. They were locked up—this was the house treasure. If you exposed a hundred detoxers to a bottle of prescription pills or cash; many would grab the pills. They would also want the cash—they weren't stupid, just addicted. They were hardwired to hit their button over and over again. He took his little pill and went to bed.

He was in a different bed than where he performed his self-hating ritual—the first time he saw that room and bed was strange. It was like seeing a scary movie you had seen as a kid that scared the hell out of you. It was just a bed. And it triggered a reel of events for him. He replayed them but the worst was the emotion that flooded him. He repeated the shame and guilt tape—the feelings dirtied him and then the chatter arrived to reinforce the state of loathing. He was talking himself down. It was horrible to be stuck in it. He had left the room and entered his new one. The tape played auto reverse perpetually.

He was a new creature. He thought back on when his mom visited him in the first days of detox. She was a good actor. It was only in the end that she cracked. Tear ducts erupted.
"I love you Arlen, Jesus will forgive you."
And that was that, she was teary inside. It stuck with Arlen for days and days.

He used what she said to throw a cog in the self-hate wheel of industry. It was hard for Arlen to change his tapes. It was horrible to be a slave to the memory stalker that circled in for the prey. It was death to the living, lack of color, and no sugar or salt. It was continual meditation of bad. It was his enemy now—it played like a friend to get the volume raised and then it clamped down and ate his flesh.

It took him a few hours to remedy the seeing of the bed. It involved the big book (the blue A.A. manual), and the promise book. One of the watchers had given him the promise book—it consisted of promises from the bible. He liked it because it was simple but hard hitting. When the fires of condemnation licked and consumed, this was one tool that seemed to make a difference. It was good, and powerful to remedy those hours of berating.

The days of detox passed toward February. The tapes and meetings helped Arlen counter his own recording loops of ruin. The word came that there was an opening for Arlen in rehabilitation. He was taking a step forward. It had taken a month but he had made it on a Friday. He packed his bag and walked over to the hospital.

REHAB

He found his way to the proper person. The place seemed huge and odd—an old institutional, hospital, recreational feel. He was shown to his upstairs room—this was old hospital for certain. His roommate was Wil, who still read L'Amour in bed. Wil stood up and shook Arlen's hand.

"You made it." Wil smiled.

"Sure," Arlen said.

"Wil, can you give Arlen a tour?" The staff person asked and walked out the door.

"Yep, I'll show him the ropes."

The room was comfortable, bathroom down the hall. They ate in the hospital cafeteria, part of a working hospital. Taxpayers made money off the sale of booze and they had to skim the profit for places such as this. Counselors' offices lined the hall. Large meeting and recreation rooms sat downstairs. It was a temporary place; you could tell it was transient.

Arlen remembered back to his physical examination triggering. There was a man before him that was seeing the doctor—he had drank photocopying fluid. He said he was lucky to live, you could barely understand him with his toasted vocal chords. Arlen thought of the desperate pursuit of discord that these residents possessed. It consumed them with a variety of approaches and speeds. It was death dressed up as a good time. Insanity clothed in happy-button-pushing clowns. Take a drink, take a pill. Find that first high. Repeat. Bring it on. Bring it down.

The weekend propped full with meetings. Arlen walked in and felt at home in his first Narcotics Anonymous meeting. He was in his immediate family. A.A. had his extended family, cousins and aunts and uncles that were in the same room but the heart was not fully shared. Arlen sat down and listened to the room chatter—there was little. These people were quiet in spirit and did not talk very much.

The meeting progressed and Arlen found himself thankful for these addicts. Some shared death's bed each time they used. They rode the edge and the experience humbled them. They were grateful to still be alive and relatively sane. They did not brag very much about the drug highs and trips. They were a different breed.

They were more affected to this moment by what they had done. You could not describe drug use as readily as alcohol. Drugs were relative and possessed more hues and shades of color, and a deeper effect on the emotion and soul. It drove them away from people; the experience was profound. Many of the drugs can be used socially yet as one progresses in the pilgrimage of addiction, most find themselves using solo. This can be said for alcohol use as well.

In the end the mirror and the pillow betray and talk back. How do inanimate objects gain such power? Perhaps because it is that addicts give such power to their drugs. The material substance world takes on more meaning and pays back to the addict in mirror and pillow talk. You lay your head on the pillow to sleep and the tapes of self-abuse begin to play. The mirror jumps out with accusations. You avoid these places with haste of dress and blackouts.

The N.A. group surprised him with the older women prescription drug users—they looked so innocent and non-addict like from what Arlen was used to. Grandmas. There they were, a different look and a different drug. When they talked, generally they were a more polite version of the said same addictive patterns.

Arlen liked to look at addicts more because they were simple, like himself. They were blown away with the present and were adjusting. They laughed funny. They did not make jokes about silly things; they did not exalt the bottle. They did not brag about the drugs they could drink. A twenty-six or forty of whiskey is pretty much the same commercially, maybe that was the difference why men would talk about their daily consumption—it was a competition.

It is all a terrible affliction and Arlen was able to hear many stories of each. The harder drugs left this violent shock that remained for a longer time. The brain damage was more serious, it took their attention vividly, and they knew they were sick on a deeper level. The alcohol left a happier gentler state of being. Even among the pickled friends of wet brain, there seemed a serene damage, a happier state.

With alcohol you are generally remained with social function. With drug use this is impaired on a deeper level—you are turned to relate with fewer people. This is a huge difference. Even the wet brain alcohol users have this social desire available.

Alcohol can talk to itself if need be. Two can be at the table and drinking and the alcohol talks, you can hear it, it may argue and fight. Put two people at a table taking certain drugs, and depending on their mental state, and drugs used, they could end up in different rooms. It confuses the mind more.

Throw in sobriety and cleanness and meetings. The two tables carry on. A.A. has a general spirit at the table of camaraderie and direction. N.A. is flat and directionally challenged but the smallest detail can have epic diversions for the individual or group. A dropped book can trip someone up or the whole group of N.A. gets on this tangent. They would probably laugh. The A.A. group would likely laugh more predictably and move on to the agenda. The N.A.'ers perhaps have deeper scarring that gets triggered to fester.

Arlen felt impure among the sanctified holy ones. They talked about being clean and sober. This included prescription drug use. This was where it became hazy. A few programmers shunned any use of prescription use. Arlen was in a conundrum. He was down in his use but he was still on drugs. They cleaned up his fuzzy head. Arlen would later realize that most people talk big and when it comes to the crunch of need, their actions are different than their ideal chatter. But this was now and Arlen waged the prescription topic in his head and absorbed the statements. The topic did not come up very often in meetings. When it did, Arlen felt exposed as a fraud. But he had tried it. His was not a case of D.T.'s—take some Librium for a while and you are set.

His was a brain chemical rusting of sorts. The cold turkey approach coagulated in fat gobules that choked his vein of reality and made it dangerous for his life. He needed the new drug and still did. A time would come soon when he could be totally clean. He could make it there. Even in this sanctuary for the addict there was a religiosity, a hierarchy of moral claim. Arlen wondered at all this caffeine and nicotine but held his tongue. He listened and took with him what helped.

WALK

He was in a twenty-one day program of drug and alcohol rehabilitation. Monday after morning meeting Arlen walked the two-mile block. He had gone first on Saturday. Wil had told him about it. It was great to take the little map and follow it through the streets. It was a simple box but it gave Arlen a taste of freedom he had not known for months. He was walking on his own and could go off the map and choose to end this rehab situation. The choice was his. The lines on the map made him feel safe—he was not ready for the whole world. The air was cool and his body was challenged by the distance.

He went again on Sunday—he took in different sights. Arlen turned the fenced corner to go north and saw it immediately a hundred feet up on the sidewalk. The hulk of a body in dark clothing lay on the snowy concrete. Arlen wanted to flee; yet a perverse frightening need to see in detail reeled him in.

The first step is to admit I am powerless over my chosen drug. I am powerless over this downed creature. Why am I the one to encounter him? I am in Rehab and walking my daily walk like a good recovering drug addict.

The time it takes to get to him is an eternity too quick. Arlen sees a slight breath in the freezing air. The blood grabs him, the ear leaks thick red. There is a beautiful side to the color—is Arlen sick?

Lysol in the cold air sickens Arlen to turn. A police cruiser rounds the corner toward them. Arlen waves him down. He parks efficiently beside them. Arlen tells him what he already knows. He thanks Arlen and tends to his business of removing the man from public-frigidity-corpse. The cop squats down and probes behind the man's ear for a pressure point that brings out a moan from his depths of chemical haze.

"Get up!" The cop pressed harder.

The moan grew urgent as the bones stirred on the cold cement.

"Come on, get up."

The dance between them intensified as pain overcame gravity.

He was out cold and now he carried his weight towards warmth. The thumb jabbed in and bothered Arlen to the point that he could feel it moving him onward, elsewhere. Wherever the thumb penetrated, his nervous skull would be, Arlen would go willingly without a peep.

Puppeted into the car, the Lysol man groaned. Rebelling the life-saving fact, he resisted his fatal liberation. Arlen wondered how many times he had silently challenged death?

They drove away. Arlen's own chill moved him forward around the big suggested rectangle of city blocks. He turned left at 20th. More cars exhaled warm clouds of spent fuel into the street. The trails of exhaust lingered and grabbed his eye.

Arlen was distant from all of this. He had been living in Banff killing his memories and pain quickly through chemicals. The beauty of surroundings soothed the process. Gravity at times threatened its assistance while he recreated stone.

Insanity and death were the final stages, they told him.

Arlen walked on embracing the cold of western Saskatoon. Its friendship shook him with closeness and showed the biggest reason Arlen felt alive.

Into the center, Arlen went back in time; it had been there for decades. How can there be so many people to keep a place like this going indefinitely? Are we all sick?

MUSCLE

The meetings and meals pass into muscle—to withstand the tempta-
tion of leaving. There is Sue, they know her as the Nymphomaniac. She
has a certain driven energy that intensely flirts. Arlen is attracted to her
and scared at the same time—he keeps his distance.

Arlen shakes with the cold that reminds him of limbs and blood. Up
to his room Arlen floats, this is surreal. Arlen thumbs his self around
detached and separate, yet willing his self here and there, as an ob-
server who chooses where to observe through the creature that is 'I'.

There is the roommate, always reading. Pale ghoul of a face that
lives it out in westerns saving the day, can you save yourself Arlen
wonders? He hopes he did not say it out loud. He keeps reading, Arlen
must not have.

Arlen lays down and the thoughts crawl in the snow, barely alive yet
throbbing, twitch.

Drug induced psychosis has the clean-up phase—a kinder place to
be than the dirt, tear down part. It twinges still with agitation.

Six of them and the counselor, Donna, sit at a round table in a cool
office for small group. Donna "Obi-Wan" elf-like has been alive for cen-
turies drinking for a hundred years and then helping us sick creatures
for at least two hundred. Arlen has never known wisdom such as hers.
She knows each of them commonly as one, herself to be one for all, an
addict, and an alcoholic. She had guided thousands of cookie-cutter,
flaky, humans through.

They are kids being guided to use the force—it is easy to see the
children and the utter trusting gaping holes of hopelessness in all of
them. Two of the guys are in their sixties, twelve year old expressions
giving their recipes of a 26 a day, a 40 a day, from twelve to sixty, to
keep the maturity away. Empathy is the only thing a human stranger
could have for these boys. Their families could tell you other words.

John went off on a tangent, blabbering about all this poor me crap.

Donna reached behind her and placed the pot on the table in front of him and told him to sit on it. The twelve year old blushed averting his eyes to the floor through his gray-haired, wrinkled face. "Pity Pot," it said in big black letters on the side of its white painted steel. The black rimmed handle and trimmed rim stood out. Arlen has seen them in museums but had never used a chamber pot. He vows silently to never get it passed to me.

The days passed, meetings blurred the walks to be a cool reprise from the ashen faces and stories of lost days. Arlen overflowed with gratitude, to be waking up here after only two decades of walking in winter. He had hope of a different life, a new way of discovery and goodness. He chose life.

MARBLING OUT

Graduation day—the marbling out ceremony was upon them. They figured they'd all lost their marbles and deserved one back to keep as a symbol of sobriety. They each got to pick one out that had special meaning and the counselor would give it to him or her and they would explain briefly to everyone why they had picked that one. What a weird grad.

Awkward smiles through uncomfortable faces exposed the challenge of not having the chosen substance coursing through your veins—surging with coolness and courage. They were a clean, ungainly crew released to the general public that day.

Arlen had searched the marble bowl for a long time and settled on a small one with twisted bands of white through it. His turn came to speak to the group.

"I chose one with some white to represent my innocence lost and maybe I can regain some to see things more clearly."

PART TWO

THE ENIGMA SOLVENT

Insanity is a gateway: create opportunity, or accept hell.

MARBLED OUT

Booze advertisements triggered salivation among the poor dogs that night. Some would succumb to the slide of death—they would relapse. Others could, and would, seek the drying of their crave. A desert would be their honorable place of earning.

The odd spring would rise up over the years and be ignored a day at a time, back to the sand. These people are everywhere with hidden worlds of desert-driven splendors. They have risen through the shit of who they were to be unknown heroes today.

Arlen's mom picked him up and he went to live in the basement for a while. It had been two and a half years since he had lived there. He had changed. Arlen spread his possessions out in the room—stuff littered the dresser in disarray. The N.A. and the A.A. books shone as beacons on the pile. Arlen thought that it looked odd and took a picture of the dresser mess.

Small town Saskatchewan was full of ground to sprout. It was community and protected. Arlen felt like he would lay low. Someone in such a place sees every move. He needed some quiet time to make sense of the last months—he was still in shock. Things had moved way too fast and now the boat still rocked at anchor. He focused on the ceiling and thought.

On Monday night, another basement in town held an A.A. meeting. The importance of meetings was beaten into Arlen at Rehab. Arlen needed this meeting like water flows down a decline. He pondered the tree skeletons on the five-block walk to the church. It was still weeks before the leaves budded. Arlen slithered down the stairs.

Smiles and warmth held Arlen. Mr. and Mrs. So and So, (Some of his parent's peers) were now Bills, and Helens, and Bobs. He had thrust his bones into a secret club on a side of town he grew up in, and never knew. These people were like the others at the city meetings, yet more stable. Coffee and nicotine hailed loud. One could imagine eastern orthodox priests circling the table, waving their incense pots to anoint the members, the hair, the clothes.

The meeting comforted Arlen with acceptance. All you had to do is show up to be cherished.

"My name is Arlen, I'm an alcoholic."

He wanted to say, "I'm a drug addict." It didn't seem like they were ready for it. This was rural drinking territory. One drunkalogue irritated him in useless bragging excess; it was the occasional price of admission. The trees on the way home looked bound for spring. Arlen trotted.

The coffee barred him from ease of slumber that night. The next morning pushed noon when the craving gnawed at his gut. This house, this town, and especially this mirror were all so plain. Arlen was straight and sober dull. He brewed a pot of coffee, let it cool and chugged it back. It filled half the needy spot; his afternoon jittered oddly content with the furnishings and scene. "A day at a time." The frequent pees moved him.

ROUND-UP

The weeks passed into spring and A.A. roundup season. And Arlen was a horse that needed an event. Graciously he was given a ride to the lake, and a room to stay in a cabin. The people had known Arlen's brother who died.

It was a half-mile to the event with hundreds of people in attendance—urns of coffee and cartons of cigarettes. Arlen did not smoke but he drank coffee. There were gatherings and meetings everywhere.

It was a circus of healing. Tapes and bumper stickers were hawked. There were sunrise and sunset and noon and midnight meetings. Arlen took it all in and drank coffee and peed. It was afternoon on Saturday when the caffeine caved within him. He stopped en route—he froze. His nerves surged and hammered yet he was not capable of movement. His adrenaline gland tweaked. His vision blurred through the slight out-of-focus lens. He was not capable of seeing people in detail, yet the whole sight was inviting. He found a quiet place and jittered down and away from coffee.

Spring found him driving tractor on a farm. It was great for Arlen to stare at the earth—the landscape soothed his thirst. The radio beer commercials played and Arlen salivated. He found himself craving; he didn't even like beer in the past. The dust billowed from the earth.

CAMP

Arlen worked a job as counselor at a summer camp that his brother Jake had arranged—he knew the director. Arlen was a new creature in Christ and this was his jungle of play. He was a counselor in charge of kids at night. During the day it was continual activities. Talk about focusing on others to help you. Arlen forgot about himself with all the children around. He loved the responsibility and the kids were great after the death of detox, psych, and rehab.

It rejuvenated his youth to be among kids. They were innocent energy. Arlen learned to water-ski. He drove a barge with the kids on it. He canoed and swam. He was the center of attention one evening when everyone gathered around the dock but left a gap approach. Arlen pedaled his bike down the hill onto the dock and jumped off the end into the water. The kids loved it.

They sung around the campfire by the water. Arlen was asked to give his testimony. He stood by the fire and looked at the water and talked of his time with drugs and struggle. He even talked about going crazy and the bed electrocuting and cutting. And how Christ had found him and he was here learning about love and peace and joy. A little girl came up to Arlen after his speech, "I wish I had a story like yours."
"No you don't." It disturbed Arlen.

It was a busy summer with no time to think of drugging. It was a second childhood for Arlen. He laughed with the kids. They loved him. An airplane flew over the playing field and dropped peanuts for the kids to pick up. The whole event of camp shocked him in a good way—it revived his seed of life. One other counselor was heading to Bible College to be a dean. Arlen liked her—she was a good friend. He would visit her.

Summer camp ended and Arlen found himself swathing and driving tractor on the farm. It was a good job for Arlen to mediate on what went down at camp: hours of driving per day with the radio as the only distraction. He cut the crop and then he tilled the soil. He loved to see the difference he was making, the look of the land changed by him being there.

On rainy nights that were too wet to work, Arlen went to town and attended A.A. It felt odd to plug back in once in a while—it was easier to attend the same meetings all the time. This occasional attendance was hard on his system, the entering of the meeting stressed him out to the point of wanting to use. The rest of the day was fine—but this performance edged him out of serenity.

He had worked the program in his own way for months now. His thinking had cleared up. He knew he was different than everyone around him. He carried this oddness within him and kept it in a secret room. He was afraid of alienating people. He drove farm implements and thought and listened to the radio.

Arlen wrote:

The tears flowed down my hands
They ran to catch someone
Down the windowpane they coursed
I reached out, through the pain
But they would not find me
I just felt cold, and dropped my hands.

COLLEGE

The fall ended with some cash in Arlen's new jeans. His brother Jake arranged a used car for Arlen. He drove it to the bible college city and visited the dean of women. It was the end of November and Arlen was impressed with the place. It was full of people just younger than him. There were girls and this was a good thing to do. He decided to go for it.

He joined classes the next week, three months late. Oh well, he could be on time next year to complete the year certificate with a new class. He decided he could not handle the dorm situation. He lived off site in a room to rent situation.

He started classes and it attacked him to realize his brain was fuzzy. An assignment was given to write a paper on the life of Christ. The project consumed Arlen: it was his entrance or exit. The condemnation rushed back to him—he had killed his brainpower and this was the end of Arlen, he wasn't capable of learning and study. He had toasted his noggin.

He disappeared into the project—he combined the four gospels with contemporary material. He couldn't leave it alone. He didn't even want to go to classes. He needed to shine in this project to prove that he could think. Arlen turned a minor project into a major test and broke through. He received the marked paper and smiled—he had validation, the teacher liked it. A perfect score.

Arlen moved into residence and embraced the full life. He played hockey, sang in choir, hung out with girls, and studied. He was a little older than the rest and felt distance but the gap filled. Arlen continued to de-age. It was a healthy existence for him.

Spring found a repeat of farm, summer camp and a bit of fall farm work and then he was back at college. He was fully adjusted now and focused more on the social than the studies.

Arlen did grow spiritually through this time. He read and studied the bible. He loved the books of Proverbs and Ecclesiastes; they were close to the A.A. material. He needed and gained guidance and support here. He now missed his father more. He needed a dad as an adult—it would be nice to share things. Arlen found this in a small way with the College President. It was a good morsel. Arlen had learned to turn crumbs into feasts of gratitude.

His attitude had transformed since the Banff daze. He was a new person. His God gave him courage and power. His first night of visiting in the penitentiary was tough. The doors slammed shut and echoed; Arlen lost count of how many doors had finalized this enclosure. Oh, but for the grace of God, he thought. This was a two-year-plus-a-day, to life served and everyone in between.

They had a meeting in the chapel with the chaplain. It was a cool economical space. They were told that the men would be on their best behavior; they were stable for years and did not want to lose this privilege. Arlen was directed to his man, N.P.. It was just the two of them in the room. It was their first time—both were nervous.

Arlen went with the flow. He walked in and picked up a bible from the desk and hit N.P. over the head with it.
"Now you've been bible thumped, we can get to know one another."
They laughed out of relief and settled into the rhythm of weekly visiting. Arlen loved to listen to N.P.'s stories of adventure. The man had lived large or was a good bullshitter. He had much cash from a marijuana grow operation and had contributed to the economy greatly by buying toys.

They had built a track outside his farm to race monster trucks and raced remote controlled trucks in the barn on a mini track. He bought a remote helicopter and mastered the flying of it through the breakings of many blades—it had a grappling hook that could right his rolled little truck. N.P. seemed to be telling the truth, as far as Arlen could tell. They were great stories.

The night came when Arlen asked N.P. what he had done to end up in there. It is a hard topic to continue to avoid. You get to know someone to a certain point—it's a missing piece.
"I don't remember what happened, he ended up dead and I ended up in here."

"Oh."

Arlen learned that N.P. had indeed quit drinking on the inside, they shared that in common and it was a bright place they focused on.

The van filled with Bible Boys at the college to play the Prison Boys at Volleyball. Larry was dressed in pink shorts, fairly short pink shorts. Pink was in a bit at this time for men to wear. The van drove to the pen and the doors opened and closed behind them.

The group was guided toward the gym. The prisoners worked out with the weights. It was a rough crowd; sweat turned the air. The college boys walked past the men who whistled.

"Umm pink."

"Short shorts."

Larry's face turned pink. He needed a wardrobe change for prison visitation. They walked into the big gym and played volleyball. They discovered that Larry was a desired man.

Arlen grew in his spiritual ways. He wanted to live the life seriously and in fullness. He wanted to bring more people to the Lord. He wanted to spread love and peace and joy. He did not like the fear and damnation preaching. He did not operate in that way. He knew Jesus to be love and goodness. Fear of hell was not for Arlen.

Arlen loved the president's classes. He blew Arlen's mind to expand. He was an open-minded man who encouraged thought. It was important to know what one believed and why. He was a wide-ranged man of knowledge.

"Perhaps there is more around us than what we can see with our senses, there is more reality than this."

Arlen loved it when he said things like that. It revived his spent brain cells. His synapses fired again in explorative ways.

The van loaded to play at the women's correctional facility across the river. It was a snowy, cool November night. They played the sport in an outdoor court—three sides were building wall and the fourth was fence. The girls were happy to see free men. The college team had two girls only. The snow soccer soon digressed into tackle soccer-rugby. Arlen was surprised to be groped in a tackle. He laughed. It was harmless service to the lord. These girls needed goodness.

Arlen found sex to be a troublesome subject to balance. The world was doing it and the church was married and had children. To be single was to be scarred and unwanted. The churches where Arlen saw older singles, they were the out-of-placers. Arlen fit in with them—it was a form of second class. Most everything was designed for the married: it was the married who did the planning.

Arlen enjoyed the choir tours—they traveled thousands of miles to sing and give testimonies. Arlen was a testimony guy. He spoke in front of hundreds and on a local cable channel. It was his gift to the church. He was so screwed up; it seemed to be something to be proud of, he was needed as the freak that came to the Lord. The choir was good—they had practiced for hundreds of hours. Arlen loved to sing and be part of something big.

Arlen met with a Christian Counselor to prepare for missions in the north. Jake and Carmen had moved to the Northwest Territories, they could use some help. Arlen met with the counselor who had done similar work decades previous. They talked of the need for scripture protection. There were strange and powerful spiritual forces at play. Arlen memorized bible verses—it was his shield.

Arlen spent December at the college helping with some maintenance work and studying old spiritual classics. He was preparing for a mission field a mere thousand miles to the north. No immunization or passport. It was a simple drive through one's own country.

Arlen wrote:

To your side
Take me
In your wounds
To see
How you love me.
I sit here
In the moment
Take my fears
Pull me heaven send.

NORTH

Arlen met with a northern mission man and learned much from him—his stories raised Arlen's eyebrows. Arlen grabbed a dozen spiritual tracts. He read them in his college room; the spiritual stories were bizarre. These trappers saw things in the bush. They had all been delivered. The stories scared and excited Arlen. He prayed, "Take me through whatever it takes to make me who you need me to be. Whatever it takes Lord."

It was hard for Arlen to leave the safe harbor of the college but his time came. Directly after Christmas, Arlen caught a ride up with Carmen's sister and family. A mini van was packed with three adults and two pre-schoolers. It was a long drive to Fort McMurray. An hour past the city the pavement disappeared and became gravel and then winter road. They hammered the van in dropping to the ice levels of rivers. There was never a curve sign on the bad corners. They would drop down the forty-five degree shore to roll across the ice.

It takes faith to drive across ice in a vehicle. In truth it is safer than the highways because few vehicles are on the road. Hundreds of miles of snow and ice and trees and rivers and lakes passed by the window and under the tires. Desolate Fort Chipewyan stood as a thriving oasis. The Athabasca Lake shoreline to the east lay flat to the horizon.

They crossed the border and arrived in darkness. Fort Smith was ready for Arlen. The first person he met had him over for Caribou Steak. Arlen liked his first impression of the north. The visiting ended and it was back to normal for Jake and Carmen and Arlen. Jake had arranged a cabin for Arlen to stay in.

It was a rustic simple shelter. It sat on a hill by a ski area. He would be there in a security deterrent role—in trade he was able to stay for free. It was twelve feet by ten feet. The roof had a foot of snow on it. The walls were made of logs. It had two small windows, a table and two chairs, a bunk bed, and a stovepipe. Jake took Arlen to the hardware store and they bought an airtight heater. They installed it and tested it to work great. Arlen bought a half cord of wood, delivered. He bought groceries and he was set with items like an axe from Jake and Carmen.

Jake resumed his drop-in center work. They were open to all comers. The rough ones had drank themselves to near death. The focus shone on the many First Nations people in the area.

Arlen lit his stove and heated the place up. Most spaces are more beautiful when you add a wood fire. He stripped his jacket off and stoked more wood. Arlen smiled at where he ended up—it was a cozy cabin to pursue his devotional life. It was his quiet cool in Christ. It was his Thomas Merton Cabin. He could worship God continually in such a place.

The fire was the survival necessity and luxury all in one. He took his outer shirt off and sat down—it was getting hot. He kicked the door open. It was a small space to be heated. Arlen had to duck to pass by the rafters. In a few days he could duck and raise his head in the right places.

Arlen found employment with a department store selling men's wear, sporting goods, hardware, and furniture. Arlen walked the mile to Jake's house before a shift—he had a choice of bush trail or road. The bush trail was packed with snowmobiles—he usually took the trail. He would shower and change into sales clothing and head to work. It was a part time job that suited Arlen fine.

He ended up with another part time position developing film for the local paper. The editor would groom Arlen to write and take pictures. This was a good deal for Arlen. He had loved developing pictures in his druggie days. They had hot boxed a darkroom and toked much marijuana and laughed the pictures out with a good stone.

Arlen was impressed with this darkroom-automated system and he had a good teacher. Chemical trays were eliminated with a machine roller. It left only one tray to stop. Arlen liked to burn features in more clearly. With a piece of cardboard with a one-inch hole in it, he would rotate the circle light to expose the face or detail that needed clarification. The smell and sights enticed him. He loved darkness and near darkness. He felt safe in it.

Arlen let his fire go out when he left the cabin. Every time he returned he would have to rekindle and start the fire. It was an advantage in minus thirty to walk and generate some heat that could carry you through these procedures. It was the five o'clock in the morning log in the fire that took some training. If he left it too long he would have to get the fire going again. It was simpler to wake while there was burning momentum and throw some logs on to make it to morning. Arlen learned to pre-make some kindling to have on hand just in case. Arlen liked this step back in time to experience harsher living conditions. He found himself joyful when chopping wood.

The cold was his greatest barrier to ease. The continual dressing and fire maintenance demanded much attention. The outhouse was challenging to embrace with a good attitude. It was best to time your movements with being dressed. Arlen found in minus thirty, you needed a certain amount of clothes to make it through the procedure. He experimented in waiting till he was going to explode—this was uncomfortable but successful in exposing the privates to a lesser time of freeze.

SETTLED IN

Arlen attended the same church as Jake and Carmen—he was an accessory to their lives. He helped out at the drop-in center, and with the youth in the church. Arlen wanted to make a difference in his new life. He tried to transform into a person that could help God.

A young man had blacked out drunk outside: Dean had crawled in the snow to his sister's house and knocked. He gave up and lay on the cold step. She had finally come to the door and found him. He was freezing to death. She got him to the hospital—it was dicey.

Arlen heard through Jake the story of the sister and Dean. It moved Arlen to action—he went to visit him. Dean was in a battered state, hazy, like he was unsure of this reality called hospital and sobriety. Arlen introduced himself and told Dean a bit about himself. The bandages appeared bright against Dean's skin. Dean was in bed; he would not be walking for a while. He might lose toes and parts of his feet. His hands should remain intact. His forearms, shins and knees were also bandaged. Arlen thought of the snow and ice crystals cutting at the flesh—it was akin to a burn.

Arlen took Dean on as his project—he would visit him daily till he left the hospital. He saw the wounds—it turned his stomach to see the frozen banana flesh. His hands appeared to be dipped in blackened wax. His appendages were pain and stiff. The dead frozen layer sloughed off. Dean was pleased to learn that he could keep his feet and toes.

They talked of Alcoholics Anonymous and Christ. Arlen tried his best to lead Dean away from self-abuse. Passing out in winter is a drinking spirit of abandon. It had a bleak future. Dean was able to take a few painful steps. This all helped Arlen to see that going back to addiction was a terrible choice.

The weeks passed and Arlen found a routine. And in the routine he prayed and practiced the presence of God: like Brother Lawrence had taught him in the book. He was in love with God and would sing and worship him with his every step and word and breath. Arlen sensed that a breakthrough of some kind was to occur. He could feel it. He embraced it for he trusted God and knew that everything had its purpose for good in the end. He was the faithful optimist.

"God, take me through everything you need to make me who you want me to be."

It is a dangerous prayer. Be careful what you pray for.

DARK NIGHT

Arlen found the days were stricken with an overall feeling of darkness, yet there was unutterable joy. He was indeed chosen by God for great things. He was used to bring Dean to Christ. Arlen felt specially chosen of God for something. He heard a song about the dark night of the soul. He slid toward its mouth.

It came on fast. Arlen submitted himself to it and held on. He worshiped and prayed. He was falling for a woman in the church and felt there was a special union for them. He was the single outsider. When he approached her, she had no inkling of passion for him.

Arlen satisfied himself in the love of God. He worked and ministered as best he could. He wished he could talk to someone, but he felt no one would understand. He kept the fire going at night and walked the town in the day. The days lengthened. It seemed like continual night on the days that Arlen worked inside in the daylight hours. The days stretched into the dark night of the soul. Arlen ached for he knew not what. A feeling of oddness prevailed.

It approached Valentine's Day and he was ripped open for a love that did not soothe his wound. He was torn asunder and needed relief. His mind slipped and missed gears. This mistaken thinking was back and this time there was no chemical trigger.

Things at work became weird—he snapped in sending a package to another store in the chain. He wrote on the cardboard, 'Bleed love on the wound, Christmas is a hoax—one big family reunion.' He had a vision that Christmas was just one of many routes to God, each tribe in history has its own route back to its father's tent. In the end it is all family gatherings and happy reunion. The person on the receiving end of the package would be informed of what they needed to know to proceed.

Arlen served a Mormon Missionary Man in sporting goods. The young man told Arlen of the paradise waiting for him and his brides for eternal life. Arlen felt ripped off that there was not even one woman for him. He faced inward and walked toward home in the dark through the trail in the trees.

It was a night with no moon. Arlen worshiped and prayed. The black tugged at him. He bounced from ecstasy to demise of doom. He focused on Christ and love and peace. "To live is Christ, and to die is gain." Arlen wished for death to end this and he could be with Jesus. He ached for it. Arlen fell in the snow and worshipped there and arose and walked on.

The days continued their focus to meet. It was coming: whatever this breakthrough or transformation was, it is near to hand. Arlen could feel its heat through the many layers he wore.

The wind howled to blow trees down but all it did was sever branches. Arlen liked winter storms, he liked to be out in them and he liked to ride them out in a warm cabin such as this. It was a short storm and the next morning the blue sky shone. The sun felt warm. It was a magical walk into town to work. Snow had drifted and shaped fingers and dunes. Arlen felt on top of the world. He was good to go. He was ready for anything to happen. He went home that afternoon through the snow. He was ready.

SUBMIT

He entered the cabin—it came upon him suddenly. He didn't start the fire, it was only minus ten Celsius, and he kept his clothes on and heeded the call. He grabbed the spiritual tracts and removed everything from the two shelves on the wall. He lined the dozen stories of demons and doom on the shelves. He locked the only door to the cabin. He turned to the colorful stories and spoke, "I will not come out of this cabin till I have experienced everything that you twelve experienced."

He didn't feel it at first. There was a change within him and about him. The cabin transpired. The composition of the air tightened. His DNA rearranged for the passage. Arlen lit a fire in the stove. The temperature climbed. Arlen removed his outerwear and waited for something to occur, but he didn't see it coming—it was a smooth adversary.

It started with the chopping of the wood on the chopping block by the entrance. Arlen thought of the scripture about Jesus stepping on Satan's head. Arlen could sense his own neck on the rough block of wood. He could feel the sole of the foot press and then he could feel the axe fall. Slice—the air changed. It was hot and the pace quickened. Arlen grabbed the tracts and re-read the unfortunate stories that all ended joyfully in Christ. He changed his mind now, he didn't want to experience the said same as these trappers and northerners. It felt wrong.

It was not with his head that he had decided in the first place. His heart had opened a door, a trap door to a cellar. Arlen spun his head, what was that? It overtook him and fluttered about. He didn't see it. Arlen are you okay in this cabin? You are certainly warm enough. Arlen grabbed his red parka and black pants and threw them and his other cold weather gear out the door. He unlocked and relocked the door; he burst his arm out long enough to cast the protective clothing to the snow.

The fact that night poised to drop did not register with Arlen. His attention was inside the cabin. There was a breakthrough at the ready. The temperature forced the clothes from Arlen. It was too warm for shirt and pants: underwear and socks remained. He paced and waited for something. He thought not to pray, he did not worship Christ anymore. He paced and ducked his head from the rafters. He waited in the wings for occurrence.

He sat down on the stump block. The fire threatened to roast his flesh. He turned to cook the other side. And then he rotated again to evenly cook all sides. It slammed into him—he reeled and flew onto the bed. The stirring began. He was a kite flown in an erratic wind. Arlen lost his feet on the ground. The events blurred from reality.

The fire peaked and fell. Arlen spat on the fire and threw the tracts inside. He pissed on the fire. It steamed and stunk. He poured his water supply on the fire and closed the lid. He threw the nearest items around the room. The windows stayed unbreakable. From the outside all looked fine except the smoke. Arlen yelled and broke things. The sound up close would have been disturbing.

The need to turn the breaker off claimed him. It was above the bunk. He found himself contorting upside down to strike his heel against the main electrical lever. Arlen felt the sharpness of the metal toggle. He lost sense of self and took a ride. He lowered himself to the bed and floor. The power was out—it was black inside.

Arlen waited in the dark and didn't move. It was quiet, and getting cold. Arlen draped a blanket around his shoulders and unlocked the door. He walked in his sock feet off the porch and onto a snow trail. He turned and faced the cabin.

Above it stretched the brightest Aurora Borealis he had ever seen. It raged and danced green, rose, and white. Arlen lifted his hands. The blanket fell from his shoulder to the snow. He found his hands leading the colors and movements. He knew the score and the lights followed precisely. It was sheer brilliance—his finest moment. It was joy in triumph. He swayed and turned and flapped his wings.

The individual pixies bounced and traced his every beckon and call. It was glory. He was the composer, and chief conductor of the northern lights. This was huge. He didn't feel big, he felt right in the moment to have this experience. He was light and air. He did not feel his wet and cold feet. He was above all this skin and ice crystals. He was in space mingling with light.

He turned and walked back into the cabin. Still in his underwear and socks he closed the door behind him. This time when he closed it, it seemed final—like something was not going to get out. Something was about to die. Arlen removed his underwear and wet socks and threw them in the stove. The fire still died and smoke billowed into the cabin. Arlen stood ready for more of something. It took him now.

To be in the same room to watch, you would never know what transpired within him. It was serious and eventful ritual and spice. He stood there naked, his penis and testes pushed toward his body warmth. Arlen did not feel the chill in the air like he should. In that manner there was a power at work here that was baffling. Why would Arlen want to stand in an ever-cooling cabin? He would eventually freeze to death. Would Jake find him curled around the chopping block? Would he be curled in bed with a blanket on him?

He had left one blanket out in the snow. Arlen took another blanket and draped it above and behind him, with the corner over his head and face. He was then able to fully step on the other corner and have excess. He swung the two sides to the middle and sat on the floor as they flapped shut. Arlen felt safe now. It was dark. And he was wrapped tight and getting tighter. Arlen worked the four points of the blanket into an intertwined joint. He was the ball in the blanket. He blew breath into his hands and held his feet. The floor was cold on his ass. He spun like a hamster wheel to get the bulk of the excess blanket union between him and the floor. For some reason, he was allowed the one blanket to spin the new world.

NEW WORLD

He did not know where he was going at first. He jumped in leaps, and bounded back in time. He watched a stint of trench warfare in World War One. The Middle Ages. It was not all war, there was the forming of new countries. Overall it was the erasing of the elapsed era. He was traveling back in time in his burrito blanket. He was cold and naked—the cabin dipped below freezing. Arlen blew his warm breath toward his core. He held his legs together and exhaled warm air to his chest.

Images flashed and carried him. He had no choice now but to follow—it had him gripped. All about him had ended—it was over. He had no memory of Arlen or any such thing as this cabin. He was in a new place, simply seeing events de-fold. Puzzles tore apart. As history rewound, nature took on a greater form. People disappeared and the earth folded back upon itself. He observed the earth being formed in reverse. The halves came apart. He was out in space. Stop.

His body broke down to the individual cell compositions and then these too separated into individual cells. He was done. His cells flew off into darkness toward the stars. He was diffused. He was nothing. He became all. It flowed in a direction. Stop.

His genetic code resurrected and the matter reformed into being.

He came back and noticed the energy flow. The halves came together and folded neatly into a sphere. The sides balanced to a whole. Stop. He saw the First Nations People—a couple, Fire and Ice. The two had great love that coursed together. They arrived on earth and lay down, and in the laying together, they died, ceased to exist. Their fluids flowed and formed earth's water. Fire and ice—sulphur. Heat, love. The bodies still marked their place on the earth with salt flats. It was nearby. It was life. Arlen watched transfixed. This was his show. He had paid admission to this great movie and had the best seat in the house.

He found himself stuck back in time and couldn't find a way back. He waited. Then it formed. He was in the garden. It was pleasure and joy and peace. It was a wonder. It was life in full. Arlen was taken care of, all was provided. Morning came in this manner out of the blanket. Arlen could hear the birds and the squirrels. It was bliss.

He did not want to come back. It plucked him out and hurled him forward in time. He became stuck at a place and could not progress. A bit of Arlen returned to panic—he had to get back. How could one travel back in time? It formed on his tongue and he spoke it, "What would you have me to do this day Lord?"

Some slight movement in Arlen took place of great strain—in this place it was a great feat. Zoom, Arlen would rush forward to the next stop.

"What would you have me to do this day Lord?"

Again he would be assigned some task of obedience and would perform it and be released to move on. Arlen thought that he could never get back.

It was tough and painful and slow. He was exhausted. He was cold and blew more air. He was dried up inside. His skin was wax and his fluids gelled. He touched his rectum and placed the finger to his nose. He could smell his shit—it gave him momentum. He was good for more tests. He was ready and needed to get back.

He hated to leave the garden. He would have preferred to stay there. That was utopia. But it, whatever ride this was, took him away from the nice temperature to this frigid testing ground to get back to this time. It was hard work. Arlen's body was on the edge of succumbing to the cold. His core temperature dropped and he became sludge.

It was all he could do to continue with the tests. The sun was full up now and the cabin's drop in temperature had leveled. He could see the lit windows through the blanket material. He missed the warmth of the garden, and the dark. He had to keep going and pushed himself. His whole body seemed to have changed. Each cell had scrambled and now struggled to regain stability.

BAD MEAT

Arlen's utopia had turned to bad meat and there was nothing to sustain himself with—he was famished of spirit and stuck in a state of wandering discord. He had slipped from a normal reality to a perceived state of existence—it was his alone to dwell in. He was not the only one yet he was there by himself—a singular experience. Sailing solo in another world.

It could be palatable if there was a team or a partner. They could lend support and get through it together. But it was a struggle to stay awake. He couldn't sleep, he would be trapped somewhere else—how would he get back if he slept? He had to get through it. He had to chop this gallows tree down. Arlen had tied the knot that held him. He had to get back to the present. It was vital to make it soon. It was daylight and he still existed before Roman Empire time.

Arlen opened the pod of blanket and poked his head out. The temperature was much colder and the air was fresh. It felt good to breathe cleaner air. The light from the two small windows screamed at his eyes. He let his eyes adjust and looked around the half dark cabin. It was a jungle of debris—the little there was, was strewn about. He stood up with some difficulties; his muscles were stiff and did not work properly.

He needed to sit down to get back in time. He took the blanket with him and sat on the chopping block. The wood was cold on his ass, but it warmed. He was awake now in the cold. Arlen clinched his teeth together and breathed through his nose. His sinuses had dried out from the cold.

He couldn't handle the cold straight in the naked self. Arlen chastised himself and threw the blanket over his head. He felt his feet on the bare floor. He lifted his feet and placed his soles on the fabric of blanket. It was a veil of comfort. Arlen reached down and held his feet cupped in his hands and blew air on them. Twenty breaths made him dizzy.

He rested and gained resolve. He pulled the blanket to fall back from his face. It fell to his feet. He was tempted to wrap it around his feet but slid it from reach. He stood up and grabbed a piece of firewood. The man-made blanket was not appropriate for the garden and the tests. He placed the wood on the floor and sat back on the chopping block. It held a little warmth—his body was able to contact itself. It was a step back toward fetal. He sat on wood and placed his feet on wood. He was ready to continue. He had to get back from this appointed time. He had to get back to the present, he felt urgency.

He struggled to remember the password. He kept thinking Lord, Lord, Lord. It flashed.

"What would you have me to do this day Lord?" Arlen whispered. His tongue tripped thick and full.

He waited for the Lord to assign the task. No task. Wait. Still no task.

"What would you have me to do this day Lord?"

The task exploded to form and Arlen performed it in his mind to jump ahead—this time it was only a night. He could see the one rotation of the moon around the earth around the sun.

He did not feel this as a defeat—it was a small step of many steps. It was progress.

"What would you have me to do this day Lord?"

The task jumped him ahead a week, he saw it in the revolutions. Larger periods of time were marked in progress of technology and civilization. Arlen had a limited knowledge of history but it was upon his knowledge that this was all based. He always had a sense of forward, a standstill, or backward; and a small or large leap in time.

INTERUPTED

He required great forward momentum when he heard the car. He knew it was Jake by the exhaust sound. It was the same Ford sedan that had transported him to detox. Arlen heard the one door open and close. He heard the footsteps scrunch in the snow. He felt the steps on the porch. He heard the latch open; he had not locked the door the last time.

The light was intense. Arlen squinted toward the door.
"What would you have me to do this day Lord?" Arlen asked.
"Shit." Jake took one look and knew the crazy visit had occurred.
Jake had sensed something was wrong in town when Arlen did not show at the house. When he pulled up and saw that the fire was out, it deepened. When he saw the outerwear in the snow, he knew the wrong waited. It had been a cold night and these were not rational signs.

Jake scrambled to find clothing. Arlen kept repeating his mantra. It wasn't working. He was trapped. He was too weak to protest. He obeyed Jake's request to put feet into legs and to stand. The fabric felt sharp on his skin. He sat back down. Jake placed feet straight into boots. It was good for Jake to have a task to perform—he was bewildered as to what to do and where to take him. Jake prayed and pleaded. He helped Arlen on with a shirt and walked the stiff brother out of the cabin. It took a while to get momentum going. His joints did not want to flow, they were afraid of movement and might shatter.

Arlen's feet flopped in the boots. Without socks, and untied, they dragged and scraped the snow. Jake opened the passenger front seat door and Arlen worked his way down and in. Jake closed the door. Jake looked at the cabin and shook his head. It was a bad idea.

The car felt hot to Arlen. He felt cold now and shook. Jake got in and started the car. Not a word was spoken. Jake thought of where to take him. He drove around to buy time. Arlen seemed to not be an emergency. He was not moving anywhere fast. Arlen thawed.

He had a hard time relaxing, he was in a zone past exhaustion. He was toast that needed to be scraped into the sink to rid the char. You scrape and the knife breaks chunks completely through and free. The black hits the sink and softens with water. You are left with a hole-ridden piece of toast. Arlen was full of holes and needed repair. Jake had no clue as to the extent of madness. When a person doesn't speak or move he can appear quite sane and sound. But that cabin scene...

Arlen thawed to pains. His toes hurt. He embraced a killer headache that wrapped his skull tight. He warmed and his delusion melted to a dose of fear. What had he done now? He was in the present, in the car. But he felt different. Something had changed. He had flashes of his trip and wanted to tell Jake about them but didn't. He would not understand. Arlen stayed quiet and watched the world out the car windshield. Arlen felt conspicuous, the world watched again but differently. It was a required event for him to be in the car, on display.

People were bundled, you saw no one without a head warmer of some kind—it was a cold morning. They drove around down town. Jake felt the scene out. He had to take him in. No choice about it. Jake drove to the hospital and stopped by the door.
"Wait just inside the door and I'll park the car."
"Yep."
Arlen moved like an old man who needed time.

It was cold; the thirty feet to the door numbed him and felt good. He waited inside the entrance. Jake joined him and guided him to the proper waiting area and talked to a nurse. Arlen's head tightened with freezer burn. They sat and waited their turn. Jake looked at magazines. Arlen held his head up. They waited and warmed. Arlen's toes throbbed and steadied to pins. His head peaked in throbbed clench.

The doctor poked, prodded, and questioned Arlen. Physically he was fine—tired, dehydrated, and recovering from cold. Mentally he was in need. And it was for this that he was detained for a bed, a room at the end of the hall. He was checked in immediately. He needed help of the psychiatric flavor; it was the doctor's opinion. He could stay here for a few days till other plans were made. He would have to be shipped south. Wrap him up and ship him to warmer climes with wards for such people.

SLIPPERS

His felt pack boots were exchanged to slippers. Jake took possession of the boots. Warm water was secured and drank.

Arlen thought of the fifth floor in Saskatoon.
"Jake I don't want to go to Saskatoon."
"You won't have to Arlen."
In the room with clean sheets and floor and walls, Arlen felt safe for a new start—his latest in life.
"Have a nice warm shower Arlen."
"Yep."
Jake left him in the room and headed to the cabin to clean and glean.

Arlen stepped into his private bathroom and figured out the shower control. The water arrived frigid. He turned the knob and waited and shivered. The cool breeze of the cold shower sent him to shaking. He had undressed too quickly. The water warmed and became too hot. Arlen leveled it to warm and stepped in. All blood rushed to the spot and sucked the warmth from the water. The rest of his body shuddered.

He steadied it to warm a greater area of his torso and worked up to his arms and legs. He turned his back to front and savored life. He was warm. His sinuses rejuvenated and produced snot. He peed. His cells were fluid water once again. Arlen flowed open.

He idled the warmth for minutes to gain a head start on the cold he knew was lurking to attack. He shut the water off and toweled immediately. Arlen shook. He wrapped a dry towel around his middle and donned the robe and slippers and opened the bathroom door. The air was cold. The afternoon light was bright through the window. He closed the door and headed to bed.

He opened the sheets and crawled in. It felt clean and fresh and smooth. And cold. He was new born flesh that shivered. He curled up on his side and huddled for warmth. He covered his head and left a gap to breathe air. His temperature dipped from the shower to bed. It felt dicey to warm up. Arlen waited and felt the glow begin in his groin and armpits. He alternated foot contact with the other foot. His hands fanned the flames of heat with his breath. He caught fire now. The key was to not move, to let the fire grow.

His torso grew warm and spread: limbs caught the glow. Arlen waited and was rewarded with a warm body. The blankets were just enough to make it. Arlen gave thanks for heat. His journey had turned to this simple dependence on others for his well being. It would be simpler in the warm summer. He dwelled in the frigid desert and needed this help of shelter.

Glimpses of the travel came through to glory in. Arlen pondered the garden, from this warm place it seemed certain—there was no denial that he had been there. It was sheer pleasure and dependence, need and want ironed together. It was sun and rain and food picked. And love. He could feel the love now as he huddled for warmth.

Now that he was warm he was afraid to get cold again. He wished the blankets would grow heavy with winter coats and furs. He needed to be covered in heaviness. He felt like he could float away under this minimal wrap.

The nurse entered and found him huddled.
"How are you Arlen?" she asked.
"Do you have more blankets please?"
"I will get you some."
Arlen waited in stillness and anticipated the weight, this weight of warmth to fall and lock in its goodness. He heard her reenter the room.
"There you go, dear."
She had a sweet voice and the laying of the blankets felt wonderful. He needed to be pinned down like a butterfly for display under glass. The two blankets she brought hit the spot. They felt like the womb, safe and secure, he was at rest at last. His mind skittered and his body rested and warmed.

The new drug began to course its way through his veins. It settled down on him and made him rest and mellow. His brain skipped and too large of thought waged battle with reality. He experienced delusions of grandeur—he was the chosen one. It did not make sense to him, but it was a need and a compulsion that pushed him. There was no denying this megalomaniac train of thought. He was the great chosen one—and could barely stay warm on his own.

END OF THE HALL

His room was at the end of the hall. The next morning he heard one raven and looked out the window in time to see it flying up to land on the corner of the roof. Arlen was special—in the spirit of Elijah, God was sending his ravens with sustenance. Arlen heard another raven and saw this one land on the roof too. Arlen closed his eyes and knew he was in the proper place. God wanted him here.

Jake planned with the family down south what to do with Arlen. He needed a deeper level of psychiatric help that was not available in the north. Flights were booked and arrangements made. Jake would fly with Arlen to Edmonton and the mother and sister would meet and deliver Arlen to the proper facility.

Arlen accepted what the ravens could only offer. It fed into his grandiose loop. It gave him energy. He walked down the hall in his robe and pajamas. At the other end of the hospital was a ward for developmentally delayed people—a residence. Some hung about in wheelchairs and pounded their elbows and hands and made odd sounds.

Arlen's healing ability came upon him and he spoke in tongues to the closest member of the clan who laughed and banged his elbows on the table. Arlen placed his own hand palm up on the elbow hitting spot. The elbow bounced higher and hesitated. The sound changed from the mouth—a frustrated sound emanated. The elbow came down harder on the hand several times and stopped. This felt wrong. Who was this man who invaded his space and softened his elbow from the hard surface? He lashed out with his tongue: was it a language? The elbow stopped. The faces met and the eyes burned.

Arlen moved to the next person and blocked and spoke. Arlen's faith was ripe. He had no doubt that they were healed. He walked back to his room exhausted—healing made him tired. He slept again. The ravens visited him in his dream, they were in a cave and he ate the bread of wisdom—he was healed.

Arlen woke when lunch came into the room. He sat up and investigated the tray—he still did not have much appetite. He survived on the raven's fare and thought the kitchen should know that. He ate the purple Jell-O and waited for the ravens to return.

The pastor came in and chatted. He was sorry that this had happened and he and they would be praying for Arlen.

"Thank you." Arlen looked out the window at blue sky.

The ravens would not come for Arlen to show the pastor. Arlen stayed quiet; he didn't think the pastor would understand.

Arlen felt ease of spirit when the pastor left. This was all complicated and he wished that it would fall into place. He needed peace of mind measured in hours and not in minutes. This fleeting and fickle peace he gained lasted a moment. One minute, he blew on the open sea taking water in his small boat with no help in sight. Then he soared with eagles looking for the ravens. It prodded him to react; he had no control but to respond. He was echo to the fickle mood.

The ravens did not return in the afternoon. Arlen was lonely now, waiting for birds. The nurse came with a bird's eggshell-colored-pill. Oh yes, this was it, Arlen thought, it was to give birth within him—he was the vessel. The pill would rise up and change. He was ready and stayed warm under the covers.

He could not walk that afternoon; he held his bladder till dark. It was vital that he stayed still and warm. He thought of little birds as he drifted to drug-enhanced sleep. He didn't dream but awoke with a start. He felt like he was falling from the heavens, he bounced into the bed.

Another meal arrived and Arlen explored it. He had forgotten the need to be still for the hatching of the pill. He had also forgotten about the ravens. He was starving and ate every morsel and licked the plates. Salt was essential—it was compulsion to explode the salt crystals of the crackers onto his tongue. He could taste food.

He couldn't remember why he was holding his bladder but he knew it was important. As darkness fell it was his only focus. The weight of the blankets pushed to threaten submerging. Arlen held the blankets up off his abdomen.

Jake entered the room.
"How was the meal?"
"Good, really good." Arlen grimaced.
"What's wrong?" Jake asked.
"Have to pee."
"Well go then."
Arlen felt proper permission was given.

His teeth swam. He carefully climbed out of bed and edged into the bathroom and let go. He ached in the release. It was pain and relief. Arlen wondered if you could hold your bladder to the point of explosion. He walked back to the bed with a free walk.

"I talked to mom, she and Jenny are going to meet us in Edmonton and they are going to take you to Saskatchewan to a better place." Jake looked at Arlen.
"All right."
Jake had expected a struggle for this but there was immediate acceptance. In the chitchat that followed, Jake realized how scrambled Arlen was—he could not stay on one subject and toward the end started to talk incessantly. He became chatter, dribble about anything in particular that had no connection to the last thing he said. Jake went home.

Arlen walked across the hall to the TV room. The Winter Olympics were on and they captivated Arlen. He watched and things became weird when Arlen noticed that all the podium winners wore wigs. He could see they looked like Muppets and their hair was an afterthought. Some were askew. It was obvious to Arlen but they were pulling it off, the public was unaware. And Arlen wondered what else they were hiding.

Arlen fled from the international event and escaped into his darkened room. He left the washroom light on with the door opened a crack. He closed the room door and shut off the lights. He listened for footsteps. Silence. He tip toed to the window and parted the curtains. He craned his neck and nose skyward to peek for the ravens. It was quiet and no black feathers played shadow tricks. His nose smeared the glass as he lowered his gaze. The window felt cold.

He looked across the street at the monolithic Catholic abandoned building. Arlen did not know if it was a residence or what, but it was huge and entered his purpose. He was intended to transform it into a utilized building again. Arlen would infuse it with vitality for the youth to use. Arlen was full of spunk and hope—he felt like he could do anything again. He was ready to be faithful—to the end and back. He knew the outcome was good.

The night passed into day. Arlen's mood elevated. He was indeed high now and had difficulty sitting still. He discovered a wheelchair and spent the afternoon wheeling around. Jake stopped by and confirmed they were flying out the next morning. This increased Arlen's flightiness. He was good to go. He felt like he could soar there on his own.

WHIRLPOOL

He asked a nurse for the possibility of a bath. She said the only option was the big whirlpool that they lowered patients into. Arlen followed her to the room. Arlen was impressed with the size of the tub. A big arm stood ready with a harness to pluck people from their wheelchairs and swing them over and into the warm bath. There was a Jacuzzi function to it.

Arlen could picture the immobilized person hanging buck naked in the harness—like a piece of meat lowered into a deep fryer—the device seemed impersonal and cold but Arlen focused on the large jetted tub.
"Would you mind if I used it?" Arlen asked.
"It shouldn't be a problem, you might want to use the chair to stay in one place, the water moves fast."
"Yep."

Arlen could not believe his good fortune; this was an event of epic proportion. The nurse showed him the controls and left him to his own devices. She showed him the products you could add for skin care. Arlen likened it to an automated car wash to put you through the wash and wax cycle.

He filled the tub and started the jets. Huge and boiling. He shook with excitement and climbed into the chair; the water was too hot to begin with. Arlen felt himself melt with the jetted hot water. He got the idea to try it chair-less and stepped out and pressed the button to swing the chair up and out of the water.

He climbed in and immediately was swept to the side. He lifted his legs and found himself to be motionless. He was in a NASA tank to practice zero gravity. He let himself roll and pitch and spin. It was tough to remain in one spot. He steadied with his hands and legs. He was flying and felt wonderful. He turned into a fighter pilot, he imagined flying to follow his foe, turning, and spinning his enemy into his sights.

Arlen finished with suspended meat-in-the-chair time. He added the moisturizer and sat to pour with the water's flow. He was sleepy and spent. It was all he could do to get out of the contraption and drain the water. It made him happy and mellow. He walked to his room and crawled into bed. He melted into the sheets and fell to sleep. The morning found Jake once again assisting Arlen in packing.

TURBULENCE

He said goodbye to the hospital and said hello to cold air and the plane. It was a wild turbulent ride, and more so for Arlen—he was sensitive to everything. They stepped off the plane in Edmonton and Arlen walked sideways in nausea to the bathroom. He looked in the mirror at the green ashen face. He wanted to puke and threw cold water on his face. The storm settled and Arlen walked out to meet his mom and sister.

Once again he was in intervention mode. He hated the role but was becoming practiced at it. He needed help. He was loved and fortunate to have family to assist in reclamation.

His family felt concerned for his health and wanted him to get better. They did not understand his behavior and mood. He was high and removed from the situation, and chatty. This whole thing seemed like nothing out of the ordinary for Arlen. It was an everyday occurrence.

The car ride turned brutal for Arlen—it teased his energy to rise up and surge. He could not understand how they could sit in the car for so long. He begged them to stop so he could walk a bit. He knew inside that he was in the process of being shut away in a gray place and this color of world rose in his heart to clamor. He had to smell the air and feel the ground underfoot. He pleaded with them to stop.

They stopped. He was like a rubber band stretched and released, he was gone down the road and up the hill. He felt like he could walk across the country—he was uncoiled released energy. He was fusion—his energy was dangerous and needed supervision.

When they got him back in the car his mood dipped—they approached Saskatoon. He did not want to go to that same witch doctor. He did not like her. They drove straight to her house office. Arlen was afraid to go in but felt invaded and attacked in the car.

His mom and sister willed him to see the psychiatrist. He entered the office and waited. The doctor saw the women and then saw Arlen by himself. She chastised him for the Christian life that he attempted to live. He silently prayed and waited for it to be through. They needed a place for him to dwell in his zaniness craze. They waited and heard the doctor loudly discussing Arlen's need on the phone. She did not want him. But she found a place that had an opening. He was going north, to Prince Albert. He was going home to the supreme college town.

DIFFERENT CIRCUMSTANCES

In the car Arlen told his sister and mom of the chastising. He was going to a better place now with a better doctor. It was good to be in Prince Albert where he knew people. But he felt shame to be coming back from the mission field wrapped in bandages that no one could see or understand.

He was wounded: spirit and holes in head. He was crazy, and heading for the nuthouse. Arlen was doomed for incarceration in the great pill and injection land. They would interject his mind to pliable mush— it would ooze back into their provided frame.

Arlen would sleep and eat and medicate. He would wake up and do it all over again. The tiny paper cups would amass—mark the times of day. If Arlen could see how much total medication he would ingest, he would run the other direction.

They stopped at a store before the hospital. Arlen danced with fear and wanted to call the counselor that prepared him for missions. It would make him feel better to go in—he was scared to enter the psych center. There had been no mention of where he was heading but Arlen assumed it to be the loony bin.

He had been into this hospital ward to visit his older brother Brandon. Arlen had been thirteen and did not understand why his brother was so medicated—his tongue was thick and his bare feet were cracked and dry. He remembered the long hallway to the ward. It took a long time to pass through its length. Arlen was about to walk another psych ward hall and enter the door. This was defeat and sorrow. This was fear and angst. This was not peace or love or joy.

Arlen got no answer at the counselor's number. Arlen called the college president who was sorry to hear the situation. Arlen told the president that he was afraid and wanted to see Counselor John. Yes he would call John and let him know that Arlen was going in. Arlen felt slightly better to get in contact with someone. They would pray and he might get visitors.

They drove to the hospital and parked the car. In admitting they were sent straight to the pschyciatric center. They were a special breed to be slipped to the back. It was a long walk through the hospital and the corridors became quieter and remote. It was safe and secure and distant from the street and the general public. It protected the innocent on both sides of the fence. Arlen thought of his dead brother who had walked these corridors.

There was a full circle here that Arlen did not know yet. He would have time to figure it out. Upon entry into this unit, time is your sticky tormentor—it slows the hands to pass to freedom.

THE VILLA

The handoff was made in the villa—it was a warm name for a facility. Beneath the Tuscan solarity the polarities of the mental sphere play out. No red peppers or fresh basil and garlic used here. The mother and sister left their Arlen with the professionals with the admittance paperwork completed. Arlen signed himself in—the key to quicker freedom.

This, and good behavior would limit Arlen's absolute incarceration to a few days with the doctor's discretion instead of potential weeks if he was involuntary. Arlen volunteered for this duty of patient, accepting the contractual agreement of admittance. He said farewell to his family and embraced his institutional siblings and caretakers.

He was shown his room and his gear was combed and documented with the fine tooth. He was interviewed in detail and given a mild sedative. Arlen waited for the counselor to appear—there he was just in time. He was a saint that soothed and comforted and pray-tucked Arlen into bed. He felt peace with the man's voice—Arlen could do this. John left and Arlen looked at the dark ceiling alone.

He stayed in bed and tried to sleep—there was much to process, much to think about and solve. He needed time and he wound himself up to the point of not sleeping. The flashlight poked hourly in the door and shone on his face. Arlen was on the verge of sleeping when the light shone his slumber away. He got out of bed and walked the hallway. The lights were dimmed and there were stragglers in the smoking recreation room. A man smoked and rocked on a regular chair.

Arlen talked to the nurse about not sleeping and received another pill. He did nod off that night. In the morning he was hyper and ready for anything; he was good to talk to anyone and zoomed around the rooms. It was a mixed bag of people; there were teens and elderly. The smiling psychiatrist made his rounds. He saw Arlen for five minutes. The nurses administered three new drugs to Arlen that day. He had his first intramuscular injection. It was a female nurse and Arlen found it erotic to lay spread eagled on the bed with his ass exposed.

The Largactyl strained to enter the muscle tissue. Like a prehistoric beast, it lumbered into his butt and lingered. Arlen soaked in a warm bath; it soothed the bump of tension. His muscle poised ready to feed the beast that he was. Too much energy coursed through Arlen. The injection dragged the anchor on the ocean floor as Arlen sailed about the ward. He was still good to go.

Arlen found a wheelchair and wheeled the gospel to anyone who had ears or the lack of mobility. He wheeled beside them. He was movement and scattered subject—he was all over the map with hyper talk. Few people could follow his track of thought. He jumped hemispheres of topic. He was a scrambled egg.

DIAGNOSES

Arlen heard his doctor state his first non drug-induced mental diagnosis, "Hyperactive Manic-Depressive with overtones of Schizophrenia." This was a serious handle to live with—it scared him. Was this really him? Could he live up to the title?

BLOOD BROTHERS

Another hyper young man named Jim is admitted. He has his guitar out at ten in the morning, swooning a girl, making up the words as he sang. Arlen gravitates toward Jim. They spend a busy day together bouncing around the villa.

Five minutes to lights out, Jim and Arlen burst upon the idea to be blood brothers. Frantically they require a sharp object to perform the rites. A paper clip is all they can find. They straighten it and started poking each other on the hand to get blood. No blood.

The lights go out in the smoking room and the nurse goes by and says it's bedtime. Just a couple more minutes are needed. They windmill their arms to get the blood ready and stab each other some more. A few drops of blood appear and mingle, uniting their manic veins in brotherhood.

They go to their identical rooms triumphant. Arlen has trouble sleeping. He gets a pill that slows. The nurse tells him to relax in bed and let it work. The whole universe stirred against his need for sleep. A bloodcurdling scream down the hall levitates Arlen from the sheet.

Arlen wages war against his furtive self. He breathes deeply, counts Loons and starts feeling heavy. Arlen is falling asleep, drug induced yet getting there just by a smidgen, when the door opens and a flashlight shines in his face. Arlen stirs awake.
"Are you having trouble sleeping?" the nurse asks.
He wants to scream.

Hours later Arlen has slept another nap and it is morning. He has a stone over from medication—mere walking is drudgery. Breakfast is served on plastic dishes on plastic trays for plastic minds. Paper cups crumple as heads tip back the pretty color pills. After the toast Arlen realizes he's smoking, he doesn't smoke. He didn't smoke before he came here—his fingers are brown.

MIRACLE

An older lady had sat the whole time in a chair. They wheeled her out like a mannequin on sale for all to see. She was past speech into the spiral. Quality of life had been traded to a bed for accountants to balance. Jim and Arlen talked to her and together felt she wanted to let go. She held on for some reason. Maybe it was the staff helping her, they latched onto the line and pulled up, and meanwhile the spiral had claimed everything else. There was nothing left.

Jim whispered in her ear and told her that it was all right to let go and die, it was a better place and she would be okay. The two manics leaned in as vultures and kissed their prey farewell. They cut the string that medicalization had inserted on her fleeting spirit. Arlen leaned in and told her that it would be a better place than this. A psych ward is a tricky place to live your days out. It does aid in the cross and mix of realities. You can just let go, let go of these people. Welcome death. They prayed for her to be brave and journey on.

The ladies hands were soft when they took them in their own. Jim and Arlen left the chair to remain. She remained on display and the boys carried on to the next urgent endeavor. It was all-important at this stage of mania. They walked in the moment fully with great powers and communication. Some people likened it to entertainment. Others did not like their energy—it was too much. But they never noticed that people shook their heads when they turned and left. It was a confined place with limited egress and venting of such energies; the bouncing continued to build and cascade back upon themselves in waves. The walls rebounded the volley of craze.

It was the afternoon of the shackled man. His personal security man escorted him from his room. This was not your typical bodyguard. This one protected others from the manacled man. Arlen stopped talking when he spotted him. Arlen closed his mouth and watched him enter the dining area. You could hear the chains; he shuffled along with short steps, his hands and feet chained together in the front.

He was amused to be walking. His upper body bulged with bellies of snapping muscles. The man wore a pair of blue pajama bottoms, and a curious smile. It was a wild smile from a different place of dwelling. This man was touched and held by a different force. He was capable of great deeds of the darker side of Hollywood productions. The steel hardware collection was a trophy of outburst.

Arlen wondered how this was good for the other patients. Could Grandma in her spiral see him? His was a look and feel that cleared a path; it would be perfect if you did not like crowds in busy places. You could get your friend to dress like the security person and you could be the sedated monster. Nobody would invade your personal space.

It was early evening when the code was announced on the intercom and the excitement brewed and focused on Granny Spiral's room. Equipment was rushed and the string of dependence could not be reattached. Granny passed on to journey; she left the baggage of her bowels and body for a mortal to deal with.

Jim and Arlen huddled together in remarkable reverence and respect; and awe of their prayers—they knew they could work but that fast? It surprised and frightened them a bit. It renewed their vigor to work miracles and prophecy to the Psychilites. The message was clear and they were the vessels of conveyance. They had worked their first miracle and were ready to move on.

PSYCHILITES

In the center of the community the chairs lined the outside wall of the room. The ping-pong table monopolized the room—the eyes stared at the dormant green and white lined table. This smoking room filled with clouds.

Jason's hair trembled nervously with twitching energy. He forced his body to sit on the seat closest to the hall. His head threw darting, furtive looks up and down the hall. He glanced down and lit a smoke with efficiency and expertise. His nicotine stained hands confirmed this training. He sucked deep; the paper cracked with excitement. Jason's eyes closed and shoulders dropped. Parts of him placated with the influx of chemicals.

Having stopped his paranoid glances to and fro Jason commenced to rock on his stool of a perch, oddly comforted in the methodical movement of meeting his parched lips, on each crest of rocking, to suck a puff stealing smoke down his windpipe. He looked at the floor now, unaware that those he had been warily watching were now his watchers.

Gene's red eyebrows danced and blue eyes twinkled. His dimples made the old ladies swoon at his goodness; he was a fine looker with those gargantuan eyes. The scarred broomball goalie traveled in other spaces. His heart pumped like the Wizard of Oz scarecrow. He was a lion with false teeth.

Gene relived his great conquest of planet Zar. He focused out the window on the evergreen trees against the blue sky. He started muttering, about Zelda on Zar that was in a Zawful mess, to the first person his dilated eyes met. Helen was a meek nervous sprite of wispy nicety. She acknowledged hearing Gene—the story arose to flutter out of the dry mouth that cracked the words.

She had heard the basics of the story before and was too considerate to interject his flow with anything but affirmations. She had nothing to say to anyone yet she listened and won converts daily to her flock of devotees. Someday she would be someone and have something to say—she waited and listened.

Clown Fred mocked scarecrow Gene, dancing behind him, to a few suppressed smirks and laughs. Helen spotted Fred and chastised him in a flash of backbone and righteous anger. Her meekness reposed her face to lamb-like quality: those who were not watching her face, only hearing her rebuke of Fred, turned to see an outraged authority, and saw a doe.

NATURE CALLS

Arlen wrote:

The highs the lows
My heart it flows
Thru ebbs and crests
Flyin thru the best
I hold on thru
The troughs
Life is all
Not the best.

Arlen liked to watch the foxes out his windows in the melting snow. Deer took their evening walks of forage. It neared spring and nature surged within Arlen to be free. He desired to walk into the bush and disappear from these people. These paper walls transmitted his neighbors' dresser drawer conflicts. What were they looking for in the same drawers over and over? Arlen felt the banging and slamming in his bed.

Arlen's least favorite noise comes in the times of utter silence and peace. It is in times when he is by himself that it penetrates most. You see no queer sadness of behavior. The walls speak peace to you: Arlen feels the serenity pool. The medication. The scream of madness reaches each molecule of existence and rips it raw. Arlen panics and falls on fight or flight—its mode of tonality drains his lake of peace and plops him on sharp rocks. He stirs to run and protect.

Arlen prefers it when more blood twisters follow. The repeated screams help Arlen to install reference points to counter his state of anxiety. It is best when he hears the scurry of staff to cover and bind and inject and insert orally the cure. It helps Arlen to know that something is being done to remedy this sarcophagus scream.

Arlen is sometimes troubled to stay in his room on such nights. He needs to see human faces after such fright. He needs the lighthouse to beacon in from the lunacy outlands. It is beyond lonely without the comfort of modern times. It is a primal place of edge without cushioning.

Arlen peers out the window and seeks the animals in the trees to rescue him into their kingdom of sun and moon and season.

ELVIS

Morning comes. The recreation guy performs his rounds and hard sells people on coming down to the gym to exercise.

"You WILL feel better."

Others such as Arlen are simply commanded to go. Arlen finds himself sauntering with a rag tag group down the narrow long hallway that separates and protects them from the normal people. They turn right through double doors into the mini gym that you would not expect to be there. Incidentally the hardwood was covered to make offices. Healthcare does not involve fitness anymore.

Arlen noticed the lines on the floor looked great. They brought the blue mats out, running into each other waking from their chemical haze.

"I am so hammered on these Tranquilizers," Arlen said to himself.

Dillon, the leader reached up and put a cassette in the stereo. Arlen was startled to hear Elvis loud. It was his thirty first morning and it still scared him.

Arlen opened his eyes to see Dillon swooning the Karaoke Elvis. He's got the moves: the hip, the lip. Arlen closed his eyes and reopened them. He willed himself to not be there. He needed to leave the building.

"Somebody please help me," Arlen whispered.

They exercised through the repertoire of Elvis and Dillon cranking the hip and lip through. Arlen looked at the others. The older ladies catch the swoon and jive silly grins back at Dillon. Suddenly homophobic and nervous, Arlen can't engage the vibe.

They work the extremities and lay down to ground stretch. This does feel good. The drug effects tightening their muscles are countered by the session. Arlen relaxes.

"Move your knees to the right," Arlen hears and then falls asleep. He wakes by a kick to the feet, with a slight rebuke.

Arlen makes it through the duration and into the floor hockey stage without sleeping any more. Arlen loves floor hockey. There aren't enough aggressive folk to play a game—they shoot hoops and bowl at one end. Arlen and Jim tie the vinyl goalie onto the net. It is a mat that covers the goal; it has a painted goalie on it with five pockets to score, with a different allotted score for each. Arlen loves to pretend he is skating and in the groove. He lets himself go to feel the orange puck enter the toughest hole. He shoots the wrist shot that spins to touch the lip of the hole. Arlen raises his stick above his head in celebration. Jim and Arlen pass the puck and pretend glory moments over and over.

ROUNDS

The doctors perform the rounds. Smiley sees each person between zero and three minutes. Arlen laughs at this smiling doctor's power—he is the door to freedom. The doctor did not talk to him today because he was not in the doctor's physical path.

This sucks. How do you anticipate someone's path to place your body in, when they are all over the place? Try and look graceful.

Arlen never did accomplish the smoothness in approach. He felt like a needy, bumbling idiot throwing himself at the tanned smiling messiah.

Weekends saw a break in the backroom ECT ritual. On the weekdays, the patient walks in behind the nurse's station and gets wheeled out. Arlen walked by when the door was open and caught glimpses of the equipment. Doctor Franken subdued and shocked the people to a submissive state. Arlen saw the post effect of the treatment—these people were indeed shocked. They looked wiped out and could not remember their favorite restaurant.

It was Arlen's secret fear—he did not want shock treatment. He had administered it to himself and he thought that was good enough. He had to get out of this place.

The paper cups added up. Jim the other bipolar and Arlen practice their hitchhiking. On passes to leave the ward they stand outside the hospital main entrance and ask people where they are going and could they get a ride? It only takes a few tries to get a ride downtown. It is much more interesting and quicker than using the bus.

MINI ROAD TRIP

Jim and Arlen left on a day pass. They should have a policy against two manic individuals out at the same time. At the entrance waiting for a ride they decide to hitch hike ninety miles to get Jim's sports car from his parent's house.

It was a rush to get out of town; an adventure of beautiful proportions to ride with strangers through the country.

Jim told his parents he had been released that morning and got the keys. Jim and Arlen acted a little goofy and his mom was apprehensive. Intuition is a beautiful thing when you act in agreement with it. Freedom is a car when you have been recently locked up.

They made it back to the ward in better time. They told the nurse signing them back in what they had done; he was concerned yet entertained. Such an adventure had to be told. In the smoke room that evening, the others lived a taste of freedom through their words of exploit. They were close to discharge. They were forcing the world to be about them.

INSTITUTIONALIZED

It frightened Arlen to leave the safe confines of the hospital. It was his emotional blanket. He could retreat to his small room—predictable and easy. The world out there was large and unruly.

Freedom from the long stay disturbed Arlen. Someone fed him, drugged him, watched him, told him where to go, what to do, and when to go to bed. He even missed the flashlight in the face when trying to sleep.

What goes up must come down. With gravity as a rule, this is a given. A manic high may lead you to believe you can defy gravity but it catches up with you. You are flesh, and the stricken one crawls to insert itself inside you. You come down and crash drag the depths. You rapid cycle—try to keep up with this mood-lag of jump start high and low fickle.

And you simply bury in gloom and despair. It covers you deep and immobilizes you. It is devoid of feeling and taste and smell. It is dry tongue for the void of conversation that dwells within you. You have nothing to contribute—you are mute. You are deaf and dumb, and blind. You are sleep and escape into dream.

Arlen sees his doctor as he slips into suicidal ideation. The doctor is afraid that an anti-depressant may send him high again. Arlen thinks that the doctor is afraid. Arlen's constant pit in his gall is death and the end of it all—he is meditation on method of finality. No need for autopsy. Death by his own hand sounds like a style choice to Arlen. He is far removed from the world in his hovel of dirt. He feels like he deserves this muck in his mouth and his stomach. He is dirt, and fallen, and trodden and cannot get up. He is study of death—the mirror does not reflect.

The weeks pass into months as Arlen simply strives to put death off till tomorrow. He applies his 'A day at a time' from A.A.. It finds him showering once every couple of days. He celebrates this achievement. He sleeps three quarters of his twenty-four. He seeks the rapid eye movement place of dreaming a better existence—anything but this place and time. He cannot time travel anymore. He is bed ridden and dream seeking for solace and escape. The movie shorts scramble and soothe his demise. He cannot rise from bed for there is no reason to stand. He falls back to the fitful sore-back, stealing images. These dreams escape paradise.

Arlen scratched out a poem:

In the spell of mediocrity
I awoke seemingly dreaming yet not aware of which it was.
Yet I craved a reason to know, to believe,
but afraid to embrace I was alone with nothing.
Not willing to commit, I faltered;
stumbling I reached out.
Was it too late?
I grasped the ground.
After all, this was all there ever was—the dirt where all things flow from.
The dust was where I needed to breathe.
By choking on the thickness of it I found myself to be full of earth and
knowing this was the start of the end of the spell of mediocrity.

SNAKE

He crawled from his hole and shed his skin. It is nine months since the cabin and his time of conduction into disorder. He has stewed and found the place to struggle from.

It is ten months from the cabin and he is feeling like himself again. He is drugged, yet his self has regained a hold on his existence. He has outlook, and hope again. He smiles at a joke and enjoys nature.

Arlen finds employment as a short order cook—a wage slave is born. The mission field is behind him and out of reach for the stricken. He is God's broken love slave. He is tired and defeated and building once more. He is poverty and hope. Arlen is Arlen.

SOAR

The time of year of the cabin comes due and Arlen slips up from the mundane to spectacular. It sneaks up on him in an enticing way so as not to let him notice the double edge. Arlen slides up and out and away. It bites him to the point of interference with peeling potatoes. He passes into the level of hypo-manic energy where everything flows in color and sex. All is glory and taste. Arlen can do anything. He is connected and makes it happen. He is synchronicity.

Arlen floats ever higher and his feet leave the ground and his existence, his reality cracks in fissures, and his sanity falters. There are glitches of thinking—he is special again; he is the chosen one. He is past the point of spending money and acting promiscuous. He is past the wild forms of dressing, past the sucking appeal of colors to wear. He is into the naked in the snow zone. Arlen needs help.

I tire of helping Arlen. It seems like he will never make it through this shit he lives in. He is brown and stinky with it. There are different people that will help him this year, and next. There will be geographical escapes and progress. There will be much needed changes of doctor. There are highs and bottoms.

Arlen loves the hypo-mania when all shines to him. He wished that he could bottle it to sell. It is much better than cocaine and it is natural. It is he who feels it to place. It is within him to flow.

REVOLVING

Arlen signs himself in again and again and comes to dread the valentine of year. It is red and he is always dippy-turve over a chick in blue. She likes Arlen and loves his zest for life. He crosses hypo-manic to advance to her side, but it turns and Arlen flips over to a crazy place that has no ground for mortal female. She is alien and flees for her own peace. His mad place of existence has no place for company.

It is a solitary pursuit: the psychotic break from reality has single occupancy requirements. It is the only option. You cannot take anyone with you; if you could take a partner, you may be spouses for certain. Perhaps the two of you would be mentally joined at the eye—the things you saw up there would sear you together to form another emotion that only the two of you share.

Everything is filtered through your shared twist. Think of the romance: lose your mind together, squander touch with your mundane existence and fling it all to the eye of the storm and ride it out together. There you are huddled as one in the trees—you are tripping to another place and time with quick fractures and meanderings, but you are warm. They steal you away and within you are lost, but together.

It is too great to exist. It would solve the need for a partner as a mentally ill person. It would secure the fit for you to share the agony and the sick beauty of insanity. Separately there is no way that you can be together fully without the common ride.

After years of healing and no further repeat psychotic episodes you could connect with someone, but in the midst you must share the plague, the scar repels or attracts. Insanity is electrical, the sane are positive and the insane are negative charges. Negatives attract and screw with the laws of electricity.

A marriage explodes with a schizophrenic discovery of the husband. He is cast to the hospital and the single bedroom subsidized apartment with time capsule furnishings. The kids visit when he is well and the mother finds a new groom.

A severely mentally ill person resides in a soulless desert where few can dwell or meet in. They are thrown into single existence for survival. They are cactuses and the sane are water. They cannot need the sane because the sane do not understand the place of dwelling—they must rush off. For most, there is separation for a reason. Few can visit and draw the cacti free. They are the angels of this world. They suffer too. The thorns of soul take their toll. Many psych wards have pictures of saint nurses on their walls.

RELAPSE

Arlen was living in the small town and had a shitty run-down apartment to be depressed in—it was the height of summer and Arlen slunk on this day, his birthday. Jim, his blood brother, came to visit Arlen and brought an older friend. The old guy had quit drinking and the three of them shared a desperation of spirit—none of their lives shone as they needed. The old guy's son had just died. They cooked perogies in butter and onions and bacon and ate them with sour cream. They smoked and drank coffee.

Jim and Arlen went out and the cure called them out to score—in the country they bought pot and toked up on the gravel road. Arlen plummeted to panic in the paranoia cave—the walls of the small town took his breath and darted his eyes. He wanted to hide to not see anyone—they knew he was stoned.

In the doom apartment the old guy chastised and coached them that they could live without the pot.

"Life is all right, you can make it, hold on a day at a time and you will make it; you don't need that stuff, the pot will get you and mess you up."

Arlen did not toke the next day, or the one after that; the scare placed him back in a day at a time.

DAZED

Arlen was in a new year in a new city in a new job. Lithium caused his Thyroid Gland to shut down.

The doctor told him, "You need a new drug to get your gland working, carry on with the Lithium."

Arlen laughed inside awkwardly and thought, "This does not make sense, where did they get this guy?"

Arlen shook freezing cold from the low functioning Thyroid. His body weighed a thousand pounds. He took a Synthroid and warmed a bit. The following days found him dragging his cold bones around as he grew through the hypo stage toward full-blown mania.

He found himself crashing into exhaustion. He had to be alert. It was dark outside and the stars shone and the streetlamps distracted the gaze. Arlen squinted his eyes and saw the heavens. He felt to be in outer space and the lights were stars from a different angle. It was a glorious sight of privilege to see the heavens from the heavens. It was a transforming of soul with new perspective.

Arlen was tired but felt desperate to not miss anything. It was crucial to stay alert and awake. He drifted to conclusion of alarm. He had to pull an act to awaken. Arlen grabbed a sample vial of cologne. It was a glass elongated tube the diameter of a narrow pen. It was the length of close to two inches. His hand swung it to his nostril and sniffed. The remnant aroma teased but he could not smell it. Arlen was losing his footing with the senses. He was past the heightened senses stage and into the dulled sensation with the body. His smell, touch, and taste paused. He had not slept. He slipped to lunacy.

Arlen's fingers slid the vial into his right nostril. The threaded part entered first with the cap removed. Resistance slowed it down. Arlen pulled his hand away and the vial stuck in place. Arlen slammed the heel of his hand into the vial bottom. He responded in voice. Arlen felt the pain and blood flowed wet. It shocked him into feeling like Arlen and not this slipping psychotic hound. It felt good to feel pain and not be dulled into monster mode. He removed the vial and the blood surged to free. Arlen pinched and leaned to clot. He could taste the blood.

A previous hospital stay reminded him that Niacin was good for the circulation. An urge threw a handful of Niacin on his tongue. He inserted the blow dryer on high heat into his mouth. The pills melted. Arlen caught a glance of the odd sight in the mirror.

A heavy metal musician exploded within Arlen and shook his head violently. He threw another handful in that melted on contact to stoke the fire. One handful more blew him to righteous rage—Arlen donned his bathrobe and fashioned a turban around his head. Arlen was to swim the ocean and slink through the desert to kill the bastard Saddam.

What is this creature in the mirror that melts more fire in its mouth? It is wrath of excess energy. It is lack of mental pressure relief valve. The boiler explodes. It is manic. Arlen paces the house in bathrobe and turban towel.

He lurks in the downstairs bathroom mixing up the needed potion to remedy the scene. It is a room and board situation that holds him here. It is his home, a room of the widowed. Arlen is not in that room. He is downstairs building a framework for supplicants. He acts in compliance with the urges of lunacy within. He takes the baby powder and shake-anoints it about his countenance.

He flashed to the Bob Dylan album he was listening to, 'Oh Mercy.' The psychotic beast of Arlen strived to recreate the portrayal of Dylan with the drops of clear liquid in the tropics. Arlen doused his torso and surrounding with water from the faucet. He drank water and grew as a frog. His torso stretched his skin. He shook and spun the scene to fact. It is void of light in room.

He touched the light switch and flicked it. The light exploded his eyes to cower and hide the imploding pupils. He shuttered his eyes and gained a gradual look. The effect of water drops and bulging frog shoulders was there. Arlen had created a microclimate of tropics in snowy winter basement. All it had taken was darkness, baby powder, water, and the crazed will to see it.

The next task claimed Arlen. He looked up. He could hear, through the ceiling fan exhaust pipe, the roof and air. The helicopter came for him. The media was ready for his Houdini escape. He was trapped. He turned comic book. It was the only way to get out of the house. He could and would rip the ceiling off the floor and crawl through the main floor and wall and main floor ceiling and house roof space and chew and scratch his way through the shingled roof. Again the sun would be bright upon him. The cameras would roll and the rotored craft would carry him off.

INTERUPTED

Arlen heard a knock, and the doorbell. He willed the person to go away. Be gone. The knock resumed and carried on to be joined by the voice. Arlen recognized the voice to be the voice of Ron. Arlen's friend Ron had come, with a feeling that something was wrong.

He would not give up with the noise. Arlen was in the belly of the house and everything resounded in intensity. Ron knocked and rang and yelled. Persistence opened the door from the inside. Arlen had not been nailed in to the house.

Arlen led Ron back into the basement and they talked by the pool table. The friend sensed Arlen's body heat eight feet away—this pleased Arlen. Arlen cut a piece of deodorant off a stick and placed it on his own forearm, it melted. Arlen was in a horrible state; the friend thought worse of what the hospital did to Arlen and the friend helped him remain.

The following day Arlen saw his doctor in his community office. The waiting room served peanuts and coffee. What an odd combination—you are nuts and jittery.

The doctor celebrated, "Your Thyroid Gland has responded to the Synthroid, I have never seen results that low."

"Way to go gland," Arlen thought.

Arlen spilled outward in his mania, oh, how does one keep it in when everything tastes, smells, looks, feels, and sounds infinitely better then normal? And he felt like he would explode.

"I'm going to Florida for a week. You should go into the hospital. I'll see you in a week," the doctor said.

"*You* should go into the hospital while *I* go to Florida." Arlen used that special tone of voice that gets the cops there in a hurry. Arlen hardly noticed the switch the doctor used. It was unbelievable response time that found the uniforms passing the nuts and coffee.

Arlen knew his defeat, raised his hands and expressed his soft diplomatic side and walked to the car. It calmed them to allow only one to drive him. Arlen crammed into the seat sideways to deal with the legroom.

Arlen talked non-stop all the way to the hospital. Back to more of the over-medicating doctor that did not like to prevent manias once he knew the pattern. Arlen deflated by talking. The handover was made from uniform police to undercover nurse. Why don't they wear uniforms? Is it too disturbing? Does it help to see normal dress? No emergency waiting, nothing, right to the ward, this is the way to go if you have short legs.

Arlen was a little excited and suddenly burned up in this air-deprived place. They left him in the TV room. He ripped his clothes off. What he truly needed was a swim in a Florida pool.

They did not know of this, yet brought him some nice pajamas and robe. He had forgotten his mission to swim the ocean and slink the desert to assassinate the evil one.

EXPERIMENT

The chemistry experiment entered another phase. Arlen could have a massive stack of little paper pill cups if he had only thought to keep them. This was the hospitalization when he learned to accept his injections. He had left prehistoric Largactyl for Modecate. Arlen loved the stone of Modecate.

It hit his missing piece perfectly and propped him to shine. It felt like a movie star drug. He would lay spread eagled on the bed breathing, anticipating the visual effect and good stone of the drug. It always felt better if a cute nurse did it.

Arlen felt his spirit crest into an extrovert naturalle. The drug lengthened his stride and pleased his flesh. It invited others to dance in the flirt. Arlen untapped raw manic that was rough and invaded the space of the women. They would respond and dance in a diverted complex way. Arlen would feel his sex sell to them and they would counter hesitations and embrace appeals to their inhibitions.

When Arlen was injected with a major tranquilizer, he was fame and glory. He was succeeding, for the time being, to surpass the main obstacle of looking into the mirror and not recognizing his own eyes and face. They were the eyes of lacquer-coated coal. The irises had moved on to saner latitudes. Pupils rebelled against their cause of stimulus.

Arlen had discussed this concern of huge pupils with his doctor. The doctor had appeased him by marketing this concept: there was a time in Europe when people would take drops to enlarge their pupils to attend parties—it attracted the opposite sex. Arlen bought into the system cash in hand without hesitation.

He could tell that women liked the pits of eyes. They trapped the glance and drew it into a snare of looking glass. It grew into a longing of exposed glare. It was a naked unabashed place of self-disclosure. There was no fear of nudity in this place.

Arlen thought and obsessed on the mission of rollerblading across the country for mental health awareness. He wanted to rally the citizens to talk and listen about mental health.

The major tranquilizer slammed the anxieties and fears of Arlen into oblivion. The drug fit and altered his state to homeland. It was peace and ease of being fucked up in a psych ward. It was beauty and pleasure. It altered his vision to see the good and quiet meditation.

CYCLE ON

The days and weeks passed through the dregs of depression and into regular Arlen mode. February approached.

Arlen drove out of province to visit a girlfriend. He flew out of sanity; it is a lost cause to have a relationship in this time period. It is too weird to continue the visit. They decided he should go back and enter the hospital. Arlen would go to the store and get a few supplies and return to say goodbye.

He drove his big station wagon through the intersection and was suddenly pulled by the church on his right. He slammed on the gas pedal and aimed for the back of the church but veered to miss the power pole by inches. He headed through the parking lot and jumped into a snowy park, maybe eight, ten inches deep of white.

The manic rush to drive through just came over him. The big "S" curves up the hill and over became beauty to perform. The pile of snow from a grader protected the edge of the road from his reentry. Arlen sped up to hit it, launching the thousands of pounds skyward and pounded down violently, barely knocking him out.

The car was at a forty-five degree angle. Arlen saw, through starry eyes, the road downwards through the windshield. The seat belt had worked. Good thing he had placed a spicy pepperoni in his shirt pocket; he reached with his mouth and bit it reviving Popeye's spinach.

Arlen was in a sorry sling. The car started but the rear wheels spun in mid air useless.
"Shit."
Arlen saw people drive by laughing and pointing. This made him really want to escape. A couple of guys came up and asked if they could help—they were getting a towrope when the police car arrived.

The cop asked Arlen to step out of the car and searched him. They admired the nice tracks in the snow. The cop then looked at the organized assembly of computer, luggage, guitar, and bike in the back. That troubled his brain further. With Arlen's identification, he checked his name to be clean.

Arlen told him that he was manic and heading back to his province to check himself into the hospital. He was just going to visit his girlfriend before leaving. He could not believe Arlen was not on street drugs. He thought it best to take Arlen to get checked out. What do you say to no ticket? His shoulder was sore. The cop said he would call the girlfriend. Arlen rode up the hill. One does get better service brought in this way.

NEW DOCTOR

This simple getting stuck in another province, was the best thing for Arlen. It cut his stay in the hospital down to two weeks from six. Frozen water crystals and strange driving freed Arlen from a life of too much medication. What a bonus a cold climate can be.

The girlfriend arrived stressed to the scene. She played the examination room instruments to attempt peace.

Arlen's new doctor had lines on his forehead that told Arlen he had a full frontal Lobotomy. Psychosis told Arlen that he himself was a shrink too, and simply needed a little de-briefing.

Every shrink was a de-briefed crazy person. This new doctor could see that he was manic. This was good service. Arlen received a wild freezing ride up to the ward in a wheelchair as shock set in.

Less medication, and he was done with Lithium and the Synthroid. The idea of roller blading across the country for mental health awareness stole his heart again—he dwelled and lived for this event. It was a compulsion. This was publicity.

He was out in two weeks and decided to move to this fair city. It became his Alberta advantage. He raised his head and walked on.

Arlen was held captive again by his old companion: a bed that floated the suicide islands.

He wrote:

MELANCHOLIA
Bewitch puppet my gloom facade.
    Betray that depth of twist
    the others might see this genuine face
    for whole skin cannot portray
    the maelstrom of malady beneath.

On withered sticks propped, float I.
Speak a trick hollow sounds tremor.
Meet on street forth gaze my eyes down,
afraid contact me expect look away.

Lay dormant cast body bed,
    molasses stuck thoughts in head,
      action sex favors offered dead.

    Rhyme a reason for the season makes no sense, just like this:
    Dull thump ache festers repeat again bewitch puppet my gloom
facade
    on withered sticks propped float I.

LUNAR

Arlen eventually floated back to his true self. He approached the New Year with trepidation and fear. It was a given pattern now that he would go manic toward February and lose the majority of his year to the high and low and mixed state and general malaise of madness. He lived as true Arlen one quarter of the year. This pursuit of life and friends and love was a seasonal position. His fiend side sabotaged his search for companionship. He stared at the full moon and felt the twist of primal compulsion.

He wrote:

Lunar Lunacy
Big whitehead
Bouncing around the world
Getting his face all pocky
And his body all with
Constellations of moles
Driving force of lunacy
Driven desire for mate
Give me lord a clean slate

Arlen rented a farmhouse. He did not know that this night would be pivotal in his future career of mania. His mania was late for its date and had a hard-on. The sheer violence of it would push him through, he would end up in another land of dwelling—he had suffered this cyclical torture long enough.

GANG

Arlen dressed for town in black jeans, a long sleeved green shirt, a leather belt, and a pair of sandals that held his manic rage. It had been building in him and searched for release. He was to explode. Arlen drove the car and took pictures with the 35 mm camera that his dad had left for him. He ditched the camera never for the evidence to be found.

The rage drew Arlen toward the core of downtown. He parked the car in the Seven Eleven parking lot in Fairview. The seat could not contain the force that opened the car door. Arlen's legs moved uselessly below, the rage carried him above the earth—conflict moved the shell of his body. His belt restrained the power within that enticed encounter and craved clash.

A group of boys cornered him and wanted some action. They spread out to surround him. They closed in jeering. He spun around and became head energy—unlimited, unstoppable surge. He stopped, crouched down a bit, and put his arms up and spread toward their eyes. He laughed heartily and looked crazily at them. They lost their group courage for such a deed as this. They started to back away; he laughed louder and looked even more out of touch with reality. This guy is nuts, they let themselves down from their self appointed violence. They retreated.

Arlen slipped into the alley and jogged through the darkness. He had to release physically after an episode.
They called out to him, safe now with his distance, "Run crazy man, run."
It surged within him to burst—he bolted.

His thoughts wandered. Any goodness that was Arlen disappeared within this defiance. Crisis loomed. He headed to the pedestrian bridge and stopped at the bridge rail and looked down at the dark river. Two shadow men clutched bottles to their chests.

"Evening officer, Peter here is getting married tomorrow and we're having a couple drinks to celebrate, we're not hurting anyone." They looked up.

Arlen wore no uniform and was no officer. The force let itself be felt outside of his body. There will be pain. Why couldn't a slice of goodness reach out and extinguish the flame?

Arlen turned from the rail and crossed the bridge. The river ice had just broken and it crunched and moaned. The water rushed to flush the ice down. He jogged to meet the downtown hustle.

DOWNTOWN

Arlen slowed to a steady walk. A drunken man grabbed Arlen's arm. He had little awareness and asked, "You got a dollar?"

The smell crawled and lingered about him. Arlen recognized the alcohol that puppeted the drunk. Arlen pummeled him with words and moved on.

No coins, no wallet; just a key to escape the rage, a car to deliver the body. This was becoming a mission to be misery. Arlen could feel the pain magnetize to his body in power and growing hurt.

Arlen entered the stripper bar and asked for a glass of ice. He stood at the back and watched a uniformed ambulance man shoot pool with a girl. Arlen looked at the tools of life saving on his belt. Arlen wanted to use the tools. Arlen crunched the ice; it hit the spot for the moment—the coolness soothed his clinched jaw muscles.

This scene was completing without him. Arlen headed for the door and deposited his empty glass. A girl had finished dancing and walked past him.

"Where you going?" she asked.

"River."

Arlen was glad to see the street scene after the bar. He had no idea what would soothe his craze. What did he have to do to complete the need? Three men exited from a truck.

"You got a smoke?" Arlen asked them.

They fumbled about and produced a smoke.

"Got a light?" Arlen asked.

It was lit and carried off. Arlen was cold and commanding. He looked mean and people let him go. He walked toward the river and took a drag of the cigarette. He threw it in the street. The smoke did not fill his gap.

Arlen glanced to 'The Bodyguard' poster in the video store. That was the attitude that prevailed. He wore that fashion.

RUN

Arlen's head swam as he approached the river. He felt like he contained the giant within—but people could see. He needed more dark and concealment. He needed night.

He turned from the street to the paved bike trail. It was forested and black. He appreciated the darkness disguise. He couldn't see the gap he walked into and had to feel the pavement with his feet. His eyes adjusted to the slightest of shadow change.

Desertion of witnesses allowed the snap. Arlen plucked his sandals from his feet and exploded in a blind sprint through the trees. The pavement blasted his bones through the black. The sense of touch kept him true to hard course. The stones on the edge directed Arlen to straight. The trail wound Arlen to run like chased quarry. He was prey and hunter combined. He was mental victim and tormentor. He was pain and hunger for meat—something to satisfy. He pumped blood to consume more of this void.

He was seeker for light. The light came of a building—it was on the large river-faced side with no windows. There were five steps that climbed onto a landing that entered the utilities building. There was a railing that prompted Arlen to enter stunt man phase. Arlen would run up the steps and vault off the railing with his hands and flip backward upward flipping over toward the darkness to land on the concrete. He became speed and focused attention.

Arlen veered at the last moment, a diverted incident spared from occurrence. He was free to dash. Arlen rushed and the river pulled him—he could hear the water run. He stopped and walked through the trees to the river. He felt his way down the bank to water's edge. Ice blocks lingered in their relinquishment to liquid summer.

CURRENT MADNESS

Arlen inserted his feet into the sandals and rolled his pant legs toward the knee—it provided spiritual protection to his calves. He removed his shirt and rolled it tightly around his upper ass, he tied it in front and bound his sacrum to his belly; it gave posture strength.

The water received the leather sandals, the cold curled the toes and the rushing liquid enforced its grip. The river reached his knees and the rocks acted like marbles. It was a challenge to stay upright. The frigid water focused Arlen's attention—this threatened to be serious, this reality of psychosis. These next steps approached vital to act upon the urge. Arlen stopped in the middle of the river—waist-deep. His scrotum sucked toward the torso.

This was it—it claimed Arlen, it felt ordained to occur this way. Arlen turned and faced downstream. He crouched and launched into the air, arcing his body backward seeking the back flip. He was spawn. Arlen's head pierced the water and gravity gained his scalp to smash on bottom rock. It struck where the hair originates direction. It slammed Arlen's head forward. The rock and force forgave not the lack of sane planning.

It was an agreement like all applied physics. It snapped Arlen's head forward and tore. The blow drove his spine to implosion. This slammed the grain of goodness that Arlen had. Arlen thought of the doom of a broken neck. It was over. The suffering was in close breathing on his face.

The current had ideas for body disposal; he floated on his back and turned to downstream. Arlen reacted to stand. His head broke the surface and pain screamed; he clasped his cervical and heard a beaver slap its tail. It was appropriate for the moment. Arlen was threat. The pain sacrificed Arlen to the cold waters. The chilling suspension delivered mild relief. Arlen bobbed and succumbed to the spring thaw.

This was an overdue situation—he had held the mania in too long. This was a serious predicament. Arlen was not thinking this at the time—he was in the moment fully, absolutely. He was sacrifice, he was torment released—here was the promised pain.

The waters cradled the hurt. Arlen lulled into the night river. He thought of the scene from the 'Mission' movie. He floated with arms outstretched in demanded submission to the pain.

He whispered, "Father forgive them for they know not what they do."

The cold numbed, the toes clenched onto the leather, the shirt held the bound about him. He soared in the current, suspended. He felt small and non-existent, lonely. It was a dark deserted crack in the earth that he fell into—hours and miles to daylight.

Arlen floated downriver headfirst. His eyes caught the bridge rail and deck. He grazed his eyebrows with his gaze and spotted the concrete support pillar. His current driven head intended to strike the column. The wound could not take another blow; the complacency that the flow carried broke with a cringe of unwanted pain.

Arlen spun around in the water, twisting and paddling his hands and kicking his feet, full-bodied reaction except for the neck—it desired silence. The sandals lowered and found the rocks. He skidded and bounced; it was like getting up on water skis. Arlen stood, clutching his neck for support. The water throttled his upper back to bounce. He had to run with the current to stay upright. He turned to narrow the drag. He faced the shore, and gave less of a target to the flow that would transport to darkness.

The neck demanded full regard. The freezing had enabled this extrication. Arlen supported it as best he could and felt for stable anchor. The current toppled the balance and pushed him over. He lost ground and sought stability. He drifted and dragged the soles on the rocks to steady. It was a slow approach to the shore. The initial inches were hard-fought and the feet soon grew in aptitude, the body angled to resist the water wind.

EXTRICATION

The river receded from the chest to the waist. The water rushed to the ground. It abandoned his waist and knees and with it the terror of extra gravity mounted an assault—full engagement of his being to deal with the pain and support of the cervical and stay balanced on ground.

Arlen stood water free on a rock bar. The shore was within grasp. Arlen reached down with alternating hands to remove the sandals. He threw them one at a time into the river, they plopped. Arlen thought it was appropriate to appease the beaver; they could use them to complete their dam.

Pain blurred through this doffing. Survival vied for attention now, yet insanity clamored for unreasonable taxation. It demanded barefoot attention to ground details. Arlen shook with frost. He grew vivid with cold and untied the shirt; primal being fell to the wet rocks. He wrung it out and inserted his arms into the wet tubes of sleeve. All the while he had to support the neck or risk the pain of recompense for look mom no hands. It was best to have one hand clasped and even better to have two hands collaring the muscles. It was too early to give thanks for the paralyzed free act.

He was on the riverbed a world apart from the city—but within it. Each step harbored sharpness and possible cradling of the arch. Arlen sought out the smooth rocks and clambered toward shore. His cold feet numbed the gruffness of the rocks. Not enough water had eroded the rocks to soft. Arlen did not have time to wait for adequate comfort of erosion. He was now and needed to get off this river—out of this void of fracture. He needed peace.

Mere survival was the guide. Hurt had dazed the insanity. Pain was his portal and the car was the mirage. He reached up one handed for the underbrush. He pulled it down and up he tripped and inched the momentum. The footing was a dry twisted version of the deepwater rocks. Arlen gripped roughness and pulled himself into the city. The underbrush tore at his hand and legs. He felt his skin repelling from nature but this was minor pain when the car was near.

In the bad part of town barefoot, in the dark, near the earth—Arlen dragged the body. The steps emphasized sluggish and mechanical. With a glance you may not grasp the closing of an event that nobody witnessed. Arlen walked slow and looked to be in pain. He supported his neck. The gravel underfoot changed to pavement and sidewalk. He felt screaming conspicuous when a car scanned its lights across his path. They drove on. Did they even notice?

It was three blocks of longsuffering. He crossed the street—he felt the automobiles harass his inability to rush out of their way. He moved slow through the crosswalk. A car arrived and pushed his angle forward and caused him more pain. He reached the oasis of the convenience store. The lights jumped into his brain and tensed his head to ache in another depth and sphere.

The car was still there. He thought of the leather necklace keyed around his neck. He did not remember tying the key in this fashion. His mind had known he would revert to rougher times. He had been prepared for this moment. The key was not lost. He removed the strand from his neck and inserted the key in lock. Anticipation yelled and promised relief. Dry bones cracked for solidity.

The door opened and the bag of flesh and bones found the seat. The seat formed a resistance, an alliance of support that was haven. It was sheer pleasure to find a base to place his platter of putty. He could build from here. He couldn't support his body further but he could drive this car.

He waited for relief to set in place. He reached up and moved the rear view mirror to see himself—his head was adorned with red tracts—a large spider reached out from the contact point. He needed time to steady the shake that grew.

He was in a foreign land of slurpees and chips and magazines. The foreigners parked their vehicles and reached for wallets and Arlen would still be there when they came out with glittering packages. Their wanton mood of consumption repelled Arlen in his waning lunacy. He sat deep and this mere consumption seemed like lifetimes ago.

He had buried himself in a hole once again: Arlen was not well and rested his torn muscles. He drove to the base of the hospital and parked in a vacant lot and pondered his fall. He knew he needed the haven of the illuminated H on the hill. He needed the uniformed and non-uniformed staff. He needed their poking and prodding and clean linen. He meditated on his need for professional help. They did not prevent the manias.

This car worked perfectly. He was amazed to ask it to do something and it listened. He liked the obedience and reliability. He could depend on it. He felt he could not depend on the hospital to help his lunacy. He required a respite. He rested and realized he had to work the next morning. He receded from the hospital entrance—it would have been easy. He drove back to his rented farmhouse.

It was a major feat to exit the car and enter the house and pass the hours till the start of work. He surged pain and craze—he used the medication he had on hand, it was a drop in his bucket head.

WORK

He met Paul at the agreed-upon location. The huge four-wheel drive tractor and cultivator grabbed Arlen's attention. They fueled up and Paul asked him if everything was okay.

"Yep," Arlen said.

Arlen spent the day tilling the land. It was freedom and Arlen lifted from the earth. He listened on the radio to the history of the word and topic of lunacy. It was appropriate; he felt pockmarked moon face in craze and love for a woman. He needed to trace the constellations on her moles. He did not even know whom—odd that it was this huge; as big as the moon.

He imagined himself flying a plane swooping back and forth across the lines of the field. He felt the vast power of the engine. He finished the field; he had worked it to his perfection. Paul thought it was over-worked but the job was done. Arlen folded the cultivator up; this was nasty on his neck to even look backward in the mirrors. The bouncing of the tractor had aggravated the muscle tissue damage. He pointed concentrated pain on task.

He exited the approach and crossed the road. He decided the ditch could be navigated straight ahead, he inched in and the line of golfers grew. They were anxious and sped to the course. Arlen was pleased to hold them up and down.

The crossing crept. Arlen inched carefully to not damage anything in the drag. It transpired perfectly. No damage and a great long line up of cars on both sides. He was in his next field and fell to fatigue.

He deteriorated. He threw his glasses onto the field and his mind flipped loops. He had not slept much these past days. He was spinning a deeper chasm; it was a trap that would trip him up. It was a matter of time till this working and no sleep caught up with him. The back flip did not help matters. He was grinding the gears of his mind. He pondered the beaver and looked at the slough that passed by. It yelled to him to heed and touch the water.

Arlen slowed the machine and lifted the tines out of the soil. He let the engine idle and stepped onto the ground. He peed and remembered that one of the Crazy Canuck Downhill Skiers trained by riding in the hub of a big tractor wheel. He walked toward the water. His feet snapped the canola stubble—it had bleached and weakened through winter. He crossed the zone he had worked up—the dust kicked and hovered about his feet.

His neck moaned and required clasping again. Arlen was stubborn mental man—he would not give up. He exited the field and entered the reeds of the marsh. He did not want wet feet and was careful to step. He let go of his neck to cup his hand under the water to crane tablespoons to lips—it tasted of wild stagnant.

That would hit the spot; he could relax tonight. If he could sleep he would get better. He cupped some liquid to his wounded head. It felt like there was no skin on the skull bone.

He listened to the radio again—there was talk of Allied aviation burn victims in World War II that were welcomed by an English village. It described the situation in detail. The villagers affectionately called them, "Their little piggies." Arlen entered in without a fuss or thought. His imagination waited, ripe and fickle to minute suggestions. Arlen cranked the heater and sweated. He was dry and burning. He destroyed the I.D. in his wallet. The plastic pieces demanded great bending and effort. He combined the pieces into one illusion. Arlen roasted. His mind smoked with the slowdown.

He resumed the combing of the land and moved toward the next field. He could go around on the road or cut through an old narrow approach through the drainage ditch. He folded up the cultivator and headed across the thin access. Arlen crossed the trail in low gear and felt the center point on the greasy road. The tractor slipped—Arlen adjusted the steering to counter, the slightest of movements were too much. It was a battle to cross. He leaned his body to the left to counter the slide into the ditch. He did not want to get this unit stuck or rolled. The six-foot tires slid and spun. Forward momentum won to place the tractor in the next field; with exhausted Arlen.

He attempted to back the cultivator into position to set it in down mode. His neck and shoulders screamed. He tried three times in vain. He felt the guns hit. He was at altitude and dropped like a boulder to the earth. Arlen felt the impact in his spine. The heater still cranked the heat to a hundred. He was on fire. The tractor idled to burn the interior. Arlen pounded his feet on the floor. It made no sense but this reaction was paramount.

It reigned over him, the capitulated victim of aviation. The farmer Paul was a hot air balloon man. The only hope was for Paul to rescue him and extinguish the fire. Arlen melted in the wait. He felt the flames and screamed.

The radio was mute but played itself out in Arlen's head. He was spineless clay. Poor Arlen. He was again fucked in the head.

Paul arrived in the field and saw the tracks of mud. He was glad that Arlen had made it through the ditch. Why was he sitting there? Something was wrong. The bumper sticker on the truck caught Arlen's eye and saved him. 'Ballooners do it with hot air.' The intervention was underway and the forces of cool fit in place. Arlen could twist anything trivial into service to support the grand delusion.

Arlen killed the great diesel and opened the door. The air washed the firebox clear. Arlen's head of red settled to lighter hues of pink. Arlen grabbed his gear and crawled down the ladder.

"You okay?" Paul asked.

Arlen thought of the fall from thousands of feet to burn on impact. He could feel the screams of pain that the aviators wore. He thought of the agony.

"Can you give me a ride to my car, Paul?"

"Sure."

The ride was eerie; Paul needed a plausible piece to hold onto.

"I'm sick Paul, I need to go home."

"All right." Paul dropped Arlen off at his car.

"Give me a call Arlen," Paul said.

"Yep." Arlen walked without moving his upper body to the car.

BOARD

Arlen drove straight home and found a two by ten inch plank in the porch. It was seven feet long and would suit the purpose fine. He placed it on the living room floor and deposited the phone next to it and took the medication he had.

In the kitchen he grabbed flour and bowl and mixed ingredients. Suddenly he was the baker god. He baked a bread earth in a jiffy—he mixed up a globe of dough and placed it in the oven. He was the mad creator who spun the axis. He dusted his head-river-contact point with flour. That would place the mend on. He felt the stagnant water claim its evil dominance over his cellular level. He was rotting, and somehow all of this was appropriate.

He walked to the board and carefully met the floor with his body. He was ache and dull throb. His discomfort spun about him to concentrate the whole world on the board. To Arlen nothing else in the world existed. It was excruciating to lower his torso and head to the plank. He used his hands to cradle the cervical. He arced his back, pain and spasm fought with movement.

Finally his body lay flat on the board. Now the pain waved and mocked the movement. Arlen breathed and relaxed—it took minutes of nailing weight to allow the body to sculpt to the flatness of the board. Arlen reached and pulled a blanket from the couch. He worked an end under his neck to support the bones. The muscles needed a holiday. Arlen let himself go to the comfort of setting.

The peaks of pain wore to flat lines of dull. He waited and realized he was stuck in this place. His mind still spun an incredible, fickle course. He willed himself to lay still and be wood. He needed the plank to restore his sinew to mend. This narrow backboard was suitable for a mental health patient, he thought. He rested for two hours.

The farmer's wife Heather came to the door, knocked and called out. Arlen struggled to arise. He made it to erect and approached the door. "We wanted to check on you, are you all right?" Heather asked. "Yes."

"Can I help you out?"
"I need more medication."
"I can go, where is it?" Heather asked.
Arlen retrieved the information and handed it to her.
"They should give it to you, they can call me."
"I'll be back."
"Thanks Heather."

Arlen found the support of the plank to rest on and struggled to the door when she returned. She passed him the bag. He thanked her. She left. He took one of each. He knew he needed something more—it wasn't in the bag. He lay on the wood and waited for the bee sting to inflict its nectar to soothe the popping in his brain. Arlen dwelled past the point of mere stings to counter the malaise; he needed baseball bats and clubs to knock him out and down.

The sting hit and left in moments. He could feel the peak and release. It covered him for seconds and not to the full required depth. That was that. He used all the doctor had empowered him with to no avail. He was meal and stew. Madness dined.

His mind rose against the vigil of prone. He balanced it with the promise of pain to rise. He had had enough—it was over, he could not move any more. Enough pain, he was done. It was time to bring in the professionals. Arlen reached for the phone and pressed 911 for the first time in his life.
"I'm a manic-depressive, I need help."
"What is going on?"
"I'm a mess."
She suggested that he seek out the hospital. Arlen wanted and felt that a helicopter should attend to the situation and airlift him in. His neck equaled pain. She suggested the psych ward and gave him the number.

He called the psych ward and talked to a nurse from the previous year. She was kind and helpful. Arlen could not convey his pain to these professionals and it frustrated him. He needed validation of his crises. He required the dignity of an ambulance. They would not give him that. He broke down on the phone. She comforted him. He waited on the plank on the carpet. He craved water.

After the phone calls Arlen thought he should have it over and lie, tell them he had fallen on his head and needed an ambulance. He hadn't told them enough about the river—he had talked about the beaver. He knew he had screwed up and accepted his place. He lay ready for healing. He was the true patient waiting, beyond helpless. He was self-induced trauma—deliverance challenged.

The kind farmers decided to check on him again. Arlen showed Dean the flour infested wound. There was empathy and a whirlwind of preparation. Paul was sought out and the two of them, straight from the field, were there to bring him in. From the farm to the city emergency ward, the car was brought into place.

Paul and Dean sandwiched Arlen to stand and walk. One stood on each side of him. Once again Arlen required others to save him. The walk to the car was tough. The crawl into the backseat turned grueling. He inched to the middle and bound himself ramrod erect. He held his neck with both hands—stiff to support the wounded shoulders and neck.

It was dark as they passed on the same roads that Arlen drove to town on.
"Weird day, I saw a goose land on the barn, never seen that before." Dean looked at Paul.
"First time?" Paul asked.
"Yep."
The large H sucked them up the hill and into place. They again helped Arlen to walk. They were his spine.

Admittance fell Arlen into bed. The manic-depressive line sends triage awareness into a different sphere. He was treated first as the unfortunate mad and a distant second physical injury. His pain was not addressed.

Arlen hurt more than his mere physical emergency entrances. This was a different approach of aloof. He was the stricken, is how he felt, a lower class than when he was primarily physically broken. He was placed on the shelf to be processed through to the unit of the mind. The plainclothes specialists would take over.

There wasn't much they could do for him. Arlen was thankful for the bed to rest in, and for the two men who brought him in. They loomed self-conscious with their work attire. They were of the land and they stood out as life to Arlen as they said farewell. Thank you. They were blooming earth against the sterile backdrop of examination room.

Arlen waited on his own now in this warehouse of suffering. The whole of this complex specialized in what was wrong with people. He was in the right place. He was wrong. His mind was loopy and frosted. The sedative danced its heaviness upon Arlen's flesh. His bones fell toward bed. He drifted off. The clubs were on deck to strike his consciousness. He was ready to be put in coach. Arlen's mind would be the ball pitched across the plate. Batter up.

PORTED

They made Arlen sit in a wheelchair. What is real and acted pain in this realm of neurosis and psychosis? What is actual and supposed? The porter wearing running shoes ported Arlen—it was his workout and Arlen's chilling. It was a long ride and Arlen was appreciative of the smoothness of wheels—what a great invention. The chair on wheels acted ease on the jarring of pain. Arlen was unit bound and once again found needing of an eggshell to house his broken yolk.

Arlen's lobotomy incision-scarred forehead shrink was out of town. Arlen was pleased to get rid of the man. He talked more about himself than about Arlen, and made Arlen wait for hours after the appointment time. Where do they get these people?

Arlen found himself with a new doctor that clicked. Something was different about this one. He was real and spoke the truth. Arlen and this Ulrich doctor were on the same wavelength. Ulrich was a straight shooter; he held nothing back and was not fazed by bullshit. He took Arlen on.

Arlen would hear the strange pride people shine with, concerning their tumors and physical ills. They like to talk about a relative that is diagnosed with a heart condition or diabetes. But when it is mental illness, all is quiet on the open front. It is in awkward whisper, if at all. It is the understood shun. It is the silent suffering without pride. We want you to be well, come back when you are better. It isn't from my side of the family.

The egg renewed and followed with mixed states of up and down. Arlen held on to the rocket and deep sea submerging. It was brutality to be high and down several times in a day. Arlen found that he could never catch up. Part of him remained in the last consequence of mood. It was unnatural, too grand of a leap to dwell on suicide and then moments later feel on top of the world. Too quick of a ride to follow. Arlen lagged in between. He saw how easy it could be to commit suicide with the rush of energy combined with the bleak feeling. The manic strands wore themselves bare.

Arlen quit his part-time massage classes. His classmates visited him in the hospital and rubbed his muscle tissue clear. It would be three months before Arlen was pain free.

Arlen could sense the anti-psychotic medication working. The brain tissue was edged and dried from misfiring. The medication felt like small warm wet fingers massaging his brain matter. It was kind and gentle soothing. The balm of digits stroking made him close his eyes and give thanks; it was relief to have his scorched brain soothed.

RELEASE TO DEPTH

Depths of depression followed. Arlen lay on his bed tucked away from humankind for three quarters of each day. He was thought on suicide and singing of method. The summer was again fresh and fierce with sun and blue sky and Arlen lay wanting. He avoided the sun walkers. Arlen became cease-and-desist from life. All was dull and great weather once again mocked his despair. Everyone was happy for summer except for him.

He forced himself to exercise. He bought a 'Bad Religion' CD and played it loud. He played his metal and punk music to fuel the energy. He laced up his in-line skates and donned his helmet and wrist pads and hooked up the tunes. This event of skating pavement trails through forest and by the river lifted his spirit.

It reattached his puppet string. It forced him to move, to react to the speed and curves and impending doom. He had to come to life to deal with the obstacles and corners. It substituted elixir for suicide. He felt free on these eight wheels.

The music pounded his thighs to burn through the trees. Arlen climbed from depression one stride at a time. He skated both sides of the river spot where he attempted the back flip. It was like looking at a site where someone else had met their death. It frightened him to face the highs. The manias were becoming more unpredictable and dangerous. He could not afford the risk of crushing the dice to play again.

PREVENTION

Arlen thought of his potential crazed states of existence. He needed to arrest them in their infancy. Abort the crazy baby while it was still cute and cuddly. Chase away the diapered self-defecating hypo-manic life-enhanced joy seeker while it was still in the everything-in-the-senses-is-brighter stage.

Annihilate the lovely that everyone adores. Corner its transposed ego and inflated sense of esteem. Kill it while it could talk to anyone and sell any idea. Wring its neck while it is horny and promiscuous. Quarter it while it wants to shop beyond all means. Disembowel it when it has no sense of consequence.

Somehow in the midst of that pleasurable heaven sent state of bliss and wonder; someway set up a warning light to self-abort the greatness, install a hardwire warning system of alarm to trigger the burning of the wonder boy. It is brutal to mercy kill your darling; to strangle the best that you have ever felt or acted or been. It is illogical after licking the shit dirt of suicidal melancholia. It is cruel to kill optimized human.

It is essential to sabotage the bowels to a slower pace before they become excited and empty forty and fifty times a day. He accepts the need to bury the mania; he cannot accept the new habits he awakes to, when he comes back to sanity. He is tired of quitting smoking when he comes down. The last couple of down cycles he has not even stopped. It is a drag to be suicidal and smoke.

Perhaps if Arlen could abandon the manias to a distant archipelago they would make a dwelling there and be happy without leeching onto, and into, his existence. They could meet other psychotic spirits and fuck with one another and have mutant offspring—it would be a grand circus.

And they could plan a subdivision for the neurotic cast-offs. There could be houses with no doors that could be built with the residents inside: build the roof over them, enclose them in bliss. The hand washers could have sinks in every room of their homes. The doors could have motion sensors that counted for them, the sensors would be set for their number and the door would only open or close with those five, or six motions. It would jar shit with authority and affirm their magic numbers power.

The suicidal suburb would have impassable daily loops of pits to drive your car into. Plenty of space to wind the car up and many fine underpass walls to implode into. The cream of the slurry in the underpass section would be the thousand ton steel block that was suspended by a crane and ready to be dropped on the burning wreckage. This would alleviate Arlen's fear of not hitting the concrete wall fast enough. His suicidal ghoul would be assured of perpetual complete annihilation.

This continent would be lost and everyone with mental cast-offs dwelling there could have parties every year to celebrate the freedom. They could hire actors to dress up like clowns and dance around. The liberated celebrators could throw food and mock the clowns as their exiled demons. They would call it their crazy day.

Arlen could if he would, prevent the heights of the highs and avoid psychotic breaks entirely; he would also prevent the depths of self-termination meditation. He would cast it to Atlantis and forget about it with the psychotics and neurotics.

THE PLAN

Arlen analyzed his cyclical highs—they seemed to be connected to winter and then a warm spell would send him high. Valentine's Day was a connection too, but this past mania was pushing April. He concluded that the winter was too long.

Arlen studied the effects of Chinooks and was intrigued by the similar winds around the world and their effects on people and history. The last several years he had felt the Chinooks of Alberta. It was the opposite ionization of the air as waterfalls and crashing surf. The friction and compression of the winds after the mountain flow did strange things to the air. It was documented that it triggered migraines.

Arlen searched for a link to mania but was not rewarded. He read of the Santa Ana, the Shiraz, and the Mistral. He read that in Europe, murders that were committed under the effect of the sharp breeze had been pardoned. Arlen knew how great he felt to be by crashing waves and waterfalls. He knew the agitation and distress that the Chinook winds administered to his cloak. He read that in parts of Europe, they treat their large buildings to counter this effect. Arlen was in Calgary at Devonian Gardens and walked from the mall shop area into the gardens of moving water and greenery. He smiled and felt at ease and happier—there was truth to these theories.

It all added up to the need for him to shorten his winter and avoid the Chinook winds. He had not tried this as a solution.

Arlen learned that he could breathe similar to snoring and it would equalize the pressure in his head. He felt the first Chinook hit—his feet lifted off the ground and scurried in agitation. Arlen lay on his bed and practiced the snore breathing to equalize the pressure. It was hard to master but he felt eased. Maybe it was just the stillness and steady breathing but he felt soothed and able to face people again. He was Arlen and not the winds' play toy.

Arlen met with Ulrich and designed a plan. This new doctor helped with new drugs supplied for emergency. Wage strategy to face the winter challenge of height. Guard sleep with a knockout pill. Face the mania down.

Arlen rose with the autumn leaves' submission to break out of his depression. He struggled back to a sense of his true self. Like an old friend that he had not seen in ages, he saw glimpses of himself grow toward and into all-day-and-night Arlen. He lived as himself again. The filter of mania and depression had lifted from his inner thoughts. The veil had fallen and disappeared. He was free and clear of the nasty adversary that controlled.

It took years for Arlen to wake to the sense of prevention and took longer to find support in preventing the mania and depression. He compared his new-enlightened doctor with his over-medicating smiley doctor and became enraged at the lost years that could have been prevented with some logic. Arlen wondered if the over-medicating doctor was pleased to have his ward full of patients. It was a steady income to grease the revolving door.

The shrink could not learn simple things in a cyclical history and strive to prevent them. Was he paid to talk to his patients a minute or two per day? Arlen thought of the suicidal ideation and the withholding of medication to ease that suffering. To withhold an anti-depressant for suicide prevention because it might send you high is wrong when you go high anyway; and then to not prescribe prevention for manic psychosis that is recognized as patterned—these are both human rights issues. Arlen thought of the human rights atrocity that he thought this doctor was. He was evil to not strive to prevent suffering. No one is god among us.

It took five shrinks to finally meet the one to help Arlen free himself. He was fortunate that destiny and fate conspired with prayer to introduce the Ulrich doctor. Arlen was pleased to seek early retirement, and save the paper cups from demanding the whole forest.

READY

There were good money oil patch jobs. He made the leap to decent money and a new industry; poverty slipped from his psyche. He could eat out if needed—when he slipped manic, he found a simple meal would slow his ascent.

Arlen worked and saved and planned the trip. It was an exciting day to meet with the travel agent. Arlen decided on Varadero, Cuba. He had two weeks of all inclusive waves and sand. Everything would be provided and he could focus on breaking this pattern.

Arlen informed his doctor of the trip. They discussed the need for sleep and the strength of Arlen's hardest drug. The doctor had performed a fine job of creating a toolbox of drugs for Arlen to utilize and implicate in the murder of his manic self. The doctor was an accomplice to the first-degree pre-meditated killing of the manic man that attempts to rise again within the gray matter of Arlen. They would shoot it down with prejudice.

They planned the medications to journey with. Arlen asked about the need for an injection to settle like a blanket over the whole blessed experience.
The doctor resisted, "I want you to enjoy yourself, just oral."

Arlen finished his last days at work. It felt great to quit the job and face the troubled time with medical employment insurance. Eliminate the stress and hopefully say adieu to the manic man—Manicma was confident that he could come out of the basement once again; Arlen ignored him. What a great day to end a job and jump fifty degrees of Celsius. Arlen was pumped to arrive in the Caribbean.

ARRIVAL

The day before departure, Arlen read over the documentation and discovered he could take his bicycle. Straight to the bike shop, sure they had boxes to transport. They dismantled the bike and Arlen was good to go with the large cardboard box.

It was minus thirty when he entered the Calgary airport. Brother Jake had transported him there. It was plus twenty when he arrived in Cuba. The dry jet air exchanged slowly through the open doors of the plane. They stepped down the stairs and Arlen was drawn to look at the jungle perimeter of the strip. The air was lubricated with water. Arlen's winter dry nasal passages adhered with the water molecules. He was happy to be freed from the plane.

They herded into the airport to face customs. The large suitcase and mountain bike in a box were tricky to move in line. Arlen looked around for machine gunned security and was disappointed to only see side arms. He slid the cardboard box on the tile, it scraped.

The line moved closer and Arlen felt he had something to hide. He could not figure what he was concealing but he had the vibe sucked into maximum. He visualized where the prescription drugs were placed with the doctor's note. Arlen had done his homework.

He slid the box forward and offered his passport. His pronunciation for bicycle was off but the point conveyed. The man wanted to open the suitcase. Arlen submitted—the man dug in his underwear and innards for a moment. Arlen felt to be on display.

Arlen repacked the excess volume to compress. The suitcase was plump and laden with giveaways for the people. He had stocked up on freebies and practical items to give to the people. He had heard this was a good idea. Consumer goods were in short supply.

Arlen zippered up and pushed the box and pulled the suitcase to the door. He shook his head that they looked in the suitcase and did not care for the box. He could have anything in there.

The taxi solicitation began. He was free and queuing for the bus. His trip was an institutional situation; he stuck with the plane people he had recognized. He muscled his bike into the cargo bin and hopped on.

It was getting dark as they performed the milk run. The strong mix of vintage American cars trapped a nuance of time warp against the newer imports. Arlen saw the other hotels that he had seen in the brochures. It was indeed tropical; the air was fine and warm. Arlen talked to a couple from Edmonton—they were ready for scuba diving in the morning. They exchanged pleasantries and the time of the route to their hotel—they were staying at the same hotel. Arlen had made his first friends.

At the hotel, the queue began to check in. The entrance and lobby were basic and adequate. He did not notice the compound effect. He would soon realize where the locals were allowed and not allowed to go.

He again scraped the box ahead. It was a topic of conversation for people. "A mountain bike," was the answer to the many queries. He noticed the diving equipment of the couple—it looked cool to Arlen.

He checked in and found that his room was across the street and up the stairs. It was good to get settled in. It was mysterious to arrive in a foreign land for adventure. Arlen felt the surge of change.

His room was away from the compound and it seemed to Arlen that there were more people on their own in this building—singles. At the ground level stairs were two attractive women who smiled at Arlen, and one man who seemed like a security person. Arlen smiled back at the two women and carried up the stairs.

It was a nice room, his home for the next two weeks. He put shorts on and didn't unpack anything else. He placed his passport and cash in the safe in the closet and grabbed his keys and headed out the door to explore.

FOREIGN HEAD

He was foreign man in a foreign land. He glided down the steps with adventure calling. One woman sat at the base of the stairs. She smiled at him and said, "Buenos." Arlen returned the, "Buenos." He clued in to the fact that she was there ready to please him sexually. It was her purpose to exist on these steps. They could have a business agreement that resulted in orgasm for him. She could pretend.

Arlen was horny and had brought condoms just in case. He wanted to be prepared for any event. He knew where the condoms sat ready for their excited tearing of box and package. He had limited cash and did not want to open the door to escorted sex. He had seen what that could do to a soul.

He had had a roommate who was addicted to prostitutes: it ruined his soul and financial picture. It was three in the morning when there was a knock on Arlen's bedroom door. It was the John with his wrists cut, it had been a feeble attempt but the sobbing was valid, he needed help and Arlen did not hold that against him.

John moved out shortly after that and forced his situation to improve—it involved imposed poverty and helping inner city people. John had trouble with depression and Arlen wondered how much of it was guilt and remorse.

Arlen turned from the woman and hit the street. He headed back into the compound first. He said, "Buenos" to the doorman; he was a large black man, dressed in white. Arlen checked out the lobby, it was entirely quiet now. He walked out and checked out the pool and bar—it was exotic in night-lights and colors. The party was rising both in numbers and noise: the rum flowed. Arlen wanted to drink, but couldn't. The prescription medication he was on did not mix well with booze—it would scramble the brain matter. He could not dive into the booze. That would throw him over the edge. He would have to let the included rum spill on someone else.

Arlen walked past the doorman and nodded, the doorman nodded back. Arlen sauntered out on the street and toward the strip. It was two blocks to the busy street. He noticed the darkness—it was pitch and things hid in the shadows.

He stopped just short of the strip and stood in the shadows himself; and watched. He observed the action. He noticed the night watchman observing the security of his area. They saw the couples laughing in love. Arlen felt the warm breeze. He listened to the palm trees and vegetation rustle and scratch. This was all a stage for the tourista to walk and drop money. It was a resort town, a strip that baited the dollars to flow. It was beautiful and exotic.

It pumped him up and his feet hurried to take in more. He walked up the strip to see the partiers on the sidewalk. He passed by groups of men sharing a bottle and playing music—it was the fire that kept them warm. They huddled around the sound that bounced their chests to beat and breathe. The music danced everywhere; it surged and wavered with the wind. It pushed Arlen to speed up.

Last night he had walked in Canada in minus thirty. Tonight, he floated in plus fifteen celsius. The locals sought warmth and Arlen wore shorts and a t-shirt. He also wore that grin that just came from a harsher clime. He wore it for all to see. The locals thought he was crazy already; he was another target that could be asked for money and goods.

The first asking threw him off—he wasn't ready for it and he shook his head and continued on. They were ruining it for him. He wanted to go get the nylons and socks and give them away right now; he wanted to give the soaps and shampoos, the crayons and books. He wanted to dump it all on the sidewalk but where would that leave him tomorrow? He had to wait and so did they. He couldn't spare any cash, he only had a hundred American, and it wouldn't go far. He had cringed to pay two dollars for a drink on the bus from the airport. He had ninety-eight left. He was a poor tourista, but these people did not know that. He was a northern man, and they all have money to visit here. They asked—that is what they must do. Arlen moved on. He was flying now: the sights, smells, and sounds fueled his ascent. The air was sexy and he embraced it.

TRY TO COUNT SHEEP

Arlen looked at his watch, time for bed. He found his way back to the room. He didn't look at the hooker. He ran up the stairs and entered his safe harbor. He closed and locked the door.

"What have I gotten into?"

Arlen was scared and sick. He was high and had within the hour changed into a different person.

This new scene was threat to Arlen—the river was nothing compared to the trouble he could bathe in here. He was in another country and mentally ill and immersing in a deeper hue of craze every minute. He took out his toolkit of drugs and logbook. He did a quick inventory. It would have to do. Arlen lay on the bed and could hear a psych nurse say, "Lay down and let it work its wonders."

Arlen lay there and missed the safety of the psych wards. He felt scared and knew nobody. He decided that he must build a support network if he were to make it through the fourteen days. He would lay low and meet people—make it without the hospital. Maybe that is what this was about, learning to look after himself without the professionals. He wished he had something stronger to beat his soaring head to the pillow.

The pill allowed him to lay prone for a full hour and that was all he could muster. His spirit rose to full height and his body followed. He stood and unpacked the suitcase. He tried to think slow and relaxed. He breathed and tried to not panic. He wanted to talk to someone. He ate half a box of the crackers that he had brought. It helped him to chew and digest. He slowed down a bit more.

He turned the TV on. No remote control here. It looked like a North American television evangelist without the trappings and the saccharine smile—it was serious Spanish talk. Arlen wondered of the revolution. He shut the TV off and listened to a mellow tape on his Walkman.

He was in a deep place without a boat. He had to swim for fourteen days, could he do it without sleep? He had the feeling that sleep would be shy. It was too much for him; he was too much for him. This scene had thrown him to manic man in hours. He was stuck in Manicma—a scary place to be on your own. He did not want to initiate helping connections with other tourists but that is exactly what he had to do, starting at breakfast in the morning. He looked at his watch, it was one in the morning—it would be a long night.

He counted the pills and separated them into fourteen piles. He could imagine the needle hit in his ass and the blanket anchor cast upon his head and shoulders. He could feel the sinking to soundness. But all he had were these mild pills. It was not enough but it was all he had—it would have to do.

He made a chart on the back of his journal book for the medication. He set the times of administration. He had been trained well by the hospitals. He wondered if the times were close to his actual hospital medicine times. He would simulate sleep by forcing himself to stay in bed from midnight to six a.m.—if he slept it would be a bonus. He would at least rest his body; he could not sustain twenty-four hours a day for fourteen days. He willed himself to not be hospitalized upon his return.

He would have to depend on his old friend, masturbation. He used it now; he thought of the prostitutes and shot his load and the release allowed him to relax fully to the bed. His mind dipped into the dark waters for minutes. All was peace. Arlen thought of sleep and that brought him above the murky waters to air. This revived him to scurry about in mind but he forced himself to stay in horizontal mode. He forced obedience.

He wrote in the journal book that he intended and needed the writing to be purposeful and not hypergraphia, not the gobbledygook that shines lucid and brilliant at the time of writing. He wanted to write something strong and relevant. He rambled and limited himself to two pages. The release of words wore him to the ground and he was able to turn out the light and be still again.

He thought about many things and tried for quiet thinking. He thought about the scripture, "Be still and know that I am God." Arlen was still thankfully in the mode of mere mortality. He was not god yet;

he hoped it would not come to that—he didn't think the Cuban authorities would understand his delusions of grandeur.

They would be ruthless with him and he would be incarcerated without medication—he would go rabid and bite and salivate. The bars would rust with the saltwater. It would rinse with his own tears and stain his face orange. His imagination stole him to the darker sides of Castro and being cut off from the United States of America.

His dependence on the pharmaceuticals scared and humbled him to pray on his knees before the multinational pharmaceutical giants for an injection of Modecate. It would fix him up proper and stretch him on this bed. It would make jelly of his muscles. It would produce a sleep of artifice that would suffice till the natural sheep arrived to range and count free.

He looked at his watch, three a.m. The night passed through a tiny mouse hole of time, there was a backlog waiting to squeeze through the hole. He thought of everything. He had to think anyway, it was his need and only pursuit. His synapses choked and sputtered as Arlen burned down, and tracked up old memories and threw new flame on them. The hours crept by on the ground and he waited for them to catch up. He was in morning mode and the rest of the world was tardy. They refused to jump ahead to coincide.

He had to fall in to the party line. He had to play by the Communist-run national policies for international tourism. He was stuck in a sleepless place in an exposed state. He needed cover in such a land. He required downtime—the stimulus was too grand of a scale. It was off his template charts for mania—no reference points to secure from. The external was hodge-podge and required Arlen to organize a sense of secure lodgings in his mind. He had to be careful and protect his self from all of this surrounding.

The fear of God and insanity rose in him. He had the respect of insanity and death burned into his dread receptors. This insanity alone could traipse to the depths of the addiction cycles in a sprint. He could be decent tonight and not sleeping and he could lose his sense of reality and do the very thing they could not handle in such a place. He would be dead in days.

Arlen wondered at the number of people each year that go crazy on the road, in other countries. To be on your own would be a bitch in places where they lock you to a bed. It would be better in parts of Europe where they house their crazies in four star hotels because it is more economical than the revolving hospital door syndrome. Arlen had not studied the treatment of the mentally ill in this fair land.

SUNRISE

Finally, six a.m. arrived and removed Arlen from his cell. He had drifted off once for a nap. The freedom of the open door erased any weakness created by the lack of zees. He walked out his door and onto the sundeck. It was tiled terracotta style and the building was white. He walked to the railing edge. He had a vantage point to see the neighborhood. The vegetation looked great and lush compared to the snowy desert he had come from. It grew light. Every sense of reality changed—exotica cranked his mood. The sun rose without him, he had to find a better spot to see the sunrise. This life is to be seen and felt to the full.

He jogged down the stairs and headed to the bright part of the sky. It was several blocks to the coast on that side of the peninsula. He jogged and looked at his surroundings. Arlen was now on the backside of the strip, away from the developed area. He stopped in his tracks to see the silhouette of a huge dump truck. He looked up to see the truck was full of bodies. Dozens of workers stood as dark shadow cut outs against the lightening sky.

Arlen jogged across the road and the sun poked up. He could see the bar of molten fire over the water. There were rows of hundreds of pump jacks pumping oil. He stood on the backside of tourism. The sun wore many shape intensities as it mirrored the water and rose to double half ball and then full double fireball. It was an opening shell. The solar half shells broke in two. Arlen semi blocked his eyes from the intensity. It was toned down by the earth's atmosphere. It lifted and separated from one double to two single balls. The one in the water danced and waved toward him. The original lifted like a kite to drive his day.

Arlen was now anointed to live. He kicked the red dirt at his feet and wondered what makes the earth red. He looked again at the well jacks lifting their horse heads up and down. They took drinks from deep within the earth. Arlen thought it would be great to work in the oil patch here.

Arlen had never been anywhere where the dirt was red. It boggled his mind. He shook his head and turned away from the industrial side. The full sunlight felt good in his eyes. He looked for other dump trucks as he crossed the road. He was thankful for his old car at home.

At the hotel, he had to wait for breakfast. He sat at the lobby bar and watched the place start to move. Staff wandered. Arlen thought of his dining room waitering days. He ordered a coffee and bought a package of cigarillos. He sat on the barstool and lit the match. The sulphur ignited differently—it struggled to prosper in the humidity. Arlen inserted the brown filter into his mouth and sucked. Has it been five months since he smoked? He took the habit on in seconds—he pointed and paid, unpackaged one, lit up and inhaled. Arlen held the smoke in to taint his blood. His head spun and he fought back a cough. He laughed with the barman. Arlen wondered if he dispenses booze this early.

Arlen held onto the stool, he felt it desire freedom from under his nicotine hit.

The coffee is placed in front of him. Arlen does not drink sugar in his coffee, but this Arlen is slipping up on us. He takes the spoon and brims it with the fine white.

He thought of his cocaine days and dipped the spoon into the black fluid—he tipped the spoon slightly to submerge the white into the liquid. The brown rushed to infiltrate the clean white. Arlen smiled and placed the spoon to his mouth. His tongue danced to receive the sweetness. Arlen rolled his eyes to the white diamond of taste. He closed his lips on the handle and pulled. His lips gleaned the crystals free from the spoon. Arlen's dimples formed. The spoon clanked onto the saucer. He lifted the coffee to his lips and sipped the rough rooted drink to mingle with the sugar. The crystals danced and spouted from every taste bud.

Arlen heaved and settled his shoulders. He sipped more coffee and cleaned the sugar free. His blood stream had something to work with now. Sugar, caffeine, and nicotine—the blessed cheap thrill trinity. It was there to serve him in a recreation sense. He took another deep drag of the smoke—rich and smooth. Arlen tried to remember what country that brand came from. It was good. He did not think to quit smoking now—it was a required prop of his state of being. He needed a tit to suck on.

Maybe it was hip but he didn't need any style enhancements— anything he wore would place him over the top. His was mania-enhanced ego. Confidence bloomed. Arlen finished his smoke and coffee. He thought of the moment and looked around. He admired the open building. A paradise without windowpanes. The foliage swayed like background dancers.

The morning bounced delightful after the long night. Arlen could interact—this hypo-manic jive man needed a crowd to work with. He worked the crowd through breakfast and into the poolside. The lounge chairs filled with tourista. The bar opened the rum to flow. Arlen met a man who had ingested a rum per hour for ten days now; as long as the bar was open, he was hooked up to it—that was dedication. Arlen celebrated this accomplishment with him. Arlen thought of the chart and medicines in his room and headed there.

Shit. He had missed his morning medication. He had to get the system straight if it was to take hold and get him through. He did not think of the caffeine. He took his meds and lit another cigarillo. His throat ached and calloused in a hurry to catch up with the rate of exposure. He lay on the bed and smoked and thought of the morning—it overflowed within him; such possibilities. He played with his changing voice. He made ah sounds and changed the pitch and depth. In between the sounds, he sucked the smoke in deep and held it to his chest to administer its medicine.

He thought of his grandpa lying down after lunch to have a rest. Arlen lay down before lunch. He could feel his body and it said rest. He forced himself to wait till twelve to go for lunch. He had to pace himself—two weeks stretched ahead. He could have stayed out around the pool all day, bouncing around to whomever would interact with him. Lucidity called and informed him to place siestas into his schedule. Shut the stimulus down and cover up in the room during the day. He decided on trying three retreats per day in the room, at eleven, three, and seven. And from eleven to six in the night, he would incarcerate himself in bed.

BEST OF IT

Arlen would have to make the best of it. He'd lifted off from the ground and had no psych ward to dock at. He had to keep it together. He was energy. He thought of putting the bike together but thought better of it. He would do it after lunch, after the beach—he hadn't been to the beach. That was first and foremost.

He slathered on sunscreen and put on his bathing suit and goggles around his neck and packed his towel in the small pack. Arlen went for lunch and sat with new people and made friends. He thought to tell them of his condition but decided they were not ready for it; he knew he was not ready.

The food sat in his stomach and made him tired. His energy soon mounted the rise and crossed him to the beach. His feet hit the floury sand and the sandals flew off—it was deep and hard to walk. Arlen walked straight to the water to touch it. He placed the water on his forehead and back of neck. He thought back to his canoe guiding days and his guru showing him how to introduce himself to rivers. "They like to know your skin, it helps them accept you in the water." Arlen anointed his head and arms with the water.

He looked up and down the beach—it went for miles in each direction. Hundreds of people blended into thousands. As far as he could see, the beach turned into resort and buildings. Arlen had nothing in the pack to be concerned about. He dropped it to the sand. He had his room key in a plastic bag in his pocket. He took the goggles and waded into the surf. It was warm and made Arlen smile. He had trained some for swimming the last few months, he had wanted to be able to be a strong swimmer in the ocean and this was test day. The waves felt sexy—they danced with him, and led.

At waist deep, Arlen dived in and soared forward kicking. Salt snuck into his mouth. He kicked to surface and opened into a front crawl. It felt great to become machine-like in movement. He was a swimmer and this was the sea he was in. It accepted him and desired to envelop itself around his every move. He kicked and grabbed at it. It moved out of his way. It made a path and allowed his passage.

He swam a hundred yards and turned left and swam four hundred yards parallel to the shore and turned left into and onto the beach. The sand felt great between his toes. Arlen had never swum in the ocean before. His lips were coated like a salt rimmed cocktail—he dabbed his tongue and spit. He walked a narrow wobble onto the sand and headed back to his pack.

He had gone for it and made it back through the surf. There was minimal undertow to contend with. Arlen looked toward the buildings and saw a woman showering on the beach edge. Arlen headed toward the shower. He rinsed the salt-water off—it felt great to stand in the sun and shower the salt free, he thought of the cold and snow back home. He smiled and stretched out on the towel.

Arlen relaxed in the sun to near sleep. He startled himself to get up and head back; he did not want sunburn. He leaned and pushed to make progress in the deep sand. He saw a couple that he had met earlier in the hotel. They said, "Ola" to him so he went over. She stood bare breasted—Arlen had a hard time not staring. It was odd to meet a stranger and then see her hours later showing her breasts. Arlen found it distracting. The woman smiled to appease the awkwardness. He excused himself and went back to his room.

Arlen pulled the bike box open and assembled the bike. He thought back to his Banff days and taking his bike apart and putting it back together; he had extra parts and took it to the bike shop to find out where they fit. Drugs and mechanics don't mix. Arlen was pleased to get the bike together. He experienced moments of peaceful sanity. The morning and afternoon were decent—he could pace and rest. It was the evening and night that threw him off and up further.

Arlen wrote in his journal, 'Act the fact and it will become.' He felt the need for sanity and willed himself to act properly when out and about. He felt free and enjoyed himself fully—but he did not need to be a freak. He needed sleep. He didn't even remember if he had slept the first night. He now wrote his amount of sleep down. He wanted to debrief with his doctor when he got back.

Arlen slept two hours the second night. He was pumped and ready to go with the flow. He noticed the coconut and palm trees swaying in the wind—it was in this time of great wind that he was driven to rage and flight. He rode the whim of nature. The wind blew and drove him into action—sheer movement and engagement of muscle and tongue. He spoke Spanish to anyone that would listen. The locals smiled, kind and gracious.

After breakfast he discovered the idea of a quadrathon. He had the energy, and it was a great weather day: he would swim first. He slathered sunscreen on his body and popped into the Speedos and headed to the ocean. Arlen safety pinned his key to his suit and embraced the water. He swam out a hundred yards and turned right. He breathed ten times to the right and then ten times to the left. It passed the time to count the bilateral. It was easier on his neck to do ten in a row before switching. He became aware of his stroke, and the small movements that perfected it. He was good to go and became lost in the pace. He felt like he could swim for hours. Suddenly it hit him—enough, and he headed to shore. It was a long walk back to his shirt and sandals. The endorphins mixed into pleasure and peace.

Arlen sat on his shirt and lit a smoke. The smoke hit him deep and washed over his back. He felt pin-pricked into a slate of submission—relaxed. He wanted to kayak next and retrieved money from his room and headed to the rental place. Once again, Arlen pushed out a hundred yards but turned left this time. He arced his shoulders to propel the boat. Arlen found the groove and lost time and place. His triceps burned and ached. Arlen turned back and slowed to make it to the beach.

He rested in his room with the door closed to shut out the sound of the breeze. He could see the leaved trees submitting to bend. A rainstorm fell. It poured. Arlen walked out on the terrace—the rain ran warm and alive with charge. Into his room he grabbed shampoo and headed back out for a downspout. He lathered in paradise and rinsed under the gutter release. Arlen was full smile with the sensual delight. His skin tingled. His fingers enlivened the scalp. After the rinse, the rain ceased. Sunshine grew to full. He was soaked to the skin with cares rinsed free. Arlen sat and dried in the sun's warmth. He closed his eyes with content.

"Ola."

Arlen looked up at a Cuban man who smiled. Arlen smiled back.
"Ola."

"Castro smoke." The man pointed and held out the box of Cohiba cigars.

"Cheap."

Arlen was open to all the universe would provide. He went to the safe and returned with the money. The exchange was made and the man left. Arlen became entranced with the box. It was grand and exotic. Arlen opened it: the native side-head relief, superimposed on the leaf beat primal in Arlen. The aroma crawled out through the musky fields and leapt to his receptors. He plucked a cigar from the bunch. The fullness of the box was perfect with one gone. This was pleasure. Arlen could not believe the size of it. Do you use two hands? He lit it and sat back on the lounge chair and mellowed to a leaf on the forest floor. He inhaled and watched the broom handle shrink. A stone fell on him to rest.

WEAR DOWN

After lunch he hopped on the bicycle and headed into the hills. The road climbed. Arlen was entertained by the variety of vehicles. It was odd to see old American cars from the forties and to see new imports.

Arlen pedaled his legs out in this third event of the day. He had the energy and headed into manic reserve. In periods of lucidity he knew the deep shit that waited if he did not get this thing under control. He did not have strong enough medication to induce sleep. The only thing Arlen could think of was to seek physical exhaustion.

On a flat section, bright colors passed on Arlen's left. It was a cycling team from Italy; they pedaled road bikes in their nation's colors. Eight of them passed Arlen with ease. Arlen surged with the idea to ride in their group. He sprinted to catch the tail of their momentum. It sucked him along in the draft of the pack. It felt incredible to be popped into this scene of bright flagged cycling through this verdant passage. Arlen pushed it two miles and dropped back. He watched the colors recede.

The climb became painful; Arlen dropped his head down and felt the heaviness of exhaustion blanket him. He concentrated on the road, the bike had been in the lowest climbing gear for miles. Arlen caught up to a farmer with a horse pulling a wagon with a large faggot of sticks. It was a tall pile; it seemed too large of volume for the lone horse to handle. The farmer was unaware of Arlen behind. The sticks stuck out the back at a perfect height for Arlen to hold and tow. Arlen sat up and held the rough wood. He balanced the bike and rested—slow but free energy. Arlen held the wood for a mile and let go. He waved to the farmer, and yelled, "Gracias." The farmer looked puzzled.

Arlen climbed with renewed vigor and pumped his legs till they burned. He slowed to a manageable pace of oblivion. He thought of nothing but this futile endurance. It felt good to think of nothing else. It was a pane of peace, a piece of pain that soothed the ravaged psychotic hound that rode his back. Arlen gazed at the four feet of road that waited patiently before his front tire.

The road ended in a gatehouse—a check stop. Arlen used his

Spanish. He was told in English, "Go, go home." They waved him back and down. Arlen turned and headed down the road but the exhaustion hit him hard. He rode into the ditch and sat down. The ground was hard and free from toil. Arlen drank water and waited. He looked down—his mind was thick with utter slop. The hound played dead.

"Ola," the voice said.
Arlen stirred his slop.
"Ola."
Arlen looked up and saw a teenager, a boy with an old road-racing bike that had seen better days. The boy smiled and seemed to be asking if Arlen was all right.
"Ci, fatigue." Arlen could not keep his limited French separate from his sparse Spanish. Arlen nodded and placed his hands in the lay your head on a pillow sign. The boy laughed and sat down next to Arlen. The boy coughed. Arlen woke up.

The kid liked the look of Arlen's bike and offered to trade for the ride down. Arlen smiled and nodded. The bike felt small and forward directed to Arlen. It had some quirks, as did Arlen's bike. Arlen thrilled to discover the sketchy brake ability, it was a bike meant for speed and the brakes were a secondary focus. They smiled and laughed at their new bikes.

Arlen noticed the kid's huge thighs; he obviously trained a lot. The kid coughed; Arlen thought of the pollution the kid was exposed to— these old vehicles smoked.

It was an easy predominately down ride to the kid's turn. They traded back and Arlen headed to his hotel.

RUN

He ate and rested and thought of the next stage. He laced up his running shoes and headed out the door. The sun painted the set. Arlen listened to the Walkman: 'The Technos' drove him through a new beat. He ran slow and steady and thought of exotica of vegetation and sea. The wind billowed the trees and Arlen felt the prodding.

He passed a nightclub where a line of people waited to enter. A woman hooked his arm and elbow with hers—he twisted and turned and straightened his elbow free and resumed the forward motion. She said something in Spanish. Arlen thought how different his run was from their revelry. He concentrated on the movement of running.

Two men mocked him for being a soldier. Arlen thought that he was only trying to fight insanity. He ran on the sidewalk toward a couple, the sidewalk was not wide enough for three. Arlen moved to the street side of the sidewalk and turned his body, embracing the street zone with his back. A bus rushed by within inches.

Arlen had not heard it nor had he looked before approaching the road. He felt the rush of forces. It whirl pooled him back onto the sidewalk. He did not think of consequences. He ran on. The beast weakened, it was broken and harnessed, but fought back.

Arlen tore his foot. He stopped with a favored limp. It was the end, his foot was pain and told him to stop. It was the weak link that ended the journey into endurance. He turned around and limp walked—it pained to put weight on. He thought of getting a taxi and paying them from the safe. It seemed simpler to walk it off; he did not want to interact with anyone. A couple smiled at him as they met, Arlen looked down at the cracks.

It was a darker dark that held the night in place when Arlen arrived back at his room. It was difficult to walk the stairs. With a bucket of ice he lay on the bed and removed his shoes. His feet stank and the bed felt great. There was no doubt that he could stay in bed for a few hours now. He was lame, a dud. It felt like his tool of wearing the energy down had broken, he was upset. He always hated to be injured on the wayside. He ironed the tissues with ice; the water dripped and ran down to his heel and other leg.

He drank water and found that he was dehydrated. He felt cold and shivered. His pee caught up with him. The floor felt cold to limp into the bathroom to relieve the bladder. He slept the most that night since arriving in Cuba.

WOUNDED BIRD

Arlen woke to the pain in his foot. It seemed serious enough—it placed that fear in his gut—if he didn't get it checked out, it could worsen. He needed to eliminate the spread to permanent wear and tear. He decided to go to a doctor.

After breakfast and research, he took a cab to a doctor. He thought of the fact he heard that doctors made less than prostitutes, and that there were many doctors per capita—it was a subject of pride with Castro. Medical and education—people were educated here.

The doctor saw him and it was merely a strain. It felt like a tear to Arlen. She advised an anti-inflammatory and something for the pain. Arlen accepted both, he felt weak.

He popped the pills at the hotel and immediately knew it was wrong. It crossed deep within him. The devil had snared him at the chemical crossroads to auction his sanity. The highest bidder took it away in a box. The void of empty shelf was filled with paranoia.

He was panic and reaction. He was fear and escape. They watched him and would take him away. Just like that, Arlen was done with the trip; the spastic creature of fear rose up and claimed him. It sold him lock stock and smoking barrel—he had to leave in the morning.

They were aware of the black market cigars that sat in his room—the 'Cohiba' contraband. He had no receipt. And they did not approve of manic-depressives in such a land. Arlen resigned himself to leave the next morning. He felt relieved in part. It had all become too much for him to handle. His head had exploded and he had no parameters for setting the fracture. He was gone.

PARTY

He panicked and grabbed all the goods he had planned to give away at the end of his trip. The large pile on the bed included his roller blades, tennis shoes, racket and balls. He left the room and limped down the business strip. He wanted one last walk through the action. He might know what he was looking for when he found it. He watched the people making merry song and dance. The air wavered with pleasure and sway.

Arlen walked past an outdoor cafe and bakery. The smell of coffee and cigar grabbed him. He checked it out. Yes this was it. Arlen saw the greatest looking cake in his life. He pointed and purchased.
"Gracias."
Arlen carried the cake, and forks and napkins back to his room and dressed for the farewell party. He did not want to be with Canadians or Europeans. He wanted to be with the locals. They had been kind to him. It was late evening when Arlen walked to the front desk with the cake. He sold his plan for the party to the staff. And he would be back in ten with the presents.

He discovered an odd painting in the back of the lobby. It stopped him to veer and daze—it was him. It was Arlen landing from the heavenlies of Manicma. There were four black spheres on both right and left sides blending into the lighter black background. Two bare reddish earthen feet centered the painting; a white minus and plus sign were above the toes. Two vertical waves held the sides of the feet. A bird like line of wing and body focused the bottom of the painting; it too was in white with two minus signs at the bottom corners above the wing tips. It blew Arlen away—he felt it was his voodoo feet that stuck in the earth. He had a wave of thought that the soaring highs were done— this painting secured his shackled ankles to the earth. His toes could feel the ground for evermore and a scratch on his foot was the cost.

It spun Arlen around to see things differently. What power did this painting hold? He remembered the party and limped to his room.

He left nylons and socks on the bed for his housekeeper. He piled the rest into a sheet and slung it over his shoulder. It was Christmas in January, and he was Santa. Eight staff members gathered to party and receive gifts. It appeased Arlen's fear of leaving the next day—he accepted departure. He opened up and gave all he could. The cake looked smooth and lickable. Laughter warmed. Arlen was in his element of mania and did not think of the oddness of the situation. It was right to give an impromptu party in the lobby. He felt like a mother and child wrapped and flowing.

The party ended with everyone having to return to work except for Arlen. He took his smile, sheet, and the remainder of the cake onto the street and floated toward his building. His foot did not hurt as much. Great, he thought, when he saw the security cop in front on his bicycle. He was smartly dressed and stoic, and wore the position of authority. Arlen could tell he was proud of his bike and gun.

Arlen walked right up to the man and offered him some cake. The stoic broke to grin and he lifted his leg from straddle and pushed the bike to the building. Arlen walked toward the steps and chairs where the prostitute displayed her patient wares. In this position, they were not allowed to say much to the rising tourists. They could just be hanging out waiting for someone if you were not attuned to the facts.

Arlen offered her some cake. She smiled and nodded. He placed a piece of cake on a napkin and passed it to her. She nodded and smiled at the goodness. Arlen placed a large piece to suit the policeman's stature on a napkin and handed it to him. The policeman, the prostitute and the manic-depressive sat and ate cake.

This was great cake made with fresh ingredients: fresh cream and fresh sugar—you could swim in the layer of cream. Arlen watched the large uniformed man and the sexy woman eat cake. They grinned at the goodness of the white frosting. Arlen ate more. It was glory. Arlen was happy. It was a reprieve from the paranoia. He wondered if this offering would lessen the severity of his extrication from the country.

The uniformed man finished and thanked him. Arlen pointed at the smudge of icing on the corner of his lip. He nodded and wiped and walked to his bicycle in a lighter fashion. Arlen waved at him, smiled at the prostitute, and climbed the stairs.

Arlen packed his bike up first. He removed the wheels and the handlebars and inserted it all into the box. He saw the cigar box—it was empty, he had given them all away. He packed the box, his clothes and assorted items. He was good to go. The bike box and suitcase waited. Arlen lay on his bed. He had a full day to chew on and ponder. He thought in recumbency. The counting of events lulled him to doze and sleep deep.

It was his Lazarus sleep. He dreamt of turkey, handcuffs and gravy. They took their turns to delight and baffle. He awoke refreshed and was surprised that they were not there yet to pick him up. He showered and put on pants and shirt—he had to unpack his bag. He had slept in till breakfast time. He was hungry and walked to eat—they could find him there, he supposed.

NEW DAY

He entered the dining room and kissed the waitress on the cheek—it was a nice custom. Arlen sat with his acquaintances from Quebec and ate heartily. It was a good morning; the cat and the dog arrived by the window and received food. Arlen and the two brothers made up stories about the adventures of the gypsy dog and cat that wandered from Peru to retire in Cuba—they liked the aroma of cigars. Arlen forgot about the authorities coming for him. They laughed and ate.

After breakfast, he remembered and returned to wait in his room for two hours in vain. The housekeeper arrived and Arlen gave her the presents. She was pleased. He asked her about Castro, and what she thought of him.

She nodded, "Good man ci."

She nodded again and pointed at the man on the TV screen and spoke a name that he was not familiar with, and she raved on for a minute. Arlen nodded and she went to work. Arlen stepped out onto the balcony and looked down on the worn red roofs and graying white walls. He remembered throwing his box of condoms off into space. He looked in vain at the ground—he could not see it.

The maid finished and moved on. Arlen lay on the bed and massaged his foot. It was sore today. He thought that the running was stupid. He didn't run anymore so why did he think he could do it? He didn't think. He found if he walked on the outside border of it, the pain was less. He grew impatient. He flushed the new drugs and found his duct tape. He taped his foot with gray and slathered sunscreen on. He was sore from the exploits of the last days and thought a swim was in order. He did not want to walk the two blocks to the beach. He would just hang out at the pool.

He had trouble letting go of the deportation. He was certain of the feeling. Was it not real? Did it happen? He could not be sure of it. He was certain of the run and the foot that cried to him. He limped to the pool—the deck chairs were filling for the day. He felt playful. The sleep had lifted the veil of psychosis enough for him to breathe.

He sat and lounged the morning through lunch, and the afternoon lay heavy in lazy holiday poolside. Arlen swam and soaked in the sun and cooled in the shade. It was lounge time. Arlen forgot about his banishment.

Arlen spotted a girl, a pretty girl who returned his look. He forced himself to approach her.

"Do you want to go for a walk?" Arlen smiled.

"Right now?" She asked and felt the spur of the moment invite her to act.

"Sure."

"Let's go." She smiled and turned to walk.

Arlen turned and followed suit. They walked slowly and talked. He explained the limp. Marie was from Montreal. She was here for five more days. They hit it off in innocence. They talked of the beauty of this place. They smiled and appreciated each other. By the time the hour passed, they held hands. It was exciting—Arlen's hand tingled with the touch. He was deprived and unaware of the need. Sparks twinkled between them.

"Another walk tomorrow?"

"Sure, what time?"

"Two o'clock?"

"Yep, same place."

"Same place at two."

Arlen reached in and kissed her cheek. Marie blushed.

MADNESS

Arlen entered his room. The reprieve of madness escaped outside. The relics of his crazed past waited patiently for Arlen to pick them up. He delved into a past relationship—the girlfriend that he could not shake. She was a love and friend that was sheer chemistry: they need to be together yet it is wrong when they are.

It promises everything you need, but is untouchable and evil. You window-shop and spot and enter and converse with the shopkeeper and purchase the item and take it home. You find out when it is just the two of you alone that it doesn't fit. You take it back and then buy it again and again.

The promise and anticipation of togetherness is fraught with conflict and dissolution. You are wrong but have to be together. It could be the state of Arlen and his illness. He remembered telling her that he would win the Nobel prize—he could not balance the uttering of this statement to the reality of sane existence. They were doomed to have paradise leanings that had no tangible outcome.

Arlen remembered the great times he and Laura had. He thought of the special connection that seemed destined. He could not get away from her. They would separate and he would find himself thinking of her more and more. Then he would run into her or she would look him up, he looked her up from time to time too. It went on for years in a twisted perennial growth. They would try to hang out together and it would fizzle and dwindle to the earth. The bulb would refocus and gain strength to reappear in another season.

Marie had turned him on. The wind picked up. It was too much for Arlen. If at first you don't succeed, medicate again till fallen. Slaughter stimulus—you're cut off from the sights and sounds of this sexy place. Arlen stood on the balcony and lavished madness with the precursors required to break in.

It came upon him fast. He shook to the core. It was a tsunami that slammed him to obsess on god and Laura and his dad—it was all about wanting his dad to die and then he did. It was horrible to be responsible for such an act.

He tried to forgive himself and did his best but there were always fragments that tripped him up in the times of insanity. His foot hurt after the walk, it was stupid to go for a walk. But it was too much sensuality; he needed a physical release when he interacted with a woman. He had to be able to move. He became sex that surged and lifted him to act. He thought of God and thought that he was to die, yes Arlen was going to die.

No, he was already dead and they were returning his body in a chopper. He could feel the pounding of the blades on his chest. It was the chopper from the river flip that had just now arrived. He was still in dire need of rescue, but he was dead. Laura was there to meet and bury him. It felt suitable to be covered with the earth, maybe then he could stay grounded and not rise up in lofty ideals and personae.

He could hear the helicopter approach and the sound of gunfire—he observed war. The balcony door was closed with the lights off. It was solitary confinement of illusions. It was a grand convincing show that he conjured.

Arlen drifted in inner turmoil and the angst rose and cracked. He twirled with image and delusion. He was grand and nothing and became endowed with hourly power that promised and delivered confusion and mistaken thinking. The hours passed into night. He was undercover of the shadows.

Arlen looked out the window and caught the door open across the block in another room—a shadow sex scene spent the flurry of desire. The faint light tore clothes and the bodies moaned with dance. Arlen turned and drew his curtain.

Arlen twirled in that dark place of sadomasochistic reflection. It claimed him and vacated the world of the sane. One never knows what goes on inside of buildings. Yes you can monitor via cameras. On a deeper level you never know what goes on inside of people.

The filter through, that Arlen massaged his miss-realities into existence and saw and acted them out, was his alone. It really happened to him and he carried the difficult task of settling the crazed real memories to rest. He needed to cremate and place them inside an urn set in a columbarium niche.

He was playing something out and was getting close. He continued with the war theme and imagined and lived the horrors of war for a while. It was the missing link to his father. His father was in World War II. His dad was a soldier: he killed people. It was horrible. Arlen became proud of his dad. Arlen broke down and cried.

It was the moment—this time of healing, over a decade past the point of actual death. The bathroom light was on and Arlen walked to the mirror on the wall by the closet. A pillar of light from the bathroom reflected on the mirror. Arlen cried and dared the mirror. He faced himself and saw lucidity. Nothing existed but this cleared channel of bird tears. He soared clean through to see his dad.

His father's eyes looked back at him and spoke, "I love you."

Arlen sobbed.

"I forgive you."

Arlen was naked in light.

"Go and live your life, I'll be watching."

The channel emptied and stayed vacuous and then became simple mirror. Epiphany eroded Arlen to be conscious of what transpired—the psychosis fizzled and reality gained a footing.

Arlen settled to bed and rested. He took his two Trilafon. His mind popped, yet there was an underlying state of solid ground. He was settling into something good—he knew it deep down. He felt his father's love and forgiveness and drifted to sleep.

Arlen woke to another shining day in paradise—this was reprieve. Somehow, he deserved the freedom from departure. This was a holiday again. He was fuzzy with the mirror conversation but took the good with him and left the bad—he had learned that from AA.. He felt better after his dad's blessing, it was what he needed. How odd was that? It had taken fourteen years to have the conversation and he stumbled upon it. Was it real or perceived? Does it matter? He was on the winding, pot-holed road to healing.

Arlen whistled as he limped to breakfast. It was all strange and good. His old self was tempted to hole up in his room for a couple of days but the goodness won out. He was set free. He limped toward coffee and mango juice.

CHEMISTRY

Arlen conserved his energy around the pool and waited for his arranged mini walk with Marie. She appeared by the pool and shook his
heart to still. He smiled and waited for his heart to settle. They talked
and fell in holiday love. They offered their ingredients to the chemical
spark—they combined to create magic by the sea. The days passed and
Marie soothed Arlen's soul to further healing.

Arlen confessed all to her. She was the compassionate love that everyone needs. They counted the days to two left. It was tragic that they
would part so soon. It was destiny that they met and providence that
kept their love at a simmer.

They progressed like teens through the hand holding and smooch-
ing and full lip locked kissing. They talked of their desire to curb their
desire—to not just have a physical union. They were at the point in
their lives that they wanted more depth. The physical priority left
them wanting. It was not enough to quench slake their longing for
companionship by skin alone. They decided to curb their tropical love
chemistry.

It was a challenge. They spread the blanket on the sand and touched
hands. It was innocent and utter sensuality—the touch of hydrated skin
on the back of hand. They reclined and absorbed the sun's warmth.
It was too much. They kissed and rolled and broke free. They caught
themselves. They stood and jumped in the ocean for a swim. They toweled off and warmed in the sun to dry.

Arlen offered a massage and Marie agreed. A sitting massage—he
straddled Marie, legs enveloped legs. He touched her shoulders. She
let go of the tension. She became loose and relaxed. Touch was inviting
and good. Arlen moved his groin closer. Marie felt the stir and invited
it—she was the moment of love and pleasure. He was desire.

He kissed her head, smelled her hair. It made him dizzy. He kissed
her ear and neck. She shivered and turned into the kisses. His hands
lowered down her back and reached. She turned and she stretched her
lips to his. He slipped his hands toward her breasts. Lips on lips, heads

lull and moan. Hands touch slopes and curves answer in groin. The kiss grows to one tongue.

Whoosh, the rogue wave flooded the groins and feet. Everything became soaked. The wave washed six inches of desire off the bottom of the couple's flesh. The water receded.

"Ah," they screamed and stood up laughing.

They were caught and receiving some help by the wave master. They giggled and held hands and smiled at their desire. It was beautiful.

They wrung out the blanket and laughed and played in the surf. It was innocent healing for the two of them. They had their teenage purity back. It was a slice of good pie. They swam and went for dinner.

To say goodbye was hard. Marie boarded the bus to the airport and Arlen stayed on. He had many days left. He concentrated on his drug schedule and the interaction with people. He was cleaning the cobwebs in his mind. He focused on swimming with his hurt foot and spent days at the poolside. He tried to read but was not able. He wrote a bit of scribble and notes and watched and talked to people.

Arlen was past his flare of craziness and it seemed that what remained was good hypo-manic energy. He was up and happy and everything was beyond rosy. It all tasted and smelled better. He watched every detail of a man making hats from palm leaves. The weaving of the strands entranced Arlen.

He thought of this trip as the weaving of the strands. It was coming together. He was capable of self-rescue. He was proving himself. It was a hat of palm that netted his head together to intact. The balm soothed and his synapses fired on cue. He settled into a piece of mind—a section of bridge that smashed the pattern.

He had obliterated the river that he fell into each winter for, was it eight years already? He had been hospitalized eight winters, and had slipped into depression eight times. It was slavery. He had fallen into a current of madness each winter that carried him to inhumane places. It had been a force of nature to be drawn and thrown into the water.

He tried to force his heels into the earth, but this was the year that breakthrough occurred. He arrived at the river, and it claimed his phoenix. The liquid doused the fiery wings from ash, the great manic bird fell into the body of current and dammed the river.

He had a bridge, he had the assertion and confidence that he could jump in the river of Manicma and stand firm. It could throw its turmoil and paranoia and grandiose delusions at him. He would frolic and play.

The dragons of lunacy could haunt his very existence and he would ignore the frontal assault, he would slipstream to the side and carry on. The slither would slime him but would not consume or masquerade his dignity.

He was free from psych wards. They had played their role in helping him but became his prison of fear and escape. The dragons would speak in his head and he would run to the pit of snakes—the concentration of madness threw Arlen for downward spirals every time. It was a fight to counter the others. One flavor of dragon is enough to combat at a time. And now Arlen was overcoming the odds, he had sought release, struggled and survived.

The rum flowed around him but not through him. He had been through the self-medicating stages and learned the bite. He had discovered that he could have the odd drink in the no-manic season and it helped him. There were no medications of consequence for it to mess with.

Arlen watched his grand Luna spirit creep into daylight and recoil. He baked in the sun and the madness shriveled. There was no longer any room for the dragons to play and claim. Arlen was open to mundane living. The regular feeling of stability was enticing him. He would give up the super cape of craze. The mad Manicma could depart, Arlen was ready, he had cleansed in the mirror.

He had finally found the words and eyes he was seeking. 'Go and live your life Arlen.' We are all tired of your life of moaning dramatics. You are simply a person who faces a challenge of sanity on occasion.

You are a person who has dignity of self. You see the world through your set of holes. Your view of the world has included madness for so long; Arlen how can you recompense this view and hold court with the sane day-walkers? Is it possible for you to return to enter the game of citizen life? You'd like to stay on poolside and ride this hyper jive through. Your days are numbered in this all-inclusive existence.

SWIM

The music filled him with comfort, unaware bliss. Arlen jumped in the ocean with his Walkman. It wound down and chattered at him and died. He gave it to a kid, and hoped that he could fix it.

Arlen taught a teen to play hackeysack. They kicked the crocheted beanbag in the air with all parts of their feet. The teen loved it. Arlen offered the bag as commerce opportunity. The boy said his mom could make them.

"Sell them," Arlen said.

The boy took the ball of beans and Arlen's enthusiasm. Arlen limped.

Arlen had made acquaintance with the front doorman—he invited Arlen to his place for a meal and wrote a note with the address in the village close by. Arlen's foot had healed enough to bike. He pedaled with the note and anticipation for the visit and meal. It was an honor to be entertained in a local's house.

Everyone he showed his note to pointed him onward. Then the pointed fingers conflicted and he lost confidence in the note's ability. Arlen became lost. He gave up and went back to the hotel. It was hard to not show up. They would be waiting. It was broken honor.

By the pool that night the games climaxed into, throw an article of clothing or footwear in a pile, stand back and then everyone runs to grab the items. Booze fizzled in the air with gaiety. It was raucous innocent fun. A man removed all his clothing and jumped into the pool and whooped and hollered.

The air changed to tense gray, this could go in any direction. Arlen did not understand the serious tone that prevailed. The night manager was there and stood on the edge of the pool. Arlen saw him waver in decision. He spoke quickly in Spanish and a towel was brought and the man was encouraged to get out of the pool and wrap in the towel, and to don his clothing. He was escorted to the exit and watched. The police were coming.

It made no sense. It was like the idiosyncrasies of Arlen's madness. One thing grew in importance when all else was dropped. This man had hit on an uptightness vein in hotel policy. For the police to bother to take him to the station meant they were serious. Bare breasts of women perked the beach just blocks away. Maybe it was male nudity. Arlen walked by the man as he waited for the police to arrive. He wore a worried countenance and managed to offer a dwindling rum-induced face of fun. It was working—they were putting the scare into him. Arlen thought that it would be a long time till this guy went in the buff poolside.

Yet Arlen was curious of the look inside the police station. What would they say to him for him to take it serious? And they would not; they couldn't do much to him. They needed these crazy tourista dollars. This included the rum waterfall, it was important to keep the barrels rolling.

IMPASSE

Arlen was already hazing to mundane. He was envious of the action that the poolman was in the midst of. Arlen headed to his room and the quietness that is domicile focus. Unlike home, he had little to counter the quiet; he had nothing to drown out the mundane, no big screen TV, and no stereo. He listened to Florida on his tiny radio and thought how odd it was for these people to listen to the surreal abundance of the States and to be cut off.

The sin island of gambling and parties was over—a regime ago. The ferries had stopped their run from Florida. It had been a stalwart standoff. Castro had waged a firm hand and Guatanamo Bay lingered as the threat reminder. The roasted pig is served. The bay is full of salt of season to taste.

Arlen wondered of the role celebration could play. He had observed that these people were more alive and dripping with culture than his TV-lulled fellow citizens. How could a place be sabotaged through martyrdom? And it holds so strong and true—how can it cling? Arlen was impressed by the will of the embargo and the firmness of martyrs. And the strange thing Arlen thought was that the redemption of the cash cow was again tourism—music, rum, cigars and pleasure.

The water is easy to cross, with the will to wager. The impasse glittered as the all mighty shone—it was the focus, and it grew. Arlen had focused on his manic times and had attracted energy to them. They always returned to prosper and tear him down.

He had crossed through the water and the deadlock dissolved. He was free to live. The challenge would be to deal with the lack of spark and the urge and desire to feel the surge of the monster rising within. He would have to kill the horrid madman that was himself.

Arlen would focus on a good life and attract the good things. The good wife and the house and the life focus that engaged, challenged and inspired him to face each day with a grin. It could all be his. Life could be lived. He had to get off this island and live it.

When Arlen approached the doorman the next day, he said that he was sorry, he had gotten lost.

"My wife had a beautiful fish." He stretched out his arms.

The doorman asked if he could come tonight. Sure he could. The doorman arranged an escort to ride with Arlen on the local bus to the village and to his home. It was mid afternoon when they walked to catch the bus.

HOSPITALITY

Arlen was ready for adventure; he pretended to be a local. It was odd to see such opulence out the window as he was transported to a rougher place. The facade faded. The bumps increased and the bus deposited and withdrew human currency to the game of tourism. The workers headed to the outlying villages.

Arlen thought of his work in Banff—there were similarities. As a tourist you can live fully within the groomed stage of the scene. You can ignore what is behind the scenes. You can ingest the pleasure and keep your back to the walls. Focus the senses onstage. Take the pictures. Enjoy yourself. Use the resources. Tip the people. Smile at the goodness that is your life. Fill your gut with pleasure to surmount the mundane of the year. Stimulate the senses to be real.

The village bleached and grayed. Arlen admired the narrow history of streets. He was blessed to be here—to make it through the madness. For some reason he caught a ride with the locals on the bus. They showed him the way, close to the earth.

His escort walked him to the door. It was like walking in a bleaching block puzzle. Arlen could tell that this neighborhood had slid from its glory years. It still remained proud and true to its self—it had nothing to hide. What you saw is what you got. Hypocrisy did not dwell here. There was no game of media-driven consumption with the Jones. No work-your-allotted-time-away for a bigger chunk of decomposing gross national product.

Survival of body and spirit, sustain the body with simple food and drink. Make music and love and live through the martyrdom. You could be a doctor, like in the house Arlen was to enter, there were three of them living here.

The door opened. He had made it a day late. Tardiness builds anticipation. Two beautiful black beams of sunshine smile with their proud daddy doorman and mom. Arlen is welcomed in. He sits and opens his pack and plays with the girls. They bounce and respond in kind to his goofy play. Arlen's latent craze raises its kid head to spin and twirl with the girls.

The meal is served. It is a glorious large fish fresh yesterday from the sea. The salad is succulent. The rice and black beans balance the perfection. It looks, smells and tastes of the earth. It is the meal to set Arlen straight on his course. He needs the basic package in life. Too much makes him regurgitate the excess. He needs to be close to the land—he is learning who he truly needs to be. The food is rounded out with a yummy cake and coffee. Arlen dived into the sugar and cream.

Arlen wondered if they always ate this good. He went to the bathroom and relieved himself. There was a bucket on the full tub edge and no water in the bowl—he primed the toilet and thought of the three doctors that lived in this house.

He thought of the tangent of back-to-the-land when he was manic. It was a recurring theme that drew him to the forest, to abandoned yard sites. He would wander about a deserted farmhouse and outbuildings and imagine staying on to restore and revive the living off the land. It showed his value through the madness. Maybe he needed to simply grow a garden and prune fruit trees.

The girls said goodnight and went to bed with their mother. Arlen went with the doorman to the arranged ride back to Varadero. It was a great evening that fizzled. Arlen did not want the adventure of life to stop. After all the crazed days, he wanted to live lucid, and large.

RETURN

It was a vintage Chevy from America—fifty years old. They were making it last. Arlen crawled in the backseat. The doorman had brought beer and offered Arlen one.

Arlen waved his hand. "No gracias."

The doorman turned and spoke Spanish to the driver. Arlen could tell that they were friends. Arlen was slipping from this fracture. He felt out of place. He was in the car but out of sync. He was concurrent with time—but these events passed him by as he struggled to be fully in this glorious moment.

The plush seats sat him back in comfort. The legroom was triumphant. The ride was solid. The windows ample. The engine rumbled a power cycle. Arlen watched the two Cubans drink their beer and take the world in. Arlen gazed out the window at the world passing through the compound island. There were gem lights sparkling, and the air was ripe with possibility. The windows rolled to admit the sweet fragrance. To ride in the old Chevy felt perfect.

Arlen had put a quarter in the horse at the mall and rode it home. It was his glory ride—he did not want the horse to stop. He wouldn't have minded if the car broke down to delay the mystery—the interest in the sublime fantasy.

Maybe he had kept breaking down for relief from the monotony of his existence. He knew he needed to be true to his inner calling. He had landed in that painting—his toenails were still marked from the earthen red. He had dragged the monster through the caverns and wore it to a mere skin that took flight and soared as an eagle. It looked for other prey unaware.

Arlen looked at the growing lights. It was darker behind them. The rolling blackouts took effect. Arlen had ridden his bike the other night and the slight-lit street had turned to black that seemed like another reality. Arlen had never seen darkness as heavy and impenetrable. He had stopped the bike and his feet found ground.

It saddened Arlen to close this ride. He had nothing to give the driver. He was sorry. It had come down to what he had given the universe and his present self. He happened to be clothed and fed. He was real and not dead. Perhaps the universe would bring fat to this growing joy and peace that he fanned. The fire within him glowed. He was warm dignity.

He gave thanks for life and took a big bite of where he was. He touched the seat and felt the heaviness of an era conundrum. The ride was ending and Arlen breathed in the meaning of the night. He was able to move on from the craziness. He savored a slice of peace. He could get out of the car. He could shed the heaviness of the Manicma and thrive with life. He believed now that he could do it.

His dad had blessed him. He was manic-depressive. He was bipolar and close to the equator. His was a mixed bliss as the old Chevy glided to a stop. The men turned as one middle to bid farewell. Arlen offered his smile and nod and open eyes.

The driver turned the interior light on—it was a flooded stage. Arlen found the handle and swung the door open. He turned.

He said, "Mucho gracias."

Arlen placed his foot firmly on the ground, and then the other with the limp.

MADNESS PAST

Thru the mountains on my knees-
scrape the valley rivers bleed.

Rains fell through my tears,
sun burned hard the fear.

Parched tongue, nor desert sands,
could speak of that my love.

Cross the ocean I must roam,
seeking saving sights alone.

Could not you speak of that for me?
Perhaps I wish you could have seen.

-Arlen